Blackberry Road

BLACKBERRY ROAD

BY

JODI LEA STEWART

Published 2022 by Progressive Rising Phoenix Press, LLC
www.progressiverisingphoenix.com

ISBN: 978-1-950560-73-8

Printed in the U.S.A.
1st Printing

Edited by: Chris Eboch

Cover Illustration: Spring Forest On A Foggy Morning, BigStock Photo ID: 77036651, Copyright: nature78
Used With Permission.

Interior Illustration: Rural Field With Ripe Wheat On Background Of Clouds. Vector Illustration, BigStock Photo ID: 1168699012, Copyright: Vectorgoods studio.
Used With Permission.

Interior Illustration: Graphic Of Branch With Blackberry Fruit, Flowers And Leaves (Rubus Genus, Black Berries), ShutterStock Photo ID: 778462003, Copyright: arxichtu4ki.
Used With Permission.

Interior Illustration: Blackberry, Made In Vector And Isolated, Black Line, ShutterStock Photo ID: 1743165482, Copyright: Karen_Remez. Used With Permission.

Cover Design by Kalpart
Visit: www.kalpart.com

Interior Design by William Speir
Visit: http://www.williamspeir.com

Books By
JODI LEA STEWART
Published By
PROGRESSIVE RISING PHOENIX PRESS

TRIUMPH, a Novel of the Human Spirit

SILKI, THE GIRL OF MANY SCARVES SERIES:
Summer of the Ancient
Canyon of Doom
Valley of Shadows

Blackberry Road

Accidental Road (Coming Soon)

The Gold Rose (Coming Soon)

Table Of Contents

"It was her habit to build up laughter out of inadequate materials."

—John Steinbeck, *The Grapes of Wrath*

A Dead Man in There

I guess it shouldn't matter why I turned into a big cusser or why, out of my eight brothers, I got my favorites... and two I kind of hate. You'll find out about that soon enough. All I know is, we were minding our own business when trouble sneaked in one day like an oily twister on a sleepy afternoon. I reckon Nowata County, Oklahoma, is still yapping how we never had a summer like 1934, and I don't blame them. Now, I want to tell you about it and how it changed everything—especially us.

But I'm getting ahead of my own self.

What's important is the murder of a good man happened right under our noses, and that started a mystery in our neck of the woods like no one ever heard tell of, and probably never will again. That situation laid open truths about some folks like a hatchet tearing into new wood. Then Allen and Tommy—that's two of my older brothers—cheated the devil hisself and didn't die when the doctor same as said they had to. Who ever heard of such things?

My story starts on May the fifth. I know the day exactly on account of we'd been out of our school term for five days on the dot. Mr. MacGregor let us out early because of some important business he had to attend to in Oklahoma City. You can look in on us that day in May, and guess what you'll see? It's me, the girl, finally done washing and wrenching and drying a peak of hell's dishes from our noon-day meal.

Just so you know, doing the dishes for that mess of ornery brothers till my hands shrivel up is worse than cutting your own switch for a switching. Sometimes, it makes me so mad I cuss a blue streak and maybe a red one, too, only I sure don't do it out loud.

I'm on the last part of my chore, which is drying the gravy skillet real good with a flour-sack towel because I don't want Mama going crazy about a speck of rust on one of her skillets. I finish drying and blow on my water-sogged fingers. They're burning bad and red as raw sausage because Mama's lye soap near eats the skin clean off them. Today they aren't so bad, but when they crack open, I sneak out to the shed and use some cow-bag balm. I don't let those eleven-year-old twins, War and Snipe, see me because they'd say I had snot on my hands since the balm's thick and kind of yellow. That kind of nasty talk makes me want to wallop the living daylights out of them, and sometimes, I go ahead and do it.

The screen door in the kitchen creaks open and Calvin, my near fifteen-year-old brother, says, "Ready, Bid?" I let out a stream of words that most assuredly would get me slapped if Mama heard, but Calvin's used to it. We do it all the time and never tell on each other.

"Hold the door, Cal, so I can throw this dadgummed dishwater out."

"Aren't you going to save it for the pigs?"

"Naw, slop bucket's near to the brim."

A few steps out the kitchen door, chickens come running

all side to side thinking I'm throwing out scraps. I turn the other direction and throw the water up in the air. Soon as it splats on the hard dirt, I swear it's like road-prisoner chains drop off my legs. It signals I'm free and don't belong to nobody, no sir, at least for the time being.

"Sammy's coming, too," Calvin says, and I already know Sammy's coming because he goes everywhere Calvin goes. Sammy's okay, and I like it when he ignores my Dad and the other boys calling him a kitchen girl when he slips in to help me with the dishes once in a while. And he ain't no girl of no type. Shoot, he can outrun any of us, but he's just got a nice streak running through him for sure. For a twelve-year-old kid, he's all right.

Soon's I prop the enameled dish pan on its edge, me and Cal skedaddle out the front room door. I'll tell you right off Calvin may be one of my most favorites, but he can be sneaky as a fox in a hen house. He's gotten me and Sammy in lots of trouble on account of he's smart and figures out plans for us that get us in trouble, but not him. Like the time he tied Sammy's legs together underneath our biggest sow so he wouldn't fall off and we were supposed to pretend Sammy was a cowboy. That fat pig bucked like she'd eaten some bad weeds, and Sammy, just five years old at the time, slid down underneath her. He was screaming to high heaven, and so was the sow. Me, too, but Calvin jumped in the pen and cut the rope before that big hunk of pork could stomp little Sammy flat as a cow patty. By the time Mama got there, Sammy was sitting outside the pen, just filthy and ruffled as he could be, with tears running down his cheeks.

"What in the Sam Hill happened here?" Mama hollered at us.

"I fell in the dirt and hit my head, Mama. It don't hurt no

more." Sam told her.

Mama didn't believe it, not one word, but we grinned at her until she walked off shaking her head. That was a long time ago, but now you see what I mean about Calvin, don't you? We never tell on him for nothing, and I don't know why we don't get mad at him, neither. That's how it's always been, even before he left us for two whole years to stay at that hospital over by Tulsa. They wanted to saw off his leg, and almost did, but he ran away. He won't talk about it, and he gets buzz-hornet mad if me or Sammy ask him to.

So here we are heading off with Mama's egg money to get her some of Mr. Leroy's Herb Whiz. She's been droopy in the mouth as of late, and I even heard her crying last night when I sneaked down the stairs to get a drink from the water bucket.

I guess that's what caused my dad to sidle up and tell Calvin and me to go get Mama some of that stuff Mr. Leroy makes and don't let the sun go down before we do it. Law, it's a smelly, goopy syrup I can't abide to look at, but that doesn't stop the women for miles around going for it like it's Sunday lemonade. It stinks like an August outhouse, no lie. Dad says it has iron in it, and I don't know why any regular person would drink metal same's on an old rusted nail, but they do.

Anyways, after Mama takes to sipping it for a few days, she starts laughing at Dad's mischiefs and does a bit of humming here and there, so he leans to her keeping a supply of that Herb Whiz around the house. Even when we lived closer to Coody's Bluff and Alluwe than Nowata, we still went right often to Mr. Leroy's little shanty house in the woods to buy his tonic.

We're walking along the path just inside the edge of the woods and I'm dreaming about those suckers Mr. Leroy gives me while my brothers are babbling about the pump house we'll be passing soon as the trees start thickening. Calvin always goes inside to touch the motors and listen to them sing, he calls it, while they pump oil. We're not supposed to mess around any pump house, but we do anyways, and that's why it's fun.

"Listen, you hear that?" Sam whispers all of a sudden. I hear it all right. It's same as we heard a few weeks ago when we were playing at Hoot Creek. Sounds like a haint, and it makes my hair bristle up. Fact that it sounds so pretty and scary at the same time gives all of us the willies.

"Is it a panther, Calvin?" Sammy's eyes are bigger than black walnuts.

"Panthers sound like a woman screaming. That there's no panther."

He's right. I'd danged near bet we're hearing something no longer living. It stops, and I see Calvin and Sammy's chests raise up and start breathing steady again.

"Ah, it ain't nothing but a Wood Ghost, you scaredy-cats," I say, skipping off, scared half to death myself but not willing to show it.

At the pump house, Sammy runs to one of those skinny rods no bigger round than a fifty-cent piece. Quick as any-thing, he's hanging on it upside down over the ditch while it goes back and forth doing its work for the oil pumps.

"Hey, Cal, I ride these pipes so good, I might go join me a traveling circus."

Calvin frowns. "I told you, Sammy, they're rod lines, not pipes."

Sammy isn't listening. He doesn't care what the real name is just so's he can ride them. I jump on one with my bare feet and fall off giggling. "Why do they have so many pump houses round here, Calvin?" I ask, grabbing a spindly tree trunk to keep from falling off while I ride another rod with my toes hanging off.

"Because Oklahoma's eat up with so much oil in the ground. Why do you think Nowata's getting so big? Those rich folks pump it out of the ground and sell it faster than I can spot a swimming hole."

I don't know how he thinks he knows so much, but the truth is, he does.

Sam lets go of the rod and stands there pointing to the side of the pump-house building facing the woods. "Looky there. The door's all funny looking."

All I ever saw before was the door shut, but right now, it's open and pulled away from the doorframe like it's busted. Calvin goes toward it with Sammy right behind. Sammy stops outside, but Calvin pushes the crooked door open and goes right on in. I can't see him on account of it's darker inside than in the bright sun. Listening to the grind of the pump and the sound of the rods, a strange feeling wiggles up my back. Same feeling like the time us kids heard dishes breaking and doors slamming in the empty farmhouse out at the old Lawson property.

Calvin comes back out looking like he's rolled his face in Mama's flour. Sammy steps toward him. "No, don't go in, Sam, it's… there's a dead man in there."

CHAPTER Two

The Law

We're running back home like a herd of swine heading off a cliff to our doom. We take the shortcut along the gravel road and my naked feet are going numb and pained on those sharp pieces of clay rock. Calvin can't go so fast since he's lame in one leg, so I hang back and let Sammy push on. He's the fastest runner I ever did see, and I can keep up with him most of the time. Calvin's face looks like he saw a haint, and I sure feel like one's breathing down our necks.

Mama is pumping water out of the cistern when Sammy runs up to her hollering about a dead man in the pump house. She sets the bucket down and puts her hands on her hips.

"What are you kids jabbering about?" she says, and I go to crying but make myself stop right quick. Bawling makes me weak in front of my brothers, so I don't do it except by myself. Mama sits down on the wooden planks covering up the cistern and looks point blank at Calvin since he's the eldest. "Were you kids in that pump house?" Her voice sounds like she's right on the edge of sending us to cut our own switches for a whooping.

Cal nods all ashamed like, but he ain't no more ashamed than a cow's head in a feed sack. He tells Mama in her ear what he saw. Mama's eyes get big. She jumps up giving orders.

"Go get your dad and your brothers, Sammy. Calvin, go to the Frosts and tell them to fetch the sheriff. You be careful too, you hear me?"

The Frosts live a few miles down the road. They have an old car that runs most of the time, and it takes them to town a lot faster than our wagons do. They're the neighbors who took me to the town doctor when I got fanged by a copperhead when I was five, but that's another story for when we aren't so torn up about a dead man.

"Biddy!" says a girl's voice, and Doodles runs to me and climbs up my legs to my arms. I swing her around and hug her close to keep her safe from the danger around us. Doodles, well, her real name is Pearl, is nine years younger than me, and she's my responsibility. Truth is, I'm so d—, I mean dad-blamed, happy to get me another girl in this family, I don't mind doing anything for that skinny little thing.

Mama hands me the bucket. "Finish filling up the drinking bucket, Biddy, and peel us a big stack of taters for supper. No telling what'll happen around here before we know it," she says, and she was right. I barely set a toe inside the house when Dad, Tommy, Allen, and Sammy show up from the fields. Sammy's walking around with his thumbs hooked in his overall straps like he's President Roosevelt just because he's brought the men news about a dead man.

I pour water in the dishpan to put the peeled taters in so they don't turn dark before we fry them. All the while, I'm spying through the piece of rusty screen Dad nailed over the window to keep the skeeters out at night. Mama's nodding her head big at what Dad's saying. He starts off walking in the direction of the pump house with three of my brothers trailing behind. Allen, who's seventeen, turns and says something to Sammy.

Sammy turns around and kicks a foot full of pebbles into one of Mama's fat Plymouth Rocks. The hen squawks and scrambles out of his way. Mama squawks too, and points to the pasture. It's a mite early to be bringing in the cows, but Mama said there's no telling what'll happen around here before we know it. Besides, messing with any of Mama's chickens always brings a repercussion.

Snip and Brownie, our stock dogs, grab at Sam's overall legs. Law, those dogs love to bring home our Guernsey and Jersey cows.

"What you doing there, Doodles?" asks my youngest brother, James, who we call Jay Bird because he's been trying to catch one since he was borned. Doodles is sitting partly on my bare feet holding a couple of big spoons and two jar lids.

"I'm cooking," she says, and Jay Bird trots to the screen door. War and Snipe, those devil-twins, crash through the door all of a sudden and knock him over. I turn in time to see Jay Bird fall backward and conk his noggin on the floor but he doesn't holler. Snipe picks him up by one arm and sets him back on his feet.

"Can I be with you and War?" he asks. He's eight, and has to beg to be with those two no goods. I don't like it because they're such a bad influence, but Snipe looks at War and War motions for Jay Bird to come on. Doodles leans into my legs while the twins tromp around the kitchen messing with everything that's none of their business. Snipe picks up a peeled tater and drops it back in the water to make it splash my arms. He looks at War to approve of it. He does that all the time like he doesn't have his own mind. War kind of hoots under his breath, and that means Snipe is doing what War likes.

War grabs a red radish from a mess of them laying on the counter and pops it in his mouth, dirt and all. He throws the green part in my clean potato water instead of the slop bucket. He swipes a piece of unwashed red-leaf lettuce and hands it to Jay Bird. Jay Bird pops it in his mouth and I hear the gritty dirt in his teeth while he chews.

"Stay out of the food," I growl in a voice I save just for War and Snipe. War sticks his tongue out and makes a face at me. Sometimes I can't tolerate that boy, like most of the time.

I finish peeling taters while War, Snipe, and Jay Bird, who doesn't know nothing yet but thinks he's big like them, snicker and go upstairs sounding like a herd of mules on the wooden steps.

"Don't bother Grandma!" I yell, but they don't listen. Grandma Massy, who's blind, was sleeping in the one bedroom upstairs, but she won't be now. It doesn't matter because Red, Pint, Moolie, and Bean, our four squirrel and rabbit hunting dogs, go to barking and whining. Guineas squawk and flutter. Geese honk. Mama's mean gander is honking loudest since he thinks he's a watchdog.

I stir the pot of pinto beans on top of the cook stove with the big wood canning stick and take a peek out the screen door. Gol, if it isn't our big sis Jean come for a visit. She's on foot, which means her husband Jack let her out on the gravel road and she walked the rest of the way, which is about half-a-mile. I figure he's making her test the waters before he shows up since he figures we most likely heard the talk about his drinking and getting rough with Jean. I don't like Jack no more since I heard that.

We don't hug or nothing in our family, but that doesn't

mean we don't like each other. Mama comes out of the chicken house with her bucket full of straw and eggs. When she sees Jean, a surprised look jumps on her face. They both stand there looking at each other, and I'm admiring my sister's white ironed blouse tucked into a straight blue and white plaid skirt. The little string of fake pearls between the collars of her blouse look so fine, and I feel uglier than sin in my old passed-down boy overalls and filthy bare feet.

Jean's got the handle of a small green travel case in one hand, and a brown paper sack with a folded-down top in her other one. "Hi, Mama. I brought you some sugar. Thought I'd come see you for a day or two."

She busts out bawling, and Mama does too. They come in the house looking down and sniffing like they got colds. I whisk up Doodles and edge past them out the door so it's like I'm not seeing nothing until Jean settles down. Jean gives my arm a pat, and nobody can stop me from seeing the big bruises on her arm when I scoot by her. I feel like taking a board to Jack. Anyways, I don't want my big sis feeling bad about crying in front of us kids.

Before the door shuts, I hear the old saggy iron bed scraping across the floor upstairs. War, Snipe, and Jay Bird are trying to hide underneath it, which means they spied Jean from the upstairs window. They know for a fact they're in for a scrubbing while she's here, maybe two or three. She near washes the skin off their dirty faces, ears, and necks, and they howl like spoilt crybabies. I laugh till I cry, I like it so much.

Soon's I put Doodles down in the yard, she starts off in the direction of the pigpen again. I yell, "Don't you go near those pigs, Doodles, you hear me?" Her bottom lip goes to quivering because I seldom raise my voice to her, but I can't help it. Everyone knows pigs might flat out eat a little kid if it falls in there with them, especially those sows when they got babies. Facts of life, that's all. Doodles has to learn how to survive around here like we did.

She comes to lean against me. I lift her on my shoulders and trot like a horse around the house a couple times to make her giggle. I sneak a look through the rusty piece of kitchen screen and see Jean finishing peeling the taters. She's half-turned, talking to Mama, who's sitting behind her at our long kitchen table. I hear the screen door in the front room groan open real slow like. Once it's back closed, War and Snipe shoot off toward Hoot Creek like someone lit a fire in their britches. I walk to the front of the house and see Jay Bird standing on the porch looking after them. He's rubbing his eyes and bawling because those hell boys told him he couldn't go with them.

Doodles wants to go back in the house. I take her in and catch Mama's eyes to see if she sees me letting go of my responsibility. I have to be sure like that since we can't let Doodles drown in a cistern like the Jefferson baby girl did a few summers ago. Or let those sows get her. Mama nods, and I go climb on top of the smoke house to think about that dead man in the pump house.

The tin roof is hot so I scoot over to the big wooden part where my oldest brother Carl patched it when we first moved here, which is a few years past. The mulberry tree spreading its branches over that spot makes it nice and cool. I lay myself back and start thinking how I ain't never seen a dead man before. I wonder if flies are crawling in and out of his nose holes like they do to the dead animals I come across from time to time. Who is that man anyways? Did he fall and split his head? We don't usually have dead people show up in pump houses around these parts. Or anywhere besides their own houses, and that's usually because they're old and decide to die from it.

A breeze jiggles the leaves above me, making them twist and turn. I trace the branches with my eyes until the dogs go to barking. I sit up cotton headed… and did I just fall asleep on that roof? The dogs and fowl are making a bigger row than usual, and I'll be switched if the Nowata sheriff hisself isn't driving his funny looking prisoner truck right on down Blackberry Road, the rutted dirt road that leads to our house.

CHAPTER *Three*

Know-It-All

I climb down off the smoke house and squat low at the corner to keep an eye out. Jean and Mama come outside and wait for the sheriff to get out of his truck. Jean dries her hands on a dish towel tied around her waist. Jay Bird and Doodles have flat noses pushed against the inside screen door, and I know Mama told them to be still and stay inside.

Grandma Massy is awake from her nap, of course, since those two hooligans and Jay Bird woke her up. She's standing behind the little kids listening to what's going on with her hands resting on Jay Bird's shoulders. Mama's eyebrows are all close together, and I take it she's either worried about the dead man or else about the sheriff finding out about Dad's corn liquor and blackberry wine in the gopher hole. Calvin says Dad's not supposed to make hooch because of taxes and stuff, and the government won't let a body do it, no sir.

"Doesn't it matter if selling it keeps your kids from starving?" I asked Calvin, and he said it didn't matter a pig's jar of knuckles if the kids starve to death and their tongues drop off and the bears eat them up. I reckoned it was pretty serious if that was the case.

Calvin pops out from the prisoner cage on the back of the sheriff's truck and plops down on the big chopping block alongside the woodpile. He's smiling pretty smug for sure.

"Mrs. Woodson," the sheriff says to Mama, touching his hat. His britches are the same color of his shirt, which is almost no color at all except for a washed-out tan. His badge is pinned above his shirt pocket, and his other pocket has a little square bulge. I'm guessing it's a pack of store-bought cigarettes. He's wearing sunglasses, and I wonder how he can afford such rich things as already made smokes and sunglasses. He's about as tall as my oldest sister's husband, Ed, which is taller than my dad or older brothers. He's not real young, and not real old, neither. I hunker in closer and sit crossed-legged on the ground by the cistern so I can hear what's going on.

"Ma'am, I would appreciate if your boy would accompany me to the pump house where he allegedly discovered the body of a deceased man earlier today."

Cal jumps up tall and important. I don't understand some of the sheriff's big words, but I get he's asking Mama if Calvin can go back to the pump house with him.

"As you know, there are numerous pump houses in this vicinity, and I can save time by going to the right one. I wanted to ask your permission because, ma'am… from this boy's account, it looks like we have a murder on our hands."

It scares me to kingdom-come hearing the sheriff say that. It scares Mama, too, because she takes hold of Jean's shoulder and covers her mouth with her spare hand. Calvin keeps on grinning like he knows everything in the world. He's happy because he loves anything that stirs things up, no matter what if it's good or terrible. He's restless in his innards, Mama says about him.

Sammy and our six Guernsey and two Jersey milk cows

come shuffling and mooing into the yard on the way to the pens. The sound of the cow bells on their necks keeps me from hearing Mama's answer, but it doesn't matter since my dad and brothers show back up. Dad goes right to the sheriff and shakes his hand, and before I can say *hog holler,* the sheriff is driving off with Dad in the front seat and Allen and Tommy scooched down in that cage thing on the back.

Mama and Jean go back inside scooting Doodles and Jay Bird back into the house. Sammy and I run to Calvin as hard as our legs will take us.

"Why didn't you go with them, Calvin? What were you doing in that cage on the sheriff's truck? Is that cage for outlaws when he carries them to jail? Did that dead man get murdered for true?" The words fly out of my mouth, and Sam looks back and forth at both of us with big cow eyes, or that's what I call them and he doesn't seem to mind me doing it.

Calvin's face is squenched up like he just bit a green persimmon. Sammy and I stay still and see if he'll talk to us or walk off. If he walks off, it means *get away*, and we do, but Calvin turns around and says, "I'm the one who found him, and I'm no baby. Hell, I'm old enough to smoke." He picks up a hunk of wood and chucks it into the wood pile. A waterfall of short logs tumble to the ground and I know Calvin isn't going to pick them up.

"Yeah, they're just stupid," I say picking up several fallen logs and stacking them back where they belong. The three of us fall into step, and it looks like we're headed to Hoot Creek. Calvin isn't talking, and I'm itching to ask him some more about that dead man. We see War and Snipe swinging out over the creek on a big rope we got tied to the oak limb. Their overalls are wadded up in a pile under the tree, and I look away fast but not before I see black leeches hanging on their white backsides.

I'm not allowed at the creek when the boys go swimming since they go naked, so Calvin shoots me a funny look and turns us in the other direction away from those fools. They'll peel the leeches off and light them on fire with matches they'll steal from the kitchen when they get home. Everything they do makes me mad.

We wind up sitting under a shade tree with none of us talking so I pull up grass blades and cover the back of a shiny green and purple beetle doodling around by our feet. Sammy laughs because he thinks lots of stuff I do is funny. "Wish we could of gone to Mr. Leroy's today because he'd give us a sucker sure as the world," I say. Sammy's eyes get big. "You never been there, have you?" I ask him. He shakes his head. Calvin ain't talking yet, so I decide to tell Sammy about Mr. Leroy's place.

"It's right there alongside Sweet Creek, and kind of deep in the woods with more trees around it than you can count. It's a one-roomer with patches on the patches, mostly wood, but a little tin, too, and clean as a whistle. It looks like he scrubs the wood it's built from, and the stones he stacks along the bottom of it don't have a smite of cobwebs or mud on them. His tin roof doesn't have any rust either, and that's a nice sight for our neck of the woods.

"His little yard looks like he sweeps it. Pretty green vines cover the whole chimley side of his shack, and two big tractor tires laying on their sides are painted white with moss roses in the inside of one and some kind of colored wild flowers in the other. In the summertime, that is."

"Gol-lee. What's it like inside his place, Biddy?"

"Truth is, I haven't never been inside because Mr. Leroy goes in by hisself and fetches us a quart jar of his Herb Whiz tonic and brings a store-bought sucker for me. Being's how we don't get any candy around here except at Christmas, my mouth goes to watering every time I lay eyes on that sucker."

Sammy giggles. I check if Calvin's ready to start talking, but he's still pouting. I fix little twigs in a square so the beetle can't get away.

"What else, Bid?"

"Well, he carries around a brown coin purse about the size of a mush melon on a strap crisscrossed over his shoulder. One time, when it was getting near wintertime, he showed me a white rabbit's foot with a fancy silver ring and chain on the end. He pulled it right out of his coin purse, and boy was he proud of it, Sam. I don't blame him, neither. I never did see such a pretty rabbit's foot like that before. Mr. Leroy's teeth were smiling white against his dark skin and it was a sight to see. Yessir, that foot makes him powerful happy, I think."

"What else, sis?"

"Most times, he says Bible stuff like, 'It shore is a God-made day full of sunshine, ain't it, Miz Woodson?' and that's Mama, of course. Sometimes he talks about the weather, like, 'That Creator outdone hisself giving us that rain yesterdee, didn't he Little Miz Woodson?' and that would be me he's talking to. Sometimes he calls me *Little Bit,* and I like it."

Calvin flops down on his stomach and lets out a breath so big it blows the grass off our beetle's back. He says, "Want to know how come Sheriff Murphy says that dead man was murdered?"

We don't get a chance to say nothing before Calvin starts telling us how come. "Because he was, that's why. His head was so bloody on one side I didn't recognize him at first, but I know who he is."

"Who?" me and Sammy say at the same time.

"Old man MacGregor, that's who," he says, and all of a sudden, I see lights flashing to the side of my eyes. I feel a pained stomachache coming on sure as sheep shires. My most favorite teacher I ever had can't be dead!

"You think you're so smart, but you ain't!" I yell at Calvin. "You made a mistake, Calvin, say it!" Calvin looks at me with big surprised eyes.

"I'm telling the truth, Biddy," he says in a low voice. He looks sorry, but I don't care.

"You're just a big ol' know-it-all, Cal," I mumble, swiping away the water starting to pour out of my eyes. I take off running, and I don't mind if any stupid mad dog chases me or a Wood Ghost kills me, neither.

Chapter Four: Bananas and Red Lipstick

My stomach is aching so bad when I get home, I slam through the door and roll out one of the mattresses stacked against the wall in the front room. My head is chock full of poor Mr. MacGregor dead in the pump house and how we won't have him teaching us no more. When our regular teacher got sick almost to death right when school got started last fall, Mr. MacGregor came to be our substitute teacher at the Armstrong School. Even before I got to know him real good, I didn't have my regular hard time talking to him like I do most strangers.

Pretty soon, he told us he was our new all-the-time teacher and that was real fine with all of us. We found out he'd retired from REDA Pump in Bartlesville, and for reasons other than he wanted to discuss, he'd taken up living in our neck of the woods. The town folk whispered that he was a big shot at that REDA Pump place and he probably had lots of money stashed away in the bank. Word was he paid cash for the Piper cabin alongside Wayne Road.

I moan and groan. Mama comes to lean over me. "What's got you all balled up like this, Bid?"

"It hurts real bad, Mama, all over my stomach and chest."

Jean comes to feel my head. "No fever. I hope it isn't her appendix, Mom. You have any paregoric?"

Mama tells her no, and I bury my head in a quilt. I hear lots of mumbling and the screen door opening and closing. I almost jump to the ceiling when something cold hits my foot.

"Hold still, silly. Your feet are as dirty as a sty. My, my they're bruised and scratched up, Biddy. Do they hurt?"

"No."

"You're going into town to see the doctor. Mom says your school shoes are too little to wear anymore, so let's get your feet cleaned up at least. We'll doctor them tonight with some salve I brought from home."

I don't like it, but it's Jean, so no use to gripe about it. Leastways, she's always nice to me and maybe she understands what I have to put up with living here with no girls except a little skinny one. While Jean is cleaning my feet, I go to thinking about the doctor. All I know is, nobody better try to cut my bloomers off like they did when my leg was all swelled up from the snake bite. I near kicked the nurse in the head back then, and me just five years old. I would have done worse if they hadn't held me down. This time I'll get it done if she or anyone else tries any such thing. I was just a year older than Doodles when that snake bit my ankle down in the field, but I remember it plain as day.

"Get to feeling better, kid," Jean tells me.

Tommy's waiting outside with the wagon all hitched up to our two work horses. I can see he's tickled he's getting out of the field work and going to town on account of he's smiling around the home-rolled cigarette dangling from his mouth. Mama doesn't allow no smoking in the house, so my older brothers smoke outside. Cal doesn't smoke, but he can if he wants to since he's near fifteen years old.

I lay on the quilt Mama has in the back of the wagon and look up at the trees overhanging the road and the blue sky behind them while our team horses take us to town. The shaking of the wagon makes my stomachache feel better. All of a sudden, I get embarrassed to be going to town with nothing but my bare feet hanging out of the bottom of those boy overalls. I tap Mama on the shoulder. "Let's go back home. I'm too old to go to the doctor with no shoes on my feet."

I mean it, too, even if I have to jump out of the wagon. It's how I am, and they all know it. Somebody calls any of us a hillbilly or makes fun of us, I take them down to the ground with my fists or run off. Wearing no shoes in town will make me feel like a hillbilly, which is worse than being sharecroppers like us.

Mama stares at me, and I think she's about to tell me to hush up my mouth and do what I'm told, but she doesn't. She pulls her coin purse with the black peeling off it from under the buck seat and counts the coins inside.

"Thomas Jr., stop at the mercantile first so I can buy Biddy some anklet socks to go to Doc Friedman's office."

Shoot, I can't believe my good luck. I lay myself back down with my belly almost feeling good again. Then I remember how Mr. MacGregor is dead, and I flip over and bawl my eyes out with my face buried in the quilt. When I shut up, I think Tommy and Mama might've heard me, but they don't act like it. My stomachache is gone, but my feelings are hurt real bad for my teacher. He was my most favorite I ever had. One time I asked Mr. MacGregor why he wanted so bad to help us farm kids catch up on our arithmetic and history and reading. He said it was on account of us working hard with our folks in the fields and having to move around so much.

He said maybe he could even the odds a little. I don't know what that means, but I do know he loved teaching us. I sure will miss that nickel he gave us for reading books he brought from his cabin. We had to give him a stand-up book report, and he'd say, "Well done."

We find out Doc Friedman isn't our doctor no more because he's done retired hisself. When the new doctor smiles at us, I can tell he doesn't mean it, and he's looking down his nose at us on account of we're sharecroppers and don't have enough money to shake a stick at. He feels around my stomach high and low and says I don't have appendix trouble, just a regular old stomachache. He charges Mama twenty-five cents and tells her to feed me overripe bananas for a few days to get me cured. I like that because we never get bananas except when Mama makes her special banana pies at Christmas time.

Me and Tommy are waiting in the wagon outside the mercantile store for Mama to buy bananas when Tommy comes off the buck seat with his fists all balled up like he was shot off a slingshot. It gives me a startle, that's for sure. I look around and see Squirrel Hobbs coming down the board sidewalk in front of the store. Tommy leaps on the sidewalk hunched over and his legs spread out like he's bow legged. "You ready?" he says through clenched teeth to the young man his same age, which is nineteen. They go to squaring off in a circle keeping their eyes dead on each other.

"You think you're man enough, Tommy Woodson? Come on!" Squirrel hollers, and they start scuffling and punching. I stand up in the wagon so's I can see better. First, my brother is on top of Squirrel. Then Squirrel throws him off, and he's got Tommy's shoulders pinned halfway on the sidewalk and half on the road. Tommy kicks a leg up and knocks Squirrel clean off him and into the road. He grabs one of

Squirrel's arms and bends it behind him, but Squirrel ducks down and throws Tommy against the side of the grocery store. Tommy wiggles out and they have each other in an arm lock. Folks are gathering to watch, and I'm mumbling, "Come on Tommy, you can take him," but I know he can't.

See, it doesn't matter if it's town, the feed store, school, or any place else… when those two see each other, they go to fighting. Thing is, neither one of them can best the other.

Mama comes out of the store and watches the last few throw downs. Both guys get up and stare each other down eye to eye for a spell. Just like that, they head off with big silly grins on their sweaty red faces. Tommy's smiling all over his face when he takes Mama's sack and puts it in the back of the wagon. His hair is ever which way, which he doesn't usually allow, and he's covered in bloody scratches on his face and arms. Mama's climbing into the wagon with a smile on her face too. I reckon she likes all that scuffling for some reason or the other.

Tommy glances over his shoulder before geeing up the horses. He whistles and says, "Gol-darn, would you look at that," and Mama and I look where he's looking. The fanciest car I ever could imagine stops right behind our wagon on account of folks are jabbering about the fight and not getting out of the street very fast.

I stare and stare at that car. It doesn't seem real with its smooshed-in nose and polished metal all over the place. I don't know how to describe what color it is—kind of gray and silver, and sparkling like a lake in the bright sun except for a ring of red-mud splatters around the bottom part.

A man wearing a white hat with a black band around the brim is driving, and I see another man in the backseat looking out the window. Another man's looking down, so I can't tell about him, but they look all dressed up like city folk. A gussied-up woman in a black hat with a stumpy brim and a white ball of fluff 'bout the size of a baby chicken on the back of it has her window rolled down and her arm leaning on the rolled down part. She's wearing lipstick redder than a rooster's comb. She smiles big at me, takes a draw off a stubby cigar, and blows two smoke rings right there in the air.

Soon's the folks get out of the way, the car gets down the road lickity-split like they're in a big hurry. The man who was looking down looks up as they pass the rear end of our wagon. I see he's got big round eyes as blue as larkspur and a face that says *don't cross me.*

Tommy drives the horses home at a pretty good clip and I think about the woman in the car. I ain't never seen a woman smoke a cigar or blow smoke circles before. None of us wears lipstick around these parts, especially red. I don't know what to think, and Mama doesn't say anything at all about it. Pretty soon I decide they must have been some of those high-falutin' oil folks from Tulsa or Oklahoma City. I ponder if poor Mr. MacGregor knew any fancy people like that when he was living in Bartlesville, and that makes me cry again.

What's War Up To?

Supper is waiting on us when we get home. Our biggest skillet on the back side of the cook stove is brimming with fried taters and onions. The pot of beans is already dumped in the gray crock bowl sitting on the table, and Jean is frying the last few Johnny cakes in sizzling bacon grease. Two bowls of lamb's quarter greens swimming in salt pork and black pepper are on each end of the table along with pitchers of cow milk. Mama's canned hot peppers and chow-chow are in the middle of the table with forks in the jars. A big pan of garden lettuce, wild onions, and radishes still wet from scrubbing the sand off them sits by Dad's plate. A paring knife handle is sticking out of the end of the pan.

"What in the merciful heavens happened to your face, Tommy?" Jean asks, looking up from her frying. Tommy just grins.

I say, "Squirrel."

"Oh," says everyone at the same time, and that's all that needs to be said about that.

Snipe says, "Jean said we couldn't eat till you got home. I'm so hungry I'm dying, and it's your fault, Biddy." From the faces looking at us, everybody is starved and about half-mad since we're so late eating supper. I shrug my shoulders 'cause, Lord knows, it ain't really my fault.

Mama tells me, "You can eat the taters and Johnny cakes, but don't eat any beans or greens just yet, Biddy." I don't get it, but then I remember how beans give everyone the gasses, so I nod okay at her. I don't want that stomachache to come back.

"Give her a dose of turpentine and sugar. That's all she needs," Dad says.

Mama doesn't answer him. She says to me, "I'll put your three bananas close to the stove tonight so's they'll be ready for you to eat by tomorrow." She lets out a big old tired sigh that lasts a long time. I reckon I'm a lot of trouble, or else she's worried about that money she spent in town for doctoring, anklets, and bananas. For sure, she needs some of Mr. Leroy's Herb Whiz we couldn't get her today on account of poor Mr. MacGregor.

War sneaks over to swipe a banana, but Mama pulls his arm away. "They're for Biddy's bellyache, Warren," she says, and he makes a nasty face at me behind her so's she doesn't see it. I grin at that boy like a barn cat with a mouse hanging from its teeth because I know what he's got coming when Jean gets ahold of him and his dirty neck and ears.

You should know our eating table about fills up the whole tiny kitchen, and we like it because this family loves eating about more than anything else. A long bench goes down the whole length of one side of the table, and the rest of the seats are cane-bottomed chairs set edge to edge around the other three sides. My dad grew up with the Indians in the Indian Territory, so he knows how to weave the cane-bottoms and fix them when they get holes.

Everyone sits down, and Jean starts the tater bowl on the end where Dad is. He looks around and takes two tablespoons of taters, a Johnny cake, a few radishes, onions, and a handful of red lettuce to rip up and drip bacon grease on to make wilted salad, and a dipper full of beans on top of everything but the salad. That's how it works. You figure out how many mouths are eating and take the right amount so's everyone can eat. If you don't respect that, you get sent from the table hungry. Usually, we have enough food to have a pinch of a second helping, but it has to be after everyone else has had their first go. When we have gravy, whoever calls dibs first on the gravy bowl gets to sop up the last of the gravy with bread.

Jay Bird takes two Johnny cakes all at once, and Dad mumbles, "Key-yoh," real low, but Jay Bird hears it for sure and puts one cake back. Dad's time with the Choctaws and Cheyennes taught him their ways and medicine, and even their dances. I don't know if he's speaking Indian with his strange words, but everyone pays attention to them.

We're all being quiet with our heads low till we get some food in our bellies except Mama asks who went down by the Groff place to gather the wild onions we're eating along with our wilted salad. Calvin raises his hand. That makes Sammy raise his too. I see Calvin look at me pitiful since I'm feeling so mournful about Mr. MacGregor. I know he took a table fork down there and pried those sweet-smelling onions out of the dirt just for me. That makes me want to blubber again so I squeeze my fists tight under the table. I'm not hungry no more, so I scrape the rest of my taters on Jay Bird's plate.

"Why'd somebody go and kill Mr. MacGregor, anyhow?" Sam asks.

"We ain't talking about that right now, Sam," Dad says. Everybody goes back to his own thinking and eating, and too soon, I'm washing those dadgummed dishes again. Jean edges me out of the dishwater, and law if Mama doesn't take a clean flour-sack towel out of the drawer and start drying the washed dishes. I wonder why she helps Jean but not me, and I reckon I might never know why. I don't pretend to understand growed-up women.

Grandma tries to help clear the table, but Jean pats her arm and says to go outside and enjoy the nice evening. Jean and Mama get to talking, and Jean scoots me out of the kitchen, too. I know they're still talking about Jack, Jean's no-good husband, but I don't care. They can talk about him till the cows come home if it gets me out of that dishpan.

I go sit on the porch with everyone else. It's still sort of cool at night, so I pull the shawl off Mama's chair and wrap it around Grandma Massy's shoulders. She reaches around and pats my hands. "Thank you, honey," she says.

The stars pop out clear and bright, and lightning bugs go to flashing down by the creek. I feel kind of good, even if it is the worse day of my life. I wish I knew more about what happens to a person after he dies, but I don't. If I did, I might not feel so bad about my teacher.

Dad pokes a big wad of Beechnut tobacco in his jaw. He's holding a Folgers coffee can for his tobacco-juice spitting. Lord help us if we ever hook a toe around that can and spill it when it's sitting on the floor. Usually, it happens when we're running somewhere we shouldn't be, like through the house or across the porch. Dad gets worked up real bad about it.

Tommy and Allen are rolling cigarettes from papers and little sacks of tobacco. They're snickering and punching each other. I listen in to Tommy telling Allen about his scrap with Squirrel and the fancy car we saw in town and the woman blowing smoke from a cigar. After that, they start yapping about the town dance coming when Nowata holds its Summer Festival. They lower their voices so's I can't hear, and ever once in a while, one of them laughs out loud.

Jay Bird and Snipe trot around catching lightning bugs and putting them in a jelly jar for Doodles. She's following them in zigzags giggling the whole time. War catches some of his own lightning bugs and squishes them between his fingers to make his fingers glow in the dark.

"Stop it, War," I say, but he ignores me. I think he's the meanest kid I ever heard tell of. Calvin's staying to hisself leaning against the side of the house looking at something in his hand. When I go by him, he stuffs it fast in his pocket. "What you got, Cal?" I ask.

"I don't know what you're talking about," he says, and goes on around to the back of the house. I don't follow him, but I think he's acting peculiar.

Jean swishes through the screen door to hang the dish rag and drying towel on nails nailed into the big tree by the porch, the one whose roots make half our concrete front porch lift up in the air. Dad stands up. "Time for bed," he says. Tommy and Allen stub their cigarettes out and everyone files in the house behind Dad. Morning milking starts around four o'clock, so my brothers don't squawk about the bed rule. Most the time, anyway.

I want to stay up longer because it's almost summer and not all dark yet, but I know better than to wag my tongue about it. Doodles runs up to me with her jar of lightning bugs flashing on and off, on and off, and I swear, she's cuter than a litter of new hound dogs. The twins pass by me mumbling to each other. I make out War saying, "… hang… neck… turn blue." Whatever that crazy kid is up to, it won't be good.

One more thing comes to me before I fall sleep on this day I'll never forget. I go to wondering why Mr. MacGregor said *the fortitude of the children at home and school is my greatest joy* about a hundred times since he came to the Armstrong school. Now, isn't that confusing, since when we asked about his own kids, he said his wife and his only girl were "passed away."

Now, he's dead, too, and I'll never get it why he said such a thing.

The Bloody Foot

"Hey-hoe. Hay-yah-gah. Hoe-hey," Dad calls through the house before light the next morning. It's what he says every morning since I can ever remember. It isn't so bad when it's summertime, but it's a sound I hate in the blue-cold winter.

Doodles is snuggled up against me on the thin mattress on the floor close to Grandma Massy's bed. When I hear the screen door slam two or three times, I know Tommy and Allen are headed out to the shed to milk the cows. "Moo," those cows grumble outside, asking my brothers to hurry since they're miserable with all that milk in their bags.

No school, so I go back to sleep. Bacon smell wakes me up, and I see Grandma sitting on the edge of the bed dressing into her rolled-up stockings and flowerdy dress. I throw on my overalls and splash water from the wash basin all over my face and dry it on the towel extra rough so Jean won't spy dirt on me. I sneak a peek at myself in the old broken mirror above the wash basin. I sure do need a new permanent because my hair's growing and going straight on the top about four inches worth.

They're the strangest things, those permanents. The first one I got was for delivering love letters from my oldest brother Carl to his sweetheart. He was home from the CCC camp in Pine Valley, and he flipped me a whole silver dollar to pay me for helping him. I was only ten, but I walked three miles to Alluwe all myself to get to the beauty shop. I had to sit there with a wooden stick and point to which metal curling rods were burning me so bad I thought my scalp would melt.

I still get a blister or two or three on my noggin when I get a permanent, and I hate that part. The beauty operator cools the hot spots down, and later my hair is all curly and I love that part.

War's been calling me Orphan Annie since I got my first permanent. I don't mind it because I saw that cartoon orphan in the funny papers once. She was okay except for her eyes. Somebody drawed them, but they forgot to put eyes in the circles. What I hate him to call me is Big Lips. I've taken him down many a time for that, but he never learns.

That's what all I'm thinking while I run fingers through my hair and watch Grandma put her special Bay Rum and glycerin hair dressing on her hair. She combs it through and pinches little pieces of hair with her thumb and finger to make curls along her forehead. She puts on the slat bonnet she wears all day every day, and now she's ready. I wouldn't guess she was blind if all I saw was her getting ready in the mornings.

"Take me to the outhouse, honey, so's I can get back and help with breakfast," she says in a gentle voice. Lord, that woman is the kindest thing on this earth. I take her arm and lead her down the narrow steps to the kitchen with Doodles trailing behind us. It's my job to take Grandma to the toilet when she visits, and I don't mind. She says I earned a prize for taking such good care of her, so she's looking to buy me a store-bought doll with eyes that shut and open back up like a real kid.

I know I'm too old for dolls now, but Doodles isn't. The only other doll I ever had was the one War threw in the fire when I got snake bit. He was so small, but he grinned about it after he did it. I watched it melt in the fire, and I cried so hard. That doll wasn't but a slip of a doll, no bigger than the front part of my arm way back then. She had painted-on eyes and brown skin, and I loved her as soon as Dad put her in my arms. He was torn up about me getting my skinny little leg fanged, so he got it for me in the dime store.

Anyways, how Grandma Massy saw that doll she wants to buy me is…oh swan, of course Grandma didn't see it because she's blind. *I* was the one seeing it in the Sears and Roebuck catalog we keep in the outhouse for wiping paper. She told me to thumb over to the doll part and see what I saw.

"What do you mean, Grandma?" I asked her.

"You pick out one you like, honey, and I'll get it for you. You're such a good girl, and you work so hard. Mind you, it has to cost under a dollar."

I didn't tell Grandma I was nigh to almost grown on account of she's so nice. I went ahead and picked one out for nine-five cents, but then something happened that still makes me so mad my ears burn. You'd think Grandma would be mad at War about it, but she isn't. Here's what he did. He sneaked around the back of the outhouse and listened to our talk about the ninety-five-cent doll she's going to buy me. Out of the blue, the outhouse starts shaking until I think we're going to fall over on our snouts, and Grandma nearly did with her bloomers down round her ankles.

I knew it was War. When I threw the door open, I saw

him and Snipe hightailing it and turning back laughing like creatures with no sense.

See there? Bet you'd cuss too with brothers like that.

Anyhow, I'm getting Grandma down the stairs, and Jean is putting two black skillets of biscuits in the oven. Mama's got some of her blackberry jelly and a pint jar of Dad's honey from his bees in the middle of the table which must be on account of Jean being here. Pitchers of cow milk sit on the ends of the table. A hill of bacon and sausage is staying warm on the back of the stove, and my stomach goes to growling like I never ate a morsel of food in my whole life. I get one of my bananas and break it in two to share with Doodles.

"What's got those dogs barking so early?" Mama says with another big sigh. "Bid, when you get back from the outhouse, you can make the gravy for us."

I don't know why everybody loves my milk gravy so much, but they do. I've been making it on top of the stove since I was so short I had to stand on a stool. Burned my belly and arms lots of times, but I still like to do it.

"I will," I say, guiding me and Grandma through the kitchen screen door and smack dab into the sheriff. I holler because it scares me, and Grandma lets out a little cry too. The sheriff backs up.

"Sorry to scare you, miss. Your pa around?"

I think to myself, *where else would he be with the sun barely up in the sky?* but I keep my tongue to myself. "He's over there," I say, pointing to the smokehouse where Dad's hammering a piece of wood to the backside of it and ignoring everything else.

I'm not liking the sheriff coming around because now he's reminded me again of Mr. MacGregor laying dead in the pump house. Back inside, I'm holding Doodles and about to sneak a piece of bacon for us when Allen pokes his head in from the front room and says, "Biddy-Kid, come outside a minute."

I hand Doodles over to Mama and stare at the platter of eggs, as many as three dozen shiny pale pink faces looking up at me. I cross the front room and crack open the screen door for a peek. There stands Calvin and Sammy and the sheriff on the porch. Dad and the older boys are standing a ways off by the walnut trees. Dad's arms are crossed over his chest. Everyone seems like they're staring at me because I'm standing part in and part out the door. My face goes to heating up, and I start reckoning on a dash to the woods. That's what happens to me sometimes when I feel like a sharecropper kid getting looked down on.

"Excuse me, miss. This'll just take a minute," says the sheriff, and I don't like it because I don't know him. I guess I'd still be standing there like Lot's wife turned to salt if Calvin hadn't motioned to me.

"Biddy," he whispers, "come on out here."

I come out twisting the straps of my overalls with both hands and stand by Calvin.

"Kids, I'm investigating the MacGregor murder. I need to find out exactly what you'uns saw yesterday at the Mercer Pump House. I believe Calvin to be a truthful young man, and he already told me how the body looked when he discovered it and how the wall was torn up on one end. Sammy gave me a few more facts, and I wrote them down. Your dad said you can talk to me too, so Rose… that's your name, isn't it?"

I nod.

"Tell me what you saw yesterday."

Lord, I don't like that man right now. He's a stranger and the law, and he's wearing those sunglasses so's I can't see his eyes. Now he's using my given name. I hear the quiet with everyone waiting for me to say something. I glance at Cal, and he kind of smiles on one side of his face, and Sammy, he doesn't know any better, he's grinning with those big happy cow eyes.

"I didn't see nothing," I say.

"What's that?" the sheriff says leaning down to me. Tears jump right into my eyes. Calvin tells him what I said. The sheriff doesn't say anything at all, and I take a step to go back in the house.

"Rose, did you go inside the pump house?" he asks me all of a sudden.

"No."

"Did you see any footprints in the dirt around the pump house?"

"I wasn't looking for no footprints."

"Did you see anything different about the pump house?"

I look at Calvin to save me, but he's shaking his head like to say go ahead and tell him. I say, "Just the door."

"The door?"

"It was off the hinges at the top, and it wasn't closed like regular, and that's all I saw."

"One more thing, Rose. I want you to look at something for me."

The sheriff takes a leather pouch with strings at the top out of his britches pocket and works his fingers in the top to loosen it up. He takes a long-nosed thing out of his other pocket. It reminds me of the pinchers Dad uses to pull the little pigs out that don't want to come into the world yet but have to or they'll make their mama die. The sheriff's pincher tool is so small it fits in his thumb and finger. He reaches down in the pouch with it and holds his hand there.

"You ever see blood before, Rose?" the sheriff asks, and I get cold chills up my back. The sheriff looks at my dad before he takes his hand out of the pouch. I look at Dad too and see his even-eyed gaze at the sheriff. Next thing I know, I'm looking at Mr. Leroy's special rabbit foot with the silver ring and chain on the end, and I want to throw up on account of the dried blood on it has to be poor Mr. MacGregor's blood.

CHAPTER Seven

Almost a Hanging

My eyes were stinging when the sheriff asked me who owned the rabbit foot, and I had to tell him it was Mr. Leroy's. Now I know he's going to blame that decent man, and it riles me like nobody's business. I know what that lawman is thinking, and he's as wrong as a corn worm in a turnip. Mr. Leroy wouldn't hurt nobody no how, and I know I have to do something—but what?

No way were all those boys going to see me bawling like a baby about it, so I took off quick as lightning. Now, here I am hiding behind the two stacked up rows of chicken nests in the chicken coop. It's a favorite hiding spot I've used since I was real little.

"You missed breakfast, so I brung you a biscuit with some smoky bacon in it," Sammy says. I don't answer, and he says, "Jean's heating some water."

I know that means she's going to scrub every neck and ear and face she says is dirty, and I have to see that for sure. I scoot out from behind the boxes and take the biscuit Sammy holds out to me. I'm hungry, so I gobble it up and wish I had another one. I take a deep breath, and it makes my chest shudder on account of I've been bawling so hard.

"Why you acting like this, Biddy? That old sheriff ain't going to put you in jail. He's just finding out who kilt Mr. MacGregor. Calvin says that rabbit foot is a big clue and probably Mr. Leroy did it."

"You shut your mouth, Sam. I mean it. Mr. Leroy wouldn't do any such thing."

"I'm just telling you what Calvin said." Sammy's bottom lip pooches out because I've hurt his feelings and I wish I hadn't talked so hateful to him.

"What makes your lips go plop, plop, plop?" I say, strumming his lower lip with my finger.

"Stop it," he says, giggling.

I don't know who made it up, but all of us do that silly thing when someone's pouting because they feel bad and we want to make them laugh it off. Sammy is smiling again, and I wonder who made the milk gravy for breakfast because it sure wasn't me.

"Well, if it ain't Orphan Annie with ugly eyes and a snotty nose," says War, who's sitting cross-legged on the kitchen floor with Calvin, Jay Bird, and Snipe. I shoot him a dirty look and I swear I'll pull his arms off if he messes with me today.

"That's very impolite, Warren," Jean says, not looking at him. "And don't say 'ain't'." She pours boiling water from the kettle into cool water already in the dish pan.

Sammy sits on the floor alongside Calvin. They're lined up for the scrubbing with no shirts on, except Calvin. He's dressed like usual. Mama's at the kitchen table dressing Doodles in a clean dress because she's already had a washing up and had her hair fixed. Doodles puts her arms out for me to take her. I sit down in a chair beside her so's I can watch everything. She crawls over to my lap and settles there.

Jean places a bar of lye soap beside some clean rags on the counter. "Biddy, you're doing really well not using the 'ain't' word all the time. Much less than before. I've been paying attention to it."

I want to say it was Mr. MacGregor who stirred me to talk better, but I don't.

War blows out an aggravated hunk of air and stands up.

"Sit down, Warren," Mama says with a finger pointed at him. Her voice is low, but it means she isn't fooling, neither.

"Who's first?" Jean asks.

The boys all point toward each other, and Cal says, "I'm not getting scrubbed because I cleaned my own self this morning, and I'm way too old anyways. I'm here to watch you take the skin off these three nincompoops." He points to the boys, and Sammy looks surprised at Calvin's words. War doubles up his fists and looks like he'd like to scuffle Calvin, but Calvin stands up tall and dares him with his eyes.

War sits back down and says, "Jay Bird's first."

Jay Bird goes to sniffling like he's not sure about what Jean's going to do to him. He's been scrubbed up before, but he acts like it's the first time every time. Right quick, Jean's running a soapy rag over Jay Bird's neck and face and digging in his ears with her finger stuck inside the rag. She wrenches out the rag and goes back over the spots. He hollers when she digs in his ears again, and she says, "You trying to grow corn in there, Jimmy?" Jay Bird smiles, probably on account of he's almost done, and maybe because Jean's kind of funny, too.

Snipe starts to cuss when Jean starts in and she slaps his lips right smart with her fingers. Not hard, but it makes his face and ears turn red because we're all watching. After that, he shuts up.

War tries to sneak out the door twice, but Mama gets a

switch and sets it on the table. That stops it. Sammy takes his turn like he does everything, with smiles and a good nature. I think he's got lots of our grandma's ways inside him.

"How come Biddy don't have to get her stupid self washed up?" War asks.

"Because she has the good sense to keep herself clean, young man," Jean says.

I'm feeling pretty proud about Jean's answer to War, but I don't like the look on his face when he walks up to Jean for his turn. His lips are tight, and the shine in his eyes sort of sets me to a chill. He does everything she says without talking, but he's acting strange. Takes the fun out of seeing it this time, no lie.

"Guess who's coming to see me, kids?" Jean said while she's doing the last rag-over on War. "Our cousin, Maggie. She's coming to spend the rest of the day."

"How do you know?" War asks in a mean voice.

"Because her brother, our cousin Henry, came this morning to borrow a saw from Dad. He was surprised to see me here, and he said he was going home and bring Maggie in the wagon to spend the day," Jean says.

Maggie is our cousin, and she and Jean are best friends. When the two of them are together, they shoo everyone away so they can talk private. Makes us feel left out, but I don't get mad about it the way the boys do. War looks over at Snipe and Sam and smiles like he knows something sneaky.

"Better get after those morning dishes, Biddy. It'll soon be time to start dinner. Jean's got some ideas for that," Mama says. She's putting on her bonnet to go work in the field with Dad. I squint my eyes till they're real little and press my lips together, but I don't let her see me do it.

I use the rest of the hot water in the kettle and put more

on the stove to heat up. Grandma says, "Put a clean towel in my hands, and I'll dry them for you, honey." Doodles gets her little play towel sewed from left-over quilt scraps and starts drying her old cup and some spoons I hand her.

Pretty soon, Henry and Maggie come in the wagon, and Jean runs out of the house squealing a little. Maggie and her dance around holding hands like kids on account of they haven't seen each other in so long. I peek through the screen on the kitchen window and see them head off arm in arm down the lane where the big shade trees are. I figure they have lots to talk about with Jack acting up like he's been doing.

I'm about done with the dishes when I hear a panther scream. No, it's a woman! I dash out the front room door and off the porch. Jean's underneath the big maple tree swatting hard at War, Snipe, and Sammy with the end of a rope. War and Snipe take off running and laughing out loud. She catches Sammy and drags him toward the house by the ear. Maggie's trotting alongside them with her hands on her hips and shaking her head real big. Her face is flushed, but not as red as Jean's. Maggie thinks our big family doesn't have a lick of sense anyhow. It's always been like that. I think she only likes Jean and would throw the rest of us out with the slop if she had to decide such a thing.

Sam's bawling something terrible and it's bothering my insides. "What did he do?" I yell over his noise and Jean's scoldings. I'm getting mad at my sister and know I shouldn't.

"What did he do? *What did he do*?" Jean hollers, getting louder and louder. She shakes a loop in the end of the rope in my direction, I know what it looks like, but it can't be true.

"This… is a noose. Those boys… tried to hang me, that's what!" Jean sputters. "And Sammy was the one who dropped the noose around my neck, isn't that right, young man?"

"Sammy?" I say, hardly believing my ears.

"I only did it because War told me I could have his pocket knife. I didn't think it would work, and Jean's feet stayed on the ground, anyhow. I'm sorry, sis, I won't help nobody hang you no more. I promise." Sammy's squalling so hard he falls face down in the dirt, but Jean says he has to get up and have a whooping.

She hauls him into the house. I stay outside on account of I don't like to see anybody get a whooping except for those two hell boys. Especially Sam. I run to the field and tell Mama about the hanging. She says, "Was Jean hurt?"

"I don't think so, but she's madder than spit, that's for true. She's whomping on Sammy right now. War and Snipe ran to the woods so they'll get what's coming to them later on."

Mama thinks about it for a minute, then just busts out laughing so hard she's wiping the tears off her face with her skirt tail. The men are gawking at her like she's lost her mind, but she keeps on cackling like a hen proud to lay a double-yolk egg.

"I'll go start dinner, Doobie," she says.

Both my Mama and Dad call each other *Doobie* and *Doob* and none of us knows why, but they do. Mama heads to the house with her shoulders shaking up and down, and I know I sure don't understand growed-up women. One thing I know, my mama needs that Herb Whiz right now today before she gets touched in the head and it doesn't go away and they take her to one of those crazy houses where you don't get to come back home.

I see Calvin's legs sticking out from the side of the smoke house when I get to the house. I want to ask him where he put Mama's money yesterday to buy the Whiz goop so I sneak up real quiet to scare him like he does to me all the time when he about scares me into wetting my britches. I stick my head around the corner, and before my *boo* has left my mouth, I see something shiny red and gold on the bottom of an upturned bucket. Calvin is pushing it around with his pointing finger real slow. He puts it to his mouth and licks it, then he rubs it on the bib of his overalls and sets it back down, shinier than ever.

"Where'd you get that, Calvin?" I say, never minding the scare I planned to give him. He jumps about a foot and crams that thing back in his pocket. He picks up an old dried corn-cob and throws it at me.

"Nothing! It ain't nothing, and you leave me alone."

He hightails it to the house, and leaves me wondering if my brother is getting touched in the head like Mama.

Poor Mr. Leroy

Sammy's in the hollowed-out part of the concrete underneath the front porch all balled up. I leave him alone because we don't like anyone bothering us after we've been in trouble. Jean's whoopings are about two or three licks. They aren't so bad, but it hurts our feelings something awful. I've never had one from her, and that isn't about to change.

Inside the house, Jean and Maggie are chattering upstairs. Grandma is in the front room singing Bible hymns she knows by heart. She finished the breakfast dishes for me, and I don't know how we got so lucky to have that good woman in our family. She's my dad's mama but not by blood. His mama died birthing him and his twin sister, Molly, and he got sent in a covered wagon to Indian Territory to live with his uncle and his wife. They raised him like their own, and now that uncle's wife is our Grandma Massy.

I go straight to Mama's milk and cream money jar, and sure enough, there's the wrinkled-up dollar bill Calvin had in his pocket yesterday. I look around feeling guilty, but I take the money anyways because it's for Mama to feel better. Besides, truth be told, I want to ask Mr. Leroy how his pretty rabbit foot got in that pump house.

I'm pushing through the kitchen door and I stop halfways out of it. Am I too scaredy-cat to go to Mr. Leroy's shack by myself after what happened to Mr. MacGregor? If I don't go our usual way, I can follow Hoot Creek to the old bridge and cut back in the woods to Mr. Leroy's shack. It'll take longer, but I won't have to see that pump house with its terrible secrets.

What about mad dogs? Sometimes they roam the roads around here and go into the trees to kill squirrels or rabbits. I'm awful fearful of those critters, that's for true. I ponder about asking Calvin to go with me, but I don't since he's been so hateful to me the last few days.

Something just raises up in my chest, and I know I'm going no matter if Calvin is being mean or if wild dogs or Wood Ghosts get me because Mama needs that Herb Whiz, and I got to tell Mr. Leroy about the sheriff toting around that rabbit foot covered in blood. I shoot off in my fastest run past the front porch and curve right so's I can take the old bridge into the woods.

In a short time, I find myself staring at the rope and plank bridge and wondering if it'll hold me. Underneath it, the creek is like a small river, kind of rough and swirly looking. I take a deep breath and run across it faster than an empty tire rolling down a hill. I skedaddle through those woods like I got wings on my feet. I hear my breath coming out ragged, and I'm running so hard when I get to Mr. Leroy's place, I forget to watch where I'm planting my feet. Dang if my toe doesn't stub out on one of those painted tractor tires full of flowers. Down I go. I'm just laying there in a pile trying to catch my breath when Mr. Leroy runs outside. I'm too wheezy and afraid from thinking about a murderer and all the scary things in the woods to say a word, so I hold my dollar bill out to him with my chest heaving up and down.

"Little Miz Woodson… Little Bit… law, you's so all tuckered out. Is something a chasing you, baby girl?" Kneeling on one knee beside me, Mr. Leroy's eyes roll huge in his face looking all around us into the woods.

"Herb Whiz… need some for Mama… please," I say, sticking the dollar bill in his hand. Mr. Leroy takes it and looks back and forth at the dollar and me. I sure don't know what's got into him, but he puts his head back and laughs a long, deep sound that echoes off the trees.

"I ain't never seen no one so eager for my tonic afore, chile. That's all right, yes sir, that's just dandy. You sure you's all right, honey?"

I nod my head and sit up. Mr. Leroy goes in his house that isn't much bigger than a cotton worker's shack and comes back out with a brown paper sack tucked under his arm. He's carrying a dipper in one hand and a peppermint stick 'bout the size of a first-grader's tablet pencil in the other. I start having a great interest in that candy now that the air is coming back in me.

Mr. Leroy brings the dipper close to my face. "Drink this water, Little Bit, and you's gonna feel revived. Here, look, I dipped you some water with a clean dipper. Go on now, drink it."

I do, and it sure tastes good and sweet.

"I puts your tonic and your coin change in my little gross store sack, and you can keep the sack. The good Lord gots you to ol' Leroy's place in one piece, didn't He? Now He's a telling me to give you this little sack and to be keeping you in my prayers. I do what He tells me, I shore nuff do. Pays to."

"Mr. Leroy, I need to tell you something. The sheriff

came to our house this morning and—"

Right then, Sheriff Murphy and two more men bounce right out of the thick trees. Scares me and Mr. Leroy so bad we grab each other's arms. The sheriff's hand is touching a gun strapped around his waist. Another man is holding a long shotgun down the side of his leg. The third man has something with round metal rings in his hands. Every one of them has on sunglasses and those ugly tan-colored clothes. The one with the metal rings has his britches tucked into the tops of cowboy boots with sharp toes.

Mr. Leroy's eyes are giant pools of brown and white and I see fear swimming all around in there. I get to my feet and take the little bag and peppermint stick from Mr. Leroy's outstretched hands.

"Mr. Leroy Abraham Jones?" says Sheriff Murphy.

"Yessir, that be me. Yes, 'tis, sheriff sir." Leroy says.

"Mr. Jones, I am taking you into custody regarding the murder of Scott Patrick MacGregor. You will submit yourself immediately to the authority of the State of Oklahoma, County of Nowata, and will hereafter be in the custody of myself and my deputies."

The man with the metal rings steps over quick-like and tells Mr. Leroy to put his hands behind his back. He snaps the rings on Mr. Leroy's wrists.

"Oh, Mr. Sheriff sir, what's that you be saying to me? Scottie… Mr. MacGregor is-is dead? Oh, my God in the Heavens, it can't be so!" Mr. Leroy's whole self starts shaking. Tears flow down his cheeks like a water fountain. He looks so pitiful I'm about to die of misery for him.

"Poor Scottie. What's to become…" more sobbing "… of the little one? Oh my Lordy-lord, who will look after…?" He turns his face to the sky and water seeps from his closed eyes in rivers.

The man who put the rings on Mr. Leroy's wrists says, "Shut up and set yourself down." And he's being rough. He pushes Mr. Leroy to the ground and steps right inside one of the pretty tires, squashing the moss roses with his cowboy boots. I know he did it on purpose, and I'm wishing I could fist his face.

"Hey, boss, who's the girl?" he asks, spitting tobacco juice right on Mr. Leroy's shoe.

"Sharecropper kid. I'll drop her home on my way back to town."

The sheriff bends down close to my face. "And what was your business here today, Miss Rose Woodson?"

Just from the way he said "sharecropper kid," I know he thinks he's high and mighty over our kind. I may be shaking scared and mad because of how they're treating poor Mr. Leroy, but I ain't letting that sheriff nor nobody else look down his nose at me. I raise myself up on tippy toes and look him in his sunglasses on account of I can't see his eyes. I say, "I'm doing something important for my mama, and I don't need you to help me get home or nothing else."

The man with the cowboy boots says, "Feisty little squirt, ain't she?"

I give him a squinty-eyed mean look and go stand beside Mr. Leroy.

"Do you have a daddy or mama for us to get word to about this, Mr. Leroy, because we'll do it for sure," I say.

Mr. Leroy looks at me so sweet, it's like he's got my Grandma Massy in his eyes. "Bless you, chile. My mama and daddy's long gone to Heaven, but wills you take my little bird with you till I be back home? Name's Charley, little Charley-Bird. He a good bird, full of sunshine and singing. Praises the

Lord hisself, that bird does. His seed's in a can right beside my flour can inside the house. It has a picher of a bird I pasted on it."

"Shut your mouth, boy!" yells the man in cowboy boots to Mr. Leroy. My fists ball up like when I'm ready to whoop the daylights out of someone—and I might be.

"Easy, Floyd," says the sheriff. He turns and looks at me. "See here, Miss Rose, my truck's parked right up yonder on Wayne's Road. I'll go inside and get the bird for you, but you're coming with me. I imagine your folks are getting worried about you."

The sheriff goes straight into Mr. Leroy's shack and comes back shortly carrying the first caged bird I ever laid my eyes on. The cage is so fancy of a little house I'm about to swoon. I can't believe there's ever been a bird so pretty—yellow as jonquil, the little thing is. Mr. Leroy's smile is sadder than drought. He nods his head, and I nod mine back, because I'm sure going to take good care of that bird for him.

"Where'd you get that from, you steal it?" growls Floyd.

"No, sir. No, sir, I promise you I didn't steal Charley-Bird nor his cage, neither."

"Why should I believe a stupid murderer? You believe him, sheriff?"

"He hasn't been charged yet, Floyd," the sheriff says, lighting up a cigarette he takes out of the package in his pocket.

Anyone can see Mr. Leroy is pained by the hateful words Floyd said. He bows his head clean onto his chest and says in a low voice without looking anywhere but the ground, "Mrs. Wright, that kindly woman, she gives it to me for making her my tonic, my Herb Whiz. She tells me it makes her feel so much better, I can have her Charley and his cage to keep as a prize. She up and went to England or someplace other, and she won't be back for a whole year. Yes, sir, that woman did such a nice thing for old Leroy."

Sheriff Murphy says, "You boys go through the cabin and report your findings to me. Especially look for weapons like I described to you earlier. Come along, Miss Woodson. We're taking the back way to Wayne's Road. Not so many trees."

He takes hold of Mr. Leroy's arm, and I hurry up to walk on the other side of Mr. Leroy. I look up at him while we walk, and I see he's weeping again but not making any noise. His face is crushed with sadness, and I think my heart will break for poor Mr. Leroy. I vow to help him, and nothing is going to stand in the way of it.

CHAPTER Nine

Cussing by Accident

Soon's we get to our yellow house, I jump out of the sheriff's truck with Charley-Bird. I never one time looked at the sheriff while we were driving. The dogs stop their barking and run up to sniff my legs. I kick at them so they don't get near Charley. Gander comes hissing up and stops. He works his head like a snake in the air and I make a loud *ssss* sound at him. I hold the ring at the top of the cage and walk to the outlaw cage on the back of the sheriff truck. It's filled up to the brim with Mr. Leroy since he's such a big man. I say, "Mr. Leroy, don't you worry about Charley. I swear I'll take good care of him till you come home, and I won't let him ever get away." I don't mean to start blubbering, but I do.

"Don't cry, Little Bit, and don't say you swear. It ain't proper. Soon's I get to make a call, I'm a calling my 'vangelist sister, Miz Abernathy. She'll pray me right out of that jail-house. Don't worry now. I'm innocent, and the Good Lord knows me real good."

The sheriff comes around the other side of his truck holding the can of bird seed and the brown sack with Mama's Herb Whiz. He touches my shoulder, and I shake his hand off and give him the meanest look I ever gave to anyone, even worse than the ones I give War and Snipe.

Mama, Jean, Allen, Calvin, Sammy, War, Snipe, Jay Bird, and Doodles, all get bug eyes seeing me walk beside the sheriff holding a rich woman's bird cage with a yellow bird inside it. Our cousin Maggie isn't there, so I'm figuring she got Tommy to take her home on account of my brothers trying to hang our sister and her thinking we're a pack of hillbillies or worse.

"Biddy, we were worried sick. Where you been?" says Mama. "You missed noon meal, and the boys were all set to take out looking for you in ever which direction." She's staring at me and the sheriff with a frown on her face. I put the cage down real careful on the plank that covers up the cistern and make sure the cage door latch is in place. I turn around and face the sheriff.

"Can I have my brown bag?" I say. Soon's he hands it to me, I give it to Mama. "I had to get you the Herb Whiz, Mama, so you don't feel worrisome or go crazy. You got change for your dollar in the bottom of the sack, but Mama, this… this…" I have to swallow because something's choking my throat, but I want to keep explaining. "This lawman's done arrested Mr. Leroy and he's got everything backasswards on account of he looks down on sharecroppers and Negroes, and that's the truth even if he won't own up to it!"

My hand flies to my mouth on account of I just cussed in front of my mama, and I didn't know I was going to. She can slap me if she wants, and I don't care. It was truth and needed to be told.

"You arrested Mr. Leroy?" Mama asks the sheriff in a voice that means she can't hardly believe it herself.

"It's because of the bloody rabbit's foot, Mama," Sammy busts out, and Calvin thumps him on the top of the head.

"Quiet, Sammy," Calvin says.

Sammy skitters away from him and keeps blabbing. "No, I ain't going to. Ain't no secret no more because he's done arrested Mr. Leroy. That rabbit foot belongs to Mr. Leroy, and it was in the pump house with dead Mr. MacGregor's blood all over it."

War all of a sudden pushes Snipe to the ground. "Shut up, Snipe," he growls, when Snipe wasn't even saying a blasted thing.

"Warren Earl Woodson! You give your brother a hand. What's wrong with you?" Mama says.

Warren puts a hand out to Snipe but he keeps staring at the sheriff like a tangle of snakes is crawling up his britches leg and it's somehow the sheriff's fault. He runs off and Snipe follows him around the side of the house. Mama calls after him to come back, but he doesn't do it. That's worse than anything except not telling the truth, so I know War's in for a whooping from Dad when he hears about it.

"Mrs. Woodson, your girl was at the home of Mr. Leroy Abraham Jones when me and my men went to arrest him. I suppose she has your permission to do so, but if I was you, I'd keep a closer eye on that young lady."

Mama draws herself up tall. "Well, last time I looked, you ain't me, so good day to you, sheriff." I feel like clapping on account of Mama's telling that man off in her own soft way.

The sheriff sets the bird seed can on the cistern by the cage. "Good day, ma'am," he says, and he looks at Jean and smiles. Who does he think he is, anyhow?

The truck drives away and we see Mr. Leroy crumpled up in the outlaw cage. It's the worst sight I ever saw, and Jay Bird, Doodles, and Sammy run after the truck waving at him. His face doesn't have a smile except a pretend one for the kids.

"What do you have here?" Jean asks, sitting down on the cistern planks. She puts her face close to the cage and makes smoochie sounds like she's calling the dogs.

"Mr. Leroy's bird, Charley. He's staying with us till Mr. Leroy gets out of the jailhouse." I'm watching Mama close to see if she's mad about me going to Mr. Leroy's place or about my cussing. She keeps watching after the sheriff's truck a long time with her lips clamped together tight. I go stand by her and look down Blackberry Road, the little dirt track that's barely a road coming up to the front and side of our house.

"They can't blame Mr. Leroy for killing Mr. MacGregor. He flat out didn't do it," I say.

"What makes you think so, sis?" Cal says. "They got evidence."

"Calvin William Woodson, you know the truth just as good as I do. Mr. Leroy wouldn't do no one harm, and besides, he didn't know Mr. MacGregor got hisself kilt till that lawman told him so. You should have seen him suffering about it. I thought he might die he was so sad. Seems to me, they were good friends, and friends like that don't kill each other."

"My, my, my," Mama says. "Biddy, watch Doodles."

Jean and her go in the house and food smells sift through the screen door when they open it. Calvin is all excited and walking back and forth. He says, "You saw them arrest Mr. Leroy? Who put on the handcuffs? How many coppers were there? Did they have their rods drawn?"

I don't feel like talking to Calvin on account of he's keeping a secret and being hateful about it too. Maybe I don't feel like talking to anyone with so many things worrying me. I grab the birdcage and Doodles' hand and go in the house.

"Bid?" says Calvin, and I ignore him.

CHAPTER *Ten*

What Mama Says

For supper, we eat leftover cooked greens with vinegar and onions on the top and cold cornbread crumbled in milk. When supper's over, Mama says she has to have a talk with me. I shrink down because I know I might get a switching for the cussing I did by the cistern. I don't believe my ears when she tells Calvin to get those boys in here to wash and dry the dishes on account of Jean has a headache and Biddy is coming to the cellar with her. I about clap my hands, but Mr. MacGregor being dead and Mr. Leroy getting hauled off to the Nowata jail means I don't feel like fun. Besides, I may be getting a whooping.

I take the last banana out of the sack on the stove and follow Mama into the cellar we call the gopher hole. The old bed squeaks when I settle on the edge. It's covered in patchwork quilts that Mama, Jean, and Ruby—my other older sister—sewed before they married and left home. Mama busies herself straightening up the gallon jugs we use to make cream into butter. I eat my banana slow to make it last and look at the dusty bottles of Dad's wild grape and blackberry wines, jugs of corn liquor, and row after row of Mama's canned fruit and vegetables bowing the wooden shelves along the wall.

Dad's best tools no body better bother without permission are hanging clean and shiny from the ceiling by short lengths of rope. That reminds me about War trying to hang Jean, and how somebody better do something about that kid before he hurts someone. Mama starts digging in the wooden box that holds crepe paper and wires she uses to make grave flowers for Decoration Day. She makes them every year and puts them in cut-off tin cans to send with her cousins up to Jay for her mama and daddy and baby twin brothers' graves. She makes more for family buried close enough to reach by wagon. My older brothers and her clean up the graves and leave cans of crepe paper flowers, and they get to eat fried chicken afterward for their trouble.

Who's going to put crepe flowers on Mr. MacGregor's grave?

"Your cousin Maggie brought us the mail today," Mama says, sitting down beside me. "I got a letter from my sister Josie's girl. You probably don't remember Evelyn. She lives in Siloam Springs out there in Arkansas. She wants to hire you for a month. Seems she's got her hands full. What you'll be doing is keeping house and tending to her baby boy. I think he's about a half-a-year old. She wants you to work in their concession stand on Lake Frances part of the day too."

"Hire *me?* What's a concession stand?"

"It's a little building, like a tiny shed, with a counter. People come up to it to buy cold sodas and beer. You take their money and give them coin change or dollars. The drinks will be iced down with a big block of ice every day."

"I ain't never done such a thing before," I whine, because I'm not liking what Mama's telling me. "Would I have to talk to anyone?"

"You ask them what they want to drink and make change for their money. You're good at your sums, so you won't have any trouble doing it."

"But—"

"You're leaving day after tomorrow. Jean's going to town tomorrow to call Evelyn and tell her you're coming. She'll call Jack to come pick her up, and they'll drive you out to Siloam Springs."

"I don't want to go, Mama! What about Doodles? She can't be without me that long."

"I'll take care of her. She'll be all right."

"But we don't like Jack no more since he's been rough-housing Jean."

"He isn't all bad. Jean ain't ready to leave him yet, so that's how it is."

"I don't have no shoes. My school shoes are too little for my big toe."

"Jean has a pair she thinks you'll about fit. We can put some catalog paper in the toes if need be."

I want to hit something or run away.

"We'll get you all fixed up tomorrow."

"What about Charley-Bird?"

"I think you might as well take him with you."

"And Grandma? I have to take her to the outhouse. You can't let those mean boys do it. It wouldn't be decent."

"I'll see to her. She leaves in a week to stay with her other boy a spell. She won't be back till fall. Biddy, Evelyn's giving you money enough for material for three dresses for school come the new term. Material's gone up to ten and fifteen cents a yard. This will help us out."

Maybe I've been dumb as a door knob, and maybe we do have hard times because Mama's saying I have to go to work now and earn wages for my own clothes.

"It'll do you good. You've been looking kind of peaked lately."

"I ain't peaked! I ran all the way to Mr. Leroy's house today without stopping, and I didn't go the short way, neither. I'm strong as an ox, too, just ask Calvin. I can lift twice what he lifts. Have you seen me hold War off at the end of my arm? He can't gain an inch. Besides, I'm supposed to go with you to fix the graves up. You promised."

"Bid, that's enough," and that's how Mama puts an end to my sassing. She looks at my downcast face and says, "I'll send the flowers I got ready with you and Jean and you can stop off in Jay and put them on Mama and Daddy and Little O's graves."

I'm so miserable, I just climb the steps and go to bed. I cry my head off, but it won't do me no good, and I know it. What Mama says goes, and that's that.

Now, who's going to help get Mr. Leroy free?

I thought the only pretty houses were in catalogs till I saw my cousin Evelyn's house in Siloam Springs. Me and Jean are standing in her front room and my eyes are rolling around my head looking at all the finery around me. There's a flowerdy divan with a matching chair just like it in the same material, two tables on the sides of the divan with real lamps—not coal oil lamps or lanterns—and a long table setting low in front of the couch. A hooked rug with flower designs sits in the middle of the floor for the furniture to set on, and the curtains on the window reach clear down to the floor. There's not a bed in sight, neither, and I figure they must be down the hall or up the stairs. I wonder where I'll sleep, and I'm feeling pretty scared being with strangers so far from home, especially rich ones.

Evelyn herself has wavy brown hair cut off above her shoulders. A piece of it keeps dropping over one of her eyes and she pushes it away with a soft, white hand with clean fingernails. Her green eyes are pretty, and she's smiling a lot. I guess we met before, but I don't remember. She looks about the age of Jean, which is twenty-one, and she's dressed nice like a town woman who never gets dirty.

I don't know why Charley-Bird picks that time to start up singing to the high heavens, but he does. Probably because he's so glad to be out of Jack's noisy old car. Took us all day to get here from Jean's little rent house in Vinita, what with stopping to put the crepe-paper flowers on the graves in Jay and all. One thing I know—I don't like being around Jack no more since he's mean to Jean.

"Goodness, what a beautiful canary," Evelyn says, bending down to look at Charley in his cage "I'm glad you brought it, Rose. Boy or girl?"

"His name's Charley," Jean says for me.

"He'll brighten up the place, and what a lovely sound. Say, they call you something besides Rose, don't they?" She's talking to me, and I can't find my tongue.

"When she was little, Mom called her Biddy, after her little biddy chickens, and it just stuck," Jean says kind of laughing along with Evelyn. I don't like them talking about me like I'm not here, but truth is, it keeps me from having to say anything. Besides, ever soul knows a biddy is a baby chick, so why explain anything at all about it?

Jean tells Evelyn how Mama appreciates this opportunity for me, and how much I help out at home. My sister graduated high school after she got married, so she talks more uppity than the rest of us. Her pink and white starched dress and oxford shoes and snow-white anklets make me feel dumb standing beside her. My last-year's dress is so tight across the top and in the sleeves, I can't hardly breathe. My hair is drooping in my eyes on account of I need a permanent. I blow it away, but it comes right back. I'm wearing a pair of Jean's cast-off flat shoes, and they're nicer than I ever had before. Mama crumpled up two Sears and Roebuck catalog pages and put one in each toe. Now they fit fine.

Evelyn says for us to go in her front room and sit a few minutes. They jabber away, but I keep staring at Evelyn's house and thinking about how sharecropping families like us live in whatever shack the land owner allows us to live in. Dad gives the owner half of what he harvests and sometimes clears the land in the first place by cutting down trees and making the horses pull out the stumps and big rocks. Us kids pick up the smaller rocks till our backs near break in two.

That's how it is. Some of the old houses we've lived in are so small, they're just a tiny room for cooking and eating and the rest is mattresses and beds end to end. Something we do is name any kind of road that leads to the house *Blackberry Road.* Mama says it makes everywhere *our* home. She says it means every road can be sweet even if it has some thorns. I reckon that's so, and we like doing it.

One time, we lived in an abandoned pump house with no motors inside, and it was the biggest place we ever stayed in. Like most of the other pump houses, the outside was tin. The windows were holes open to the weather, so Mama taped and nailed cloth, cardboard, and wood over them. Someone had already glued newspaper to the inside walls to make them warmer in the cold winter, and we did that sometimes, too.

That place was downright ugly, but it was what we had. The yellow house we live in now is nicer than any other we've been in, but don't compare it to Evelyn's house because you can't. I guess we been there starting on three years, and that's a long time for sharecropper families to squat.

That gets my mind to wondering if Evelyn thinks I'm like one of our distant hillbilly relatives we don't talk about—the ones living in the mountains who shoot at strangers before they even know who's trying to come visit them or why they're coming. Mama's not proud of those relatives, that's for true. Thinking I might look that poorly knots up my stomach and makes me want to jump in a salt barrel and never come out.

CHAPTER Eleven

Stubborn Ain't Bad

One thing you might have figured out about me is I'm stubborn. When I make up my mind one way, it's hard to talk me into some other way. Mr. MacGregor used to tell me I was strong-willed from living with all those boys and having such a hard life. I guess I didn't know about our hard lives since we always have something to eat, and Mama makes sure we each have a pair of new shoes from Sears and Roebuck every term before school starts.

She won't let us go around with rips in our clothes or buttons missing neither like some of the other sharecropper and farmer kids do. I'm thinking we might have that hard life Mr. MacGregor mentioned because look at me working to pay for the material for my new dresses for the next school term. Still yet, it's easy working in a pretty house.

But about that stubborn streak I have, I didn't know it was so powerful till one afternoon after I'd been working for Evelyn for three weeks. Things were going all right, and I didn't hate it so much as I figured I would. Fact is, I kind of enjoyed myself, even if I did miss Doodles and going to Hoot Creek with Calvin and Sammy. Shoot, the fact is, I missed the whole d—, I mean dadburned bunch of them, but I wouldn't say it if they asked.

At night, when I was all tucked into a bed on a mattress firmer than feathers but just as soft, I thought about Mr. Leroy. I wondered if his sister Miz Abernathy came to get him out of the jailhouse and take care of things like he said she would. Who killed Mr. MacGregor anyhow? My head would get to spinning pondering all that and then I'd fall asleep.

Here's how it works in Siloam Springs. Evelyn and Tony—that's Evelyn's husband—get up and eat their breakfast before going to the clubhouse to rent out boats and sell soda pop and beer to folks enjoying Lake Frances. While they're gone, I clean the whole house, wash up their six-month-old baby named Joey, and cook dinner—which they call *lunch* here at Evelyn's house.

When I have the noon meal cooked, I take Joey down to the docks to meet up with Evelyn and Tony. I give Joey over to Evelyn and she takes him back home while they eat their lunch and rest up for the afternoon. I sell beer and soda pop to whoever rich folk wants it, but I don't rent boats to no one. It was terrible hard to talk to strangers at first, but I sort of got used to it after a few days. I didn't get a choice in it, so I had to forget myself and do it anyways.

When Evelyn and Tony are through with their resting, they come down to the docks and give Joey back to me. I take him home and clean up the lunch mess and play with Joey before he sleeps again. I start supper and finish it, or Evelyn does, and I do the supper dishes.

Those dishes don't amount to piddly with just the three of us eating, so I don't mind it, especially since she doesn't use lye soap to wash her dishes. Evelyn uses soap flakes from a box in a real sink with faucets that bring the water inside the house. One of the dangedest things I ever saw is a scratchy pad with soap already in it. I didn't know what it was sitting there by the sink in a little bowl till Evelyn showed me about it. You don't use it on your iron skillets, but it sure makes fast work of scrubbing pots and pans. Evelyn calls them S.O.S. pads, and I wish we could afford such rich things at our house. Especially those nice soap flakes that don't eat up my hands.

It's easy work, and Evelyn is as nice as fresh jam, so I'm sorry something happened like it did, but it did, and it ain't my fault. I'm going to tell you about it, and you'll see how I found out my stubborn streak is as big as Oklahoma and maybe bigger, and why I'm sitting in Evelyn's fancy front room with Charley beside me in his cage. My bag is packed with my nightgown and my overalls and shirts inside, and I'm waiting for Jean and Jack to pick me up a week earlier than they were supposed to.

I won't keep you waiting, because here's what happened. Tony's parents, Mr. and Mrs. Borino, come down from Tulsa to watch someone's house for two months while the owners went gallivanting off somewhere because those house owners, of course, are rich. The house the Borino's are watching out for is across the lake, and they get paid for taking care of it.

Mrs. Borino kept to herself, but Mr. Borino hisself came to see us every day. He was real nice and talked to me while I cleaned and cooked and took care of Joey. He followed me around the house and watched most everything I did, if it was making beds or cooking or sweeping the floor. I didn't mind, but sometimes I wished he'd go help Evelyn and Tony rent boats or sell cold drinks. Seems like every turn, there was Mr. Borino grinning at me and asking me questions about how I did things.

One day, Evelyn says she needs some sugar to bake a pie

for supper and she says Mr. Borino said he'd take me for my first boat ride across the lake to borrow sugar from Mrs. Borino in that house she's watching. Mr. Borino seemed happy to help me go borrow that sugar for Evelyn, so we go to the dock and get us a rowboat and start across the lake.

I'm looking all around at the scissortails flying over the high bluffs outlining the lake and cupping my hand in the water while we row through it. I haven't never been in a boat before, and I'm liking it for sure. I can't wait to tell Calvin and Sammy what I did when I get home. I lean over and see shiny fish swimming away so fast on account of they're scared of our boat.

Somewhere in the middle of the lake we stop. I look over at Mr. Borino to see what's the reason. His hands are still on the oars locked into the sides of the boat and his eyes are shining bright over a crooked smile.

"You don't think I can go fishing, do you? I have to get back and take care of Joey for Evelyn," I tell him in case he forgot.

Mr. Borino doesn't answer me, just comes and sits down beside me on the wood seat. In a little bit, he says, "Hey, honey, you're a mighty fine gal. Pretty, too."

His words make me feel uneasy. I lean away, but before I know it, he's got his hands around my waist pulling me over on his lap. I try to get up, but he goes to slipping his hands everywhere they don't belong, even across my privates. I ain't going to lie, I've never been so upset in all my borned days. I don't know what gets wrong with his face, but he doesn't even look like the same Mr. Borino no more.

Even when I start cussing every bad word I ever heard in my life at him, he keeps smiling like he's gone dumb in the head. I scream at him to stop it, but he doesn't stop, and he tries to unhook my overall straps. I know then and there I'm going to have to jump in the lake to get away. Trouble is, I don't know how to swim.

Out of nowhere, my stubborn streak tells me that man ain't going to gain an inch on me, no sir. I get so mad my head feels dizzy. My face burns hotter than Mama's home-canned peppers. My fists start aching to bloody Mr. Borino's face.

I charge him like our goat rams his head into the side of the shed. I'm beating and kicking him everywhere I can land a fist or leg, and I'm aiming to kick his privates like my brothers taught me to do in a dangerous time, but he dodges my knee or foot every time. I'm screaming at the same time, and you can bet I'm calling him some doozy names. He's shielding himself from my fists and making squeaky noises when he slithers away quick to where the oars are. It reminds me of one of those blue racer snakes that go sideways so fast they look blurry.

"Okay, okay. Take it easy, Biddy," he mumbles, and I go ahead and tilt my head up and scream some more to the high heavens. Another boat is in earshot now, and they shout over if everything is all right or not. I stand there in the boat with my fists in knots and my chest going up and down on account of I'm still so terrible mad at Mr. Borino.

Mr. Borino waves at them and hollers out everything is fine. He takes hold of the oars and rows us away from the other boat lickity-split. "Sit down, Biddy," he says but I don't. I ride the rest of the way standing up giving him the dirtiest look in creation. I know better than to take my eye off a snake, and Mr. Borino is a poison one for dadgum sure.

"I'll wait right here for you while you get the sugar from my lovely wife," he says all nice like. "Then I'll take you back to Evelyn's, honey. I won't bother you anymore. No need to get into a fit about it. This can be our little secret, okay?"

I can't even look at him because I hate him so bad.

Let me tell you, I jumped out of that boat and ran to borrow the sugar from Mrs. Borino like ghosts were after me. I was too ashamed to tell her how the man she's married to ought to be burning in hell. Wild horses couldn't make me go back to that boat, so I ran all the way around the end of the lake over the high bluffs on sharp rocks and never stopped until I was back to Evelyn's house.

I gave her the sack of sugar and stood there trying to catch my breath and looking at her before I ran outside behind the house to have me a big bawl-baby fit. No one ever treated me like Mr. Borino did. Well, except at that carnival when Mama and I were standing in a bunch of people and a big ol' man backed up to me and tried to feel my chest and everywhere else. Mama and I both hammered his back and hollered at the top of our lungs at him. He took off running, too. My older brothers tried to track him down and beat him half to death, but they couldn't find him.

Now, here was something even worse.

I felt ashamed of myself and I didn't know why. I was laying flat on my belly crying into my arms when Evelyn showed up. I didn't want to tell her what went on in that boat, but she was so sweet to me that I blurted it out. She sat down beside me and cried as hard as I ever did. I got the feeling she'd been carrying Mr. Borino high, but now she never would again. She told me she was desperately sorry and that she'd call Jean as soon as she went in the house, and she did.

After that, she doctored my feet on account of they were bleeding from the sharp rocks I ran across to get to her house. She told me to go pack my clothes, which didn't amount to much of anything, and to wait in the front room. All the while she was talking, she was sniffling and patting my shoulder off and on. She gave me a big square of yellow cake to eat, but I wasn't hungry. I wrapped it up in a piece of wax paper to take home to Doodles.

Now you know why I'm sitting in this fancy front room with Charley Bird and my little wad of clothes waiting for Jean and Jack to pick me up a week early. I'm having a talk with myself right now, and it's sounding like this:

You ain't never going to be ashamed again for what that damned man tried to do to you. Mr. MacGregor was right—you're strong-willed, and you mean to stay that way.

"That's right," I say out loud and feeling kind of growed up since I didn't let that man gain nothing on me. Jean comes, and I'm sitting here smiling and ready to go home. I know Evelyn told her about Mr. Borino, so she probably thinks she'll find me bawling my head off.

Nope.

Because I'm stubborn, and I guess that ain't bad.

Guess What Else?

Sammy and Jay Bird are grinning like cats in cream in the back of the wagon parked by the filling station when you first come into Nowata. Allen's handling the buckboard this time and I'm thinking maybe it's because Mama doesn't want Tommy having it out with Squirrel again.

Jean's already told me this morning that Jack was driving me as far as Nowata. I know he doesn't want to face our family on account of his drinking and everything. I'm still not talking to him. Shoot, I'm not even looking at him. I spent the night at Jean's house in Vinita, and I stayed right next to her about every minute except when I was sleeping.

"Biddy!" Sammy yells when I step out of the back of Jack's old car. Jay Bird looks down, then up, then down because he's shy like that. Allen smiles his regular smile, and I like to see it. I'm feeling the strangest thing about my family. I haven't never been away before, and I sure am glad to see them. I ruffle Jay Bird's hair and smile at my other two brothers while Jean tells them howdy and sits Charley's cage in the back of the wagon. She covers it with the flour-sack towel Mama gave me to use before I left.

Jack gets out and leans against his car door. Jean looks like she's about to cry, and that gets me all worked up. "Hey, Bood," she says in a low voice, just to me. *Bood* is what she and Mama and Ruby call me sometimes. "Here's the money for your work at Evelyn's. She put in a little extra over and above your dress material. She wants you to have a new pair of shoes and maybe something else nice this summer."

Jean hands me an envelope bent in two and rubber-banded on the outside. She moves a piece of hair away from my eye. "You did really well handling that despicable man like you did. Don't let that old codger get under your skin, okay?"

I nod.

"I'm proud of you."

She turns away, and I swear she's bawling. She waves at us over her shoulder and gets in the car. Jack, who hasn't said a blessed word to none of us, looks at us squinty-eyed like the sun's in his eyes, but it isn't. He draws on his smoked-down cigarette and tosses the butt in the road. He nods at Allen and gets in the car. Watching that car go down the road gives me the most lonesome feeling. I climb up on the front buckboard seat holding my envelope tight in my hands. Allen flicks the reins.

"Giddup, you hosses," he says.

I turn to check on Charley. "Jay Bird, you hold that towel over Charley's cage for me, will you?" He puts his arm over the towel and goes to smiling to have a job so big as keeping Charley safe.

"Guess what, Biddy? Mama didn't have to take the wagon to the graves today. She rode in Ed's boss's car. She said she'd be back for supper, but did you hear about those outlaws getting all shot up and kilt in Luzianna?" Sammy says.

"What're you talking about?" I say, but I'm still watching

the car carrying Jean away from us. I'm feeling powerful low about her somehow.

Allen says, "Bonnie and Clyde. Bank robbers. The Texas Rangers and the Louisiana sheriff got them. Good thing, since they been robbing banks all over the country."

I ain't never heard of any Bonnie and Clyde, so I say, "Well, whoever cares about that? Oklahoma's been eat up with robbers robbing banks since I can remember."

Allen says. "Sure, Biddy-Kid, but this is big stuff. It's all over the radio, and everyone's talking about it. They got shot up like nobody's business. They say some of those gang guys are still on the loose, but they got the big'uns."

"Yeah, and Calvin and I been acting like we're them getting kilt. He makes me play like I'm Bonnie during the shootout, so don't tell War and Snipe." Sammy looks at Jay Bird. "You don't say nothing, neither, or I'll give you an arm burn, you hear?" Jay Bird shrinks down. Sammy pats Jay Bird's head.

"Where's Calvin?" I ask.

"He's in trouble. He couldn't come to town with us."

"Cal in trouble? Why's that?"

"On account of what he did to Necky."

"Necky?"

"A new kid that wants to hang out with us and be part of our gang."

Our gang is Calvin, Sammy, and me, and sometimes the two Bower boys from across the field. A new kid might join us until his folks move or they get tired of Calvin's tricks. Calvin thinks up names for new kids like *Squirt*, *Snaggle Tooth, Bug Eyes*, *Hoppin' Joe*, and now *Necky*.

"What happened?" I ask, scared to find out on account of Calvin's too smart for the rest of us, and sometimes he comes up with flat-out scary ideas.

"He told Necky if he wanted to be part of us, he had to prove he was worfy."

"*Worthy*, Sam," Allen says.

"Yeah, worthy, so he says Necky has to have good aim. He tells him to sit on one of them capped off oil-well pipes and do his business. Necky said that wasn't hard, so he dropped his britches and sat on the pipe. Calvin lit a match behind Necky, but Necky didn't see him do it. Pretty soon the fumes got to smelling that match and BOOM! Necky flew off the pipe about four feet in the air. His behind got burned and it made a red ring on it about the size of the pipe."

Allen is giggling, but I'm not.

"Biddy, listen to this," Sammy says. "Necky still wanted to be part of our gang, so next up, Calvin tells him to get in the well bucket at the old Groff place. He said Necky can't be afraid of spiders or the dark. Necky said, shoot, he ain't afraid of no spiders nor nothing else. Calvin puts Necky in the well about eight feet and ties the rope off.

"Calvin says to me, we're leaving, and we ran home. I don't know how Necky got out of that well, but he did. Pretty soon, here he comes to the house with his dad. Oh, law, his dad was mad! Calvin had to own up, and Necky puts his hand out and says he still wants to be friends. Calvin shakes his hand, but he's in trouble because you can see it on Mama's face.

"Soon's Necky and his dad are out of sight, Mama goes to hollering at Calvin and almost got a switch after him, but she didn't, since it's Calvin and… well… his leg, and everything. He ran off to the woods and didn't come home till dark. He didn't eat no supper, neither. That was yesterday, and that's why he can't come to town."

"I'm ashamed for both of you," I say, and I am. I hate it when my brothers are mean, and Calvin especially, since he knows better. "That isn't right, Sammy."

"I know. I'm feeling kind of poorly about it. Leastways, Calvin ain't hisself since he found Mr. MacGregor dead in the pump house, and he's hiding something, too. I see him hurry up and hide it, and he gets mad at me if I get anywheres close when he's looking at it.

"And guess what else? Everybody says Mr. Leroy shorely kilt Mr. MacGregor because they ain't got no more proof besides that bloody rabbit foot. Supposed to have a… a…"

"A trial," Allen says.

"Yeah, that's it. A trial. Soon's the circle judge gets here."

"The circle judge?"

"Circuit judge," Allen says.

"Guess what else, sis—"

"Hush, Sammy. I don't want to talk no more."

We're about halfways home by now, and my head is swimming with Sammy's talking. I didn't think about Mr. MacGregor so much when I was in Arkansas, but now I am, and it's giving me a bad feeling. Throwing poor Mr. Leroy in that jail and accusing him of what he didn't do urges me like I ought to do something about it. I make a plan to do some hard thinking tonight when I'm laying in the bed and looking at the stars outside the window.

The Secret Thing

A big black cloud coming over us says we're about to get a drenching. Allen hurries the horses along, and I'm glad when I see our yellow house in front of us. Rain starts spitting just when we climb out of the wagon.

Charley Bird is happy to be back upstairs in my little bedroom I share with Doodles, Grandma, and who knows who else if they need it. I know he likes it because soon's I take the towel off, he flaps his wings till feathers and dust fly around his cage. Durn if he doesn't look like he's smiling! I bring a dipper with a little bit of water and fill up his tiny catch-all. It only holds a dribble, like about four thimbles full. Charley gets hisself a drink, then goes to singing to the top of his voice. Doodles's eyes light up like a lantern. I give her the hunk of yellow cake I saved for her so's she can eat it and watch Charley at the same time.

The little bedroom seems quiet without Grandma Massy and her things in it. Doodles and I get the bed till she comes back unless company comes. I'm feeling good about coming home, and everyone was smiling at me when I got here. Except War. He was off somewhere or other, but Snipe was hanging around the house. Calvin looked like he was near to crying to see me, and he's got some secrets, that's for sure. I see it in his eyes. Eyes give away anybody's secrets.

Mama left orders for me to start supper early, and I wonder how she knew I was coming home a week early. It's raining cats and dogs now, but Dad's had the boys gather some cabbage, peppers, and squash from Mama's garden on the backside of the house before I got home. I get busy frying up cabbage and onions in bacon grease with just the tip of one of Mama's ungodly hot peppers in it. I boil up a mess of crookneck squash in salted water with some of the green onion stems and wash the lettuce and radishes for wilted salad. I have the cornbread almost mixed up and the grease sizzling and ready to go in the big iron skillet when the dogs and geese make a racket. I can't look out on account of all the pots and pans I have working on the stove.

Mama and Ruby come busting through the kitchen door sharing a sweater over their heads to keep the rain off their heads. "Hey, sister!" my oldest sister hollers, and Mama smiles at me, too. We all stare and grin a little bit, which is our way of saying we missed each other. Ruby says, "I'll wash up and set the table."

"Mama, how'd you know I was coming home?"

"Jean telephoned Ed's boss at the pump house company and he told Ed and he told Ruby and she told me when they got here. We got finished at the graveyard early so we could be home in time for supper. They're spending the night with us, so you and Doodles come down and sleep across the end of my bed with a quilt."

I don't mind getting run out of the bedroom upstairs because I haven't seen Ruby in so long. She's not as strict as Jean, and she always jumps in to help every living soul. About then, Ed comes in with rain all over his brown felt hat.

"Ed, drain your hat brim back outside the door," Ruby says, and she goes to wiping the dust off a quart jar of pickled beets Mama already had on the table. "Here, open this for me," she says, handing the jar to Ed when he finishes shaking his hat out the kitchen door.

Supper's kind of quiet at first because we're so hungry, then Dad says, "If it ain't raining, somebody better go pick some of those dewberries by the Y-spring tomorrow."

"This early, Doobie?" Mama asks.

"Blackberries are still green, but some of the dewberries are coming on right now. Birds will get them if we don't. Saw them yesterday when I went to check on the spring. Probably a big enough mess there to make a good-size cobbler." A big old grin goes around the table with us thinking of a first-out dewberry cobbler.

"Warren, you ain't been up at the spring bothering those berries, have you?" Dad asks.

War shakes his head. I figure he learned his lesson from that whooping he got last summer for eating most of the first ripe ones and stomping on some of the ground vines just to be ornery. Truth is, he didn't cry during that licking, and it made me bawl because it was a tough one. Dad is serious about food for his family, and War shouldn't have done what he did. Still yet, I cried for that no-good brother of mine.

"Biddy and I can go pick them first thing in the morning," Ruby says. She eyes Ed. "Oh, stop worrying. It won't take long. We can head back right after."

"Allen, I need you to bring the mules in from the pasture tomorrow morning. Mr. Gottschalks sent word he might be interested in buying one or two," Dad said.

Allen nods, and Tommy thumps him on the head.

"What's that for?" Allen asks, but he's smiling on account of Allen and Tommy tease each other all the time.

"Just reminding you to hurry up and get back to the fields when you finish your woman's chores in the morning. Me and Dad can't do all the men's work around here, you know." Allen puts his hands around Tommy's head and pretends to squeeze it hard. Tommy bugs his eyes out like he's dying and all the kids laugh because we like to see them acting up.

We dang near eat ourselves sick lapping all that supper up, and Ruby tells me I sure am a good cook. I feel awful good hearing that. Mama never tells me that kind of thing. Ruby helps me with the dishes after supper, and then I don't do any thinking about poor Mr. Leroy's situation because Doodles and I fall asleep across the end of Mama's bed as soon as our heads hit the pillows.

Next morning, it isn't raining, and I'm hanging around the bottom of the stairs and waiting for Ruby with two pans. I hear her moving around in the bedroom upstairs, and my mouth is watering thinking of dewberries hanging dark on the vine.

"Biddy?"

I turn around and Calvin is there with his hands in his pockets. "Guess you heard about Mr. Leroy getting charged with Mr. MacGregor's murder, right?"

I nod and feel my lips getting tight.

"I think I best talk to the sheriff," Calvin says.

"Why?"

"Because I got something… something I reckon he ought to see."

I know Calvin's talking about that secret thing he's been hiding every time Sammy and I come around. Thoughts fill my head like maybe it's Calvin's fault Mr. Leroy is in jail, and

Calvin is too big for his britches, and all sorts of mad-at-Calvin things swirling around in there. Ruby comes down the stairs and stands looking at us.

"Well, look who's up bright and early and not even a smile for the new day. Morning, you two. Let's get a leg on, Bood. I got to hurry before Ed gets out of sorts. He frets all the time, you know. Just his nature. Let's go to the shed and douse our legs and arms with coal oil. Can't let those chiggers eat us entirely to death."

Ruby starts outside, and I stare at Calvin. His eyes are making me promise not to say one word to Ruby about what he just said, and I have a mind to scream it out at the top of my lungs. My heart is banging hard in my chest while I follow Ruby out the door looking back over my shoulder at Calvin.

A Kick in the Head

Ruby and I follow our Blackberry Road that starts by the house and is mainly dust and ruts to the real gravel road just as the sun is poking its head up over the treetops. The rain we had the night before makes the tree leaves look greener than green ought to look. The birds are flying here and everywhere making so much racket, it's downright noisy. Squirrels race up tree trunks swishing their tails. They know for a fact we don't have any dogs to chase them or boys to slingshot them. And rabbits? We must have seen about a dozen of them hopping all over the place and none of them in any hurry. The world is so full of itself this morning, it'd bust its buttons if it had any.

If Ruby hadn't been talking me to death, I might have worried about picking dewberries because the truth is, the Y-spring is just a bit of woods and a hill or two from Mr. MacGregor's cabin. I keep answering her questions about Grandma Massy and Doodles and the rain we've been having. All the while I'm thinking in the back of my mind that Ruby is steering me away from talking about anything about the murder, but I can't put my whole mind to it because I'm concentrating on not thinking about Mr. MacGregor or Calvin's secret.

We go off the road, cross a ditch, and walk over a few hills. We come to the thickets at the Y where Hoot Creek and Sweet Creek join up. The cold-water spring bubbles up from the ground there and feeds the two creeks. Then it becomes a bigger creek people around here call Dub Creek. Ruby and I fill our empty pans with some of that cold water from the spring and slurp our heads off. It's good drinking, let me tell you.

"You hear that?" I say as we're walking out of the thicket. Ruby stops to listen.

"No. What did you hear?"

"It sounded like a whistle that wasn't a bird."

Ruby looks all around. "Just your imagination, sis." About then, a woodpecker starts up hammering a tree not too far away. "There you go—that's what you heard."

We soon come to the old bob-wire fence sagging same as it always has. It's covered in thick blackberry vines hanging full with green berries and some starting to turn reddish purple. Running along the ground and reaching up into the blackberry bushes are the dewberry vines with green, red, and black fruit. Looking at it, I think Dad's right—we should get a good mess out of what's there. I can almost taste Mama's cobbler sweetened with the sugar Jean brought her. Ruby and I grin big at each other and drop to our knees. "Watch those thorns, Bid. They're mean."

I'm picking and have my pan more than half filled up when I see something white shoved into the blackberry vines. I finally get my arm poked through the thick bush, getting eat up with thorns scratching and bloodying my arm. Heck if it isn't an enamel bowl with a red stripe around the top and a few black chips where the metal shows through. It's heaping full to the top with ripe dewberries. Anyone can see they've just been picked.

I start nosing around and see barefoot tracks in the sandy dirt powder around the bushes. I follow them till they disappear in the woods, but I sure ain't going in there right now.

"What're you doing, Biddy?" Ruby calls. I walk back to her with the bowl of berries in my hand. "Where'd you get that?"

"In the blackberry bushes. There's barefooted tracks going into the woods. Not too big, about Sammy's size of feet."

"Well, I'll be swan," she says, looking about as mixed up as me. "Guess somebody ran off and forgot it. We'll leave it here in the shade of the bushes in case they come back. They better do it quick. Those berries won't last too long in the heat once they've been picked. Kind of strange, that's for sure."

She can say that again.

We pick our pans full while the sun climbs higher in the sky. Ruby says, "Oh, that Ed is going to be a pacing around like a nervous mama cow with a calf. Guess we'd better call it a day, Bid."

"Let's go back along the creek and wade some. I'm hot."

Ruby likes that idea, and soon our berry pans are sitting on the bank brimming full of fat dewberries while we're tromping in the shallow part of Hoot Creek. Ruby always wears dresses, and right now, hers is tied up high on her legs. My overalls are rolled so high, I have to roll my bloomers up too. Ruby splashes water on me and I screech and splash her back. We go to laughing and having a good old time making lots of noise.

Soon's we stop our laughing and splashing, that's when we hear the loudest, most pitiful moans you ever did listen to.

"What on earth?" Ruby says, and the moaning gets louder. She points to a tangled-up bunch of bushes and trees further up the creek.

"Over there," she says, and we're already splashing through the water to see what's happened to some poor soul. We climb out of the water and run around the bushes and you'll never believe what we see next. There's Allen on the ground holding his head and groaning and moaning the likes of nothing I ever heard in my life.

"Allen, what's happened?" Ruby screams. She drops down beside him. It's hard to make out Allen's words with all that suffering noise, but finally we do, and from it and the looks of him, we know he's been kicked in the head by a mule, and he's probably dying. He's rolling and twisting, and Ruby looks at me with tears gushing down her cheeks. She doesn't have to tell me nothing because I already know what to do. I take off running to the house with the fastest feet in Oklahoma.

He Won't Live Anyway

When I come banging through the front door, I see Mama's cooked a big breakfast of hen eggs and some of her red-hot stone-jar sausage for Dad, Ed, and Tommy. Seems late to be eating breakfast, but then I recall Dad was going straight to the fields early this morning before it rained again. He works up a powerful appetite when he works in the field before eating.

Tommy has a heap of torn-up biscuits on his plate doused in milk gravy, and I don't know why I'm seeing everything around me so clear at such a time, but I am. I scream out what terrible thing's happened to Allen, and Dad's fork falls from his hand and hits the wooden table top. The look on his face would scare a haint. "Where?" he asks, almost in a whisper, and I yell it out where Allen is because I can't quit hollering even if I try.

Soon's I tell where Allen is, all three men take off running. Sammy's behind them, and I'm right behind him, followed by Mama, War, Snipe, Calvin, Jay Bird and Doodles. Behind me, I hear Mama yell for Snipe to go back to the house with Jay Bird and Doodles. Close to the creek, we hear Allen's pitiful cries.

The rest of what happened isn't so clear. I remember just parts of it. Dad and Mama and Ed hunker down over Allen. Next thing I remember is the men carrying Allen home, and Allen's screaming out to Heaven to take him quick being's how he can't stand the way his head's hurting. Mama is crumpled up into herself while she hurries along, and I know she's sobbing her heart out in her quiet way. Seeing my Mama suffer and knowing poor Allen—who's good all the time and wants to be a teacher and join the Army, too—may have got hisself kilt, danged near does me in.

I remember looking up and seeing War's eyes so full of water his eyeballs were near to drowning. When he sees me looking, he shoots me the meanest look and runs off to walk behind Dad and Tommy carrying Allen.

The whole time, Ruby is wailing and praying out loud for God to save our brother. Ruby is the most religious of all of us, and now I'm thinking she's cashing in on that close friendship with the Almighty. I bawl, too, but no sound comes out except a low whine that doesn't make sense.

How I find myself in that dishpan again washing up the late breakfast dishes, I can't tell you, but I am. Allen, Ruby, Ed, Mama, and Dad are all gone to Nowata in Ed's boss's car. I'm feeling a cussing streak coming on when I see, out of the corner of my eye, Cal, Sammy, Snipe, and Jay Bird scooting in close to where I'm working. Pretty soon, they're sitting on the floor against the wall with Calvin holding Doodles on his lap. Every last one of them have the saddest faces I've ever seen. Even Calvin does, who's smarter than all of us. I don't feel mad about the dishes no more.

"Hey," I say without looking at them. "If you boys go fetch the pans with the dewberries Ruby and me left by the creek, I'll wash us up a little mess of them and sneak a few sprinkles of Mama's sugar on top."

I don't turn around, but it sounds like horses run across the wood floor. In a minute, I look and there's just Calvin holding Doodles. She's playing with something that looks like a short nail but fatter, with a bigger head. It's shiny gold with a red top like a jewel. Nobody has to tell me Doodles is playing with Calvin's secret thing because I already saw him with it by the smokehouse that time.

Before I can get over there to look at it, Tommy steps up to the kitchen screen door. "Hey, Cal, let's do something for the folks. Dad and I were planting the kafir corn field this morning. It'd sure be nice if we had it done when he gets home. Give me a hand?"

Calvin stands up so fast, Doodles topples on the floor with her legs over her head. She lets out a cry. Calvin crams his secret thing back in his pocket and limps fast out the door to go with Tommy. I could cuss a blue streak over it, but it wouldn't show me that secret thing now would it?

When I finish my dish washing, I fluff up the feather beds in Mama's room and upstairs in my iron bed and tuck in quilts around the edges. I roll up the straw mattresses in the front room and sweep the wood floor. After that, I go pick messes of vegetables for supper. I fix the boys some of those dewberries and sugar and heat up leftover pinto beans for our noon meal. I'm worried sick over Allen, but I don't act like it.

When Sammy brings in the cows for milking on the early side of evening, Doodles and I go out to the porch. I've already fixed our supper, and it's waiting on the stove with lids on the pans to keep it warm. I'm sitting rocking and troubling over Allen's predicament when Ed's boss's car rolls up to the house kind of slow like and stops. Who gets out of the car is Ed, Ruby, and Dad.

"Where's Mama and Allen?" I ask, and I'm afraid what they're going to tell me. Ruby gives me a lot of comfort with her big smile. She climbs up the steps to the porch and sits down on the concrete.

"Sit by me, Biddy, and I'll tell you all about it." She pulls Doodles onto her lap and kisses her neck real loud until Doodles starts cackling. Ed and Dad sit down on the other side of the porch edge with their legs dangling off. Dad hands Ed a chaw of Beechnut. I sit by Ruby and enjoy Doodles laughing her head off.

It's been a worrisome day, and Calvin never did come back to tell me nothing. He and Tommy worked in the field till about an hour ago, came home for a bowl of beans, then went off somewhere else and who knows where.

I hear Snipe and War sneaking in behind the part of the porch that's hollow underneath. I know it's them because I hear Snipe snicker. They always do that when they think they're pulling something off, but War's quiet this time. Ruby sets Doodles on the other side of her, and says, "I'm not too fond of that new doctor in Nowata, that's the first thing."

"Me neither," I say.

"He took one look at Allen and said he wouldn't live the night and we should just keep him comfortable with medicine and let him slip on out to eternity. Mama near fell to the floor when she heard that."

I suck in my breath. "You mean—"

"I shore didn't put up with that sucker, did I?" Dad says, his back to us.

"No, Dad, you—"

All of a sudden, up pops War from the side of the porch looking like a panther's about to gobble him up alive. "Allen's going to die?" he says in a little voice, and he starts howling. All of us just stare at him because War never acts like he cares about nobody.

Ruby goes over to him and whispers something in his ear. It takes him a minute or two to stop his squalling to listen, but when he does, he says, "W-w-what?" Ruby tells him again in his ear, and a big grin breaks out on his face. He looks at us like he's never seen us before, all teary-eyed but blank in the face except for his mouth full of that grin. All of a sudden, he takes off hopping and making all kinds of hooting noises. Snipe follows him doing everything War does. It's a sight to see, and none of us talk for a few minutes.

"What did you tell the boy, Ruby?" Ed asks.

"That's for War and me and the Good Lord to know." After a minute or so, she says, "So, Biddy, let me tell you what our dad did when that Doc Silvers said Allen wasn't going to live. Dad gets in real close to the doctor's face and tells him he better try and fix his boy and stop talking like that else he'll whoop the daylights out of him."

Sammy's been listening through the front screen door and now he pushes through the door. "You said that to him, Dad?" His eyes look like stars they're so shiny.

"Yes, I did. No Old Sawbones is going to give up on my kids without a good, humble try." He spits a stream of tobacco juice far into the dirt yard.

"What'd he do then?" Sammy asks.

"He got scared bug eyes, is what," Ed says. "I think he was about to wet his educated britches." Ed goes to laughing, and that sets all of us off on a laughing fit. I can't get my breath I'm so doubled over.

"Well, did the doctor fix Allen?" I ask, wiping tears off my cheeks with the back of my hand.

Ruby says, "He called in his nurse and told her to call the Bartlesville hospital. He himself called a young man who isn't a doctor yet, I think his name is Jim… or John. Anyways, the Doc tells him to jump in his car and get to doc's office pronto because they were headed to Bartlesville.

"Now, Allen doesn't know any of this is going on because the doc has knocked him out with a shot. That's a relief for all of us, don't you know. Pretty soon, they're all loaded up in the young man's car to take Allen to surgery in Bartlesville. They fixed Allen up in the back seat with pillows and blankets, and Mama rode up front with the young man. I think his name is John. Yes, that's it. Well, Ma was happy to ride with John and stay away from that doc."

"But how far is Bartlesville?" Sammy asks.

"Oh, nigh to twenty miles," Dad says.

"Where will she sleep?" I ask.

Ruby pats my hand. "The nurse said they have a little accommodation room and Mama can stay in there on a cot with a pillow and blanket. Anyways, the last thing the doc did before heading to the hospital was stick his head out of the car window all smug and say, 'He isn't going to make it, Mr. Woodson. I'll remove the crushed brow bone and other pieces and keep him comfortable, but he'll be gone by morning.'"

"You should have seen that doctor trying to get his window rolled up with Dad charging at him like a bull!" Ed says. He and Ruby start giggling again, but I don't.

"Is it true? Will Allen be dead by morning, Ruby?"

"No, he will not."

"But how do you know?"

Ruby looks into the early evening sky. "Because I know, peanut."

A few lightning bugs flash down by Hoot creek. I say, "Well, isn't anybody hungry? Supper's cooked."

That causes a charge to the table. No sooner than we settle down to the table when Tommy and Calvin come through the kitchen door.

"Dad, War told us Allen's going to be all right," Tommy says.

Dad looks over at Ruby. She nods her head all certain like. "I reckon so, son, but it wouldn't hurt to say a word or two in his behalf… you know, to…" Dad looks up at the ceiling and I know he's talking about the Almighty.

"Yeehaw!" Tommy throws his straw hat in the air and catches it. He grins so big I see every tooth that boy owns. He washes up in the dishpan and tells Calvin to do the same. Soon's he sits down and gets his plate piled high, he says, "I need to take Cal into town in the morning, Dad."

"Why's that?"

"He's got some powerful evidence for the sheriff in the MacGregor case."

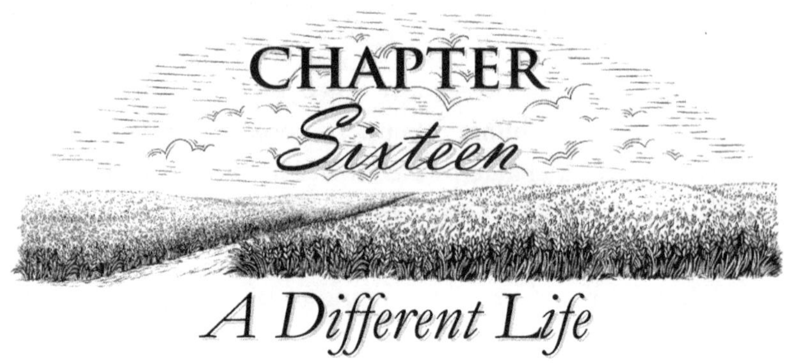

CHAPTER Sixteen

A Different Life

Three days go by and I'm still not having much to do with Calvin. Now I know what he found in the pump house and he should have spoken up right quick, but he didn't. I'm gathering eggs with Doodles when John-who-isn't-a-doctor-yet drives up and parks close to the cistern on the side of the house. Us kids gather around as Mama gets out of the car looking tired but smiling big at us. Soon's we see John open the back door of his car and loop one of Allen's arms around his own neck, we go to cheering and clapping.

"I reckon that proves Old Sawbones is as dumb as upside-down taters!" I yell out to anybody who wants to hear it.

Calvin and Sammy rush out to help John and they near carry Allen inside. Mama turns the quilt and sheet down on her own bed, and they lay Allen in it. The whole time, John's telling Calvin how to help him, and I wish he was our doctor, even if he isn't a doctor all the way yet. Sammy runs off to tell Dad and Tommy that Mama and Allen are back.

War comes running up with Snipe right behind. He takes one look at Allen's bandaged head, and I can't believe I see him knuckle tears off his face. He doesn't want anyone to see it, so I pretend I don't. War hasn't been in any trouble for three days. It's stranger than a cow with six teats, and we have one of those cows named Granny, so I know how strange it is.

"Son, would you fetch my black doctor bag from the jump seat so I can check Allen's vitals?" John says to Calvin.

Allen makes grunts that sound kind of like, "Haw kweeds" and "Dangle ol mool."

"Don't tax him," Mama tells us on account of we're all wiggling in to look at him close up.

John says, "Mrs. Woodson, Allen should be kept as quiet as possible. Keep the windows shaded, and be sure he drinks plenty of water. I'm leaving you some pain syrup for this week. He'll use a bedpan for at least another week or ten days. Don't let him get up or walk around. Give him soup, broth, juice, or a small square of cornbread and milk made into a mush. That's all. Get ahold of Dr. Silvers if he takes a turn."

Jay Bird snickers. "Allen has to use a slop jar," he says, and War slugs his arm. "What did I do?" Jay Bird asks, and I tell him to hush and go outside.

Mama nods her head at all of John's advice, and I see dark rings under eyes. Before we know it, John is gone and Mama shoos us out of her bedroom and warns us not to make any noise. We don't even want to make any ruckus because we're so tickled to have our brother back and not dead.

"Why didn't you put him in the gopher hole bed, Mama?" I ask.

"Cause I can't hear him in there if he hollers out. I can keep a strict eye on him here."

I meet Dad and Tommy outside and tell them everything I just heard and how we have to let Allen rest and he can't have any fried taters or gravy or nothing. Tommy goes inside. Dad sits down on the porch edge and rubs his face in his hands. Mama comes outside and sits down in her chair.

"Go find something to do, Bid," she says.

That means they want to talk private with no kids around. I usually like it since it means I can run off and play. This time, it makes me so curious I go around the side of the porch and lean against the house. Pretty soon, Mama's saying she's so relieved Allen is alive, and her and my dad start bawling. Now, that's a thing I ain't never seen before. Big old tears start pouring out of my own eyes.

"Doobie, all Doc Silvers did was take the crushed bones out and sew him back up. He kept on telling me Allen wouldn't live very long. If it hadn't been for John…" Mama's quiet. I peek around the corner. She's rocking back and forth with her face in her hands. Dad is looking off so's I can't see his face. After a while, Mama takes a hanky out of her pocket and blows her nose.

"They didn't rebuild his eyebrow at all, Thomas. I don't care a hound's collar how it'll look, but can Allen be strong about it? He won't look like before."

"Course he will, Doobie. Don't make a girl out of him. Ain't nobody more strong-charactered than Allen is."

Mama sniffs. Dad spins around to face her and I duck behind the house.

"I got some ideas how to pay all those bills, too."

"Do you, Thomas?"

"Yes'm. Been thinking about it. We're going to throw some of those chili dances like we used to. Remember how folks loved coming to them? Besides that, I'm hearing about mule rodeos getting popular around these parts. Listen here, those cowboys love their hooch, and I make some of the best. I can rent out some of our mules and run the corn liquor. You know I'm selling that young mule that kicked our boy's head in. He's young and wild, but he'll bring a fair price. We'll make out all right."

"What if you get caught, selling the liquor I mean?"

"I'm not going to. Cowboys ain't going to let no one stop their fun. You'll see. Stop your fretting now."

I know I shouldn't have listened to their private talk, but I'm glad I did. I skip off and run smack into Calvin. "You been eavesdropping, haven't you?" he says.

"You don't know anything about what I do," I say.

"I saw you."

"So what?"

He laughs. "I was eavesdropping on the other side of the house."

I punch him in the gut, and not too light.

"What'd you do that for?"

"Because you deserve it."

"For listening to the folks? You did it too."

"No, for you not telling the sheriff about that thing you found in the pump house."

"I told you I gave it to him for evidence. See, I don't have it anymore." Calvin pulls the inside of his pockets out to show me they're empty.

"What if it doesn't help Mr. Leroy now?"

"Sure it will. A fancy cufflink at the scene of the crime? It's a huge clue, Bid."

"Still yet, Calvin. I'm ashamed of you for holding out."

Calvin hangs his head, and by the way he looks, I'm thinking he might really be ashamed.

"I just… well, it made me consider about the way I want to live someday."

"Yeah, how's that?"

"I want to be somebody besides a farmer with a bunch of

hungry mouths to feed and no money and working in the dirt every damn day and never knowing if it will rain too much or not rain at all and everything will be ruined and I have to move my family to another shack and can't buy anything nice or go anywhere—"

Calvin is talking faster and faster, and now he stops altogether. He sits down on a stump by the wood pile. I plop down beside him. "See, every time I pulled that cufflink out, I pretended it was mine, and I lived somewhere like Oklahoma City or maybe even St. Louis. I acted like I worked in a city office and owned a car like the one you told me you saw in Nowata. Maybe I wore one of those town suits and had a pretty wife like Dick Tracy has with yellow curly hair, and I bought my food and milk in a store."

"You're too young to have a wife."

"Don't be ignorant. Sure, I am now, but I won't always be. I turned fifteen while you were in Siloam Springs, and Mama married when she was one year older than me now."

"Yeah, but Dad was twenty-three. You aren't near that age. And don't call me ignorant." I give Cal a look so he knows I mean what I say. He raises his shoulders like he doesn't care.

"Biddy, that cufflink means somebody has a fancy life and I don't… and I want one."

I sit down on the ground. I feel sorry for Calvin for some reason, so full of ideas for a different life. We're quiet for a spell, and then I say, "Well, who in the world wears one of those things around here? I don't even know what the dumb thing's for."

"Cufflinks holds your sleeve cuffs together when you wear a town shirt."

"That's what buttons are for."

"No, there's a hole in both sides of the sleeve to put the cufflink in. No buttons."

"That sounds like a bunch of corn cobs, Cal. Anyways, nobody in these parts is that rich. Maybe some of those oil people you talk about. It sure doesn't belong to Mr. Leroy."

"I know. That's why it's such a big clue. It was right there behind Mr. MacGregor's head, Biddy. It had a few specks of blood on it, but I cleaned them off."

"That makes me sick."

"I didn't tell the sheriff that part, just that I found it inside and kept it because I didn't know how important it was until my big brother said so."

"You knew it before then, Calvin."

"Yeah, I did." Calvin looks off in the distance.

"Maybe that cufflink thing belonged to Mr. MacGregor," I say.

"I considered that, but why would it be in the pump house?"

"I don't know. What was he wearing?"

"Coveralls. Hey, something I about forgot to tell you. Mr. Leroy's sister, Miz Abernathy, is living in his shack right now."

"How do you know?"

"Tommy and me saw Mr. Leroy when we went to the sheriff's office."

"And you didn't tell me?" I jump up and plant my feet all mad like.

"Settle down, Bid. I was meaning to. See, Mr. Leroy's right there in the jailhouse, and that's where we found Sheriff Murphy when we went to Nowata. He let us go in and talk to him. He's not such a bad guy."

"Mr. Leroy?"

"No, the sheriff."

"I don't believe it."

"Anyways, Mr. Leroy's sister's living in his place for a time, and he says she's going to get everything all straightened out and not to worry none because the Good Lord is on her side or something similar."

While I was thinking on that, Calvin said, "Don't tell anyone, but I asked him something while Tommy was talking to the sheriff. Just under my breath so nobody could hear."

"What did you ask?"

"I asked him why his rabbit foot was there by Mr. MacGregor's head all covered in blood."

"You didn't neither."

"I did too."

"Well, tell me what he said and hurry it up!"

"I said, 'How'd it get out of your own keeping and in that pump house, sir?' He started telling me how he keeps it in a different place in the summertime, but we didn't get very far after that. Had to shut up on account of Tommy and the sheriff said it was time to go."

"They didn't hear you talking to him about it?"

"They weren't paying any attention. They were yapping about Allen getting kicked in the head. Oh, something else. Mr. Leroy said he was worried about that deputy named Floyd."

"He's terrible mean, Cal. He hates Mr. Leroy."

"Yeah, well, he's been saying some bad things to Mr. Leroy and telling him he doesn't need to worry when the trial is since he won't live to see it, and that's all I found out, since Mr. Leroy was telling me right quick as the sheriff was saying how he had to go check on something and it was time to lock the jail door." Calvin's eyes look like dew drops while he's telling me all this news about Mr. Leroy.

"Aren't you going to tell somebody else? That's dangerous talk."

"Already told Tommy. He says he was putting his thinking cap on about it."

Sammy comes around the corner. "What are you guys doing?"

We're not telling no one about our private talk, and we seal it with a hard stare at each other.

"Nothing," I say.

Calvin stands up and stretches. "Damn, I miss that cufflink," he says.

Annie Over

You never knew such good kids the next few days. We tiptoed through the house and peeked in on Allen with not one fight or squabble. The boys, even Tommy, helped me with the dishes on account of they wanted me to hurry and not make any noise. Dad didn't shame the boys or call them *kitchen girls* for helping me, neither.

The kitchen is on the other side of the wall where Allen is staying in Mama and Dad's bed. I didn't know what to think of my good luck with those dishes, and once I wished Allen would be sick in the bed for a long time so I could keep getting help like that. I was ashamed for the rest of the day for thinking such an awful thing.

Neighbors bring us bowls of cooked food and messes of garden vegetables and butter and even cottage cheese like we must be starving because Allen was kicked in the head by a mule. I never saw anything like it, and Mama is always tending to Allen so happy and sweet and singing in the garden while she hoes around the pole beans, cabbage, and beets early in the mornings or just before dark. I sure am glad I got her some of Mr. Leroy's Herb Whiz before all this trouble broke out.

Today is the fifth day since Allen came home, and I'm outside hanging up washed clothes on the clothes line and on the fence. I'm about finished when goldarned if I don't spy our neighbor Mrs. Russell and her girl Rebecca walking down Blackberry Road to our house. Mrs. Russell is carrying what looks like a long pan, and Rebecca's got her arms circled around a pot like it's real heavy.

I clamp on the last pieces of washing with clothes pins and run to tell Mama we got company. She's having Allen lean up so's she can fluff his feather pillow. After she smooths his quilt and tucks it around him, she brings him a bowl of barley soup. He sticks out his tongue once she's turned around. I about bust out laughing, especially seeing Allen with his head all bandaged and the parts not bandaged just bruised to high heaven. I reckon he's tired of all that soup Mama's making him eat. I saw War sneak him a pork chop last night, and I didn't tell. War's been tolerable lately, and I don't want any pork chop ruining it.

Doodles is on the end of the bed watching over Allen like she has since he got home. "Allen says I'm Dr. Doodles," she says again. "Allen, drink your medicine." She hands him a bottle cap and he pretends to drink it with his swollen lips.

I head outside where Calvin's yapping at Mrs. Russell, but he's really eyeing Rebecca. She's as pretty as a picture, that's for true. She has brown curls that shine in the sunshine, and dark lashes around her big brown eyes. She's a few years older than me and helps the teacher with the younger kids, but she still likes to play games with all of us during recess.

Mrs. Russell follows Mama in the house chattering about the sugar spice cake and pork stew she brought and she hopes they help us out and Allen can eat some of that stew since it's really soup, after all, and she heard…

The screen door closes behind them and we all stand there looking at Rebecca, but I'm not lying, the idea of that sweet cake Mrs. Russell brought us is stuck in my mind. We never have cake except at Christmas when Mama makes her candy cake with the melted candy frosting.

"Hi, Rose."

"Hi, Rebecca. Want to see my canary?"

"Canary? One of those yellow birds people keep for pets?"

"Uh-huh. It's Mr. Leroy's. I'll give it back to him when he gets free again."

Rebecca looks at me with a blank stare.

"Never mind that. Let's go see Charley-Bird."

"Does he sing?"

"All the time."

Rebecca claps her hands together. We don't make it all the way in the kitchen door when Sammy yells, "Rebecca, want to play Annie Over with us? We ain't got a ball or a pig's bladder, but we can throw a matchbox over the roof."

"She's too grown up for that, Sammy," Calvin says.

Rebecca smiles big at Calvin and says, "No, I still like to play Annie Over. I'll be right back after I see the canary." Rebecca goes on inside, and I stop a minute and watch Sammy and Calvin doing contortions all over the place and Sammy jumping in the air, and I reckon those boys have gone simple in the head on account of Rebecca being so pretty.

Jay Bird follows us when we go back outside, and Sammy goes to walking on his hands the minute he spies Rebecca. The stick-match box is filled up with rocks and sitting on the cistern. Calvin's sitting on a stump waiting for us. He says, "We'll go on the other side, and you girls throw it over the low part of the house. No use to run all over the place and try to tag each other with just a dumb old match box. You start, Rebecca. When me and Sammy get on the other side, holler out 'Annie Over' and see if you can get it over the roof. If you do, I'll say 'Over!' Then I'll throw it back and you guys say 'Over!' If it doesn't get over the roof two times by one thrower, the other side wins."

"That's not the rules, Calvin," Sammy says.

"Well, it's not even Annie Over, is it, Sam?"

"What do you mean?"

"It's really Ante Over, and you have to have a ball to play it right. So, hush up, and let's play."

"Can I play?" Jay Bird asks.

"You're not big enough," Calvin says, and Jay Bird goes to pouting with his bottom lip pooching out.

Me and Rebecca wait for the boys to get on the other side. The low part is over the front room. Just a small part of it is okay to throw the box over on account of just to the left of that part is the bedroom window where Allen is.

Rebecca yells, "Annie Over!" and tosses the matchbox way over the roof to the other side.

Calvin yells, "Over!" and the matchbox comes hurling back to us over the roof lickity-split. I pull Rebecca out of the way so's it doesn't hit her.

"Over," I yell. "You have to watch out, Rebecca. Those boys throw it harder than hammers. They're probably showing off, too."

I'm ready to throw the box when, all of a sudden, there's Dad showing up from the cornfield and he looks mad. "Biddy, stop throwing that box. You kids are going to break a window."

"But we're playing Annie Over."

"You heard me," Dad says and goes in the house to eat his noon meal.

"Okay, I'll throw it once and then I'll quit," I tell Rebecca. She smiles and I wind up my arm like I'm going to throw a killer throw and wham! I throw the box of rocks straight through the bedroom window. My mouth goes drier than a pecan shell hearing that glass shatter into pieces. By the time Calvin and Sammy run around the house to see what happened, Dad busts through the front room screen door, down the porch steps, and straight to me with his hat in his hand.

"I told you to stop, Bid, didn't I?" he says, his face red. He swats me across the rear three times with his hat, and I'm dancing around like he's killing me. He heads back in the house mumbling, "When I tell you kids to stop, you best stop."

I'm standing here with my face burning hot and my feelings bruised to all consumption and tears leaking out like rain. My dad never hit me before, and pretty Rebecca and all the kids saw me get whooped.

I take off running, and I don't care if I ever stop.

CHAPTER Eighteen

The Wood Ghost

The only place to hide except for the woods is up here in the biggest elm tree away from the house and alongside the creek. I'm kneeling on the wood planks the boys hammered in it last summer so the branches and leaves make me invisible. My head is as stuffed thick as Mama's feather pillows, and my own soul is aching. I can't never show my face to Rebecca again, and those boys saw me get a licking from Dad. Nothing ever felt so bad except for Allen almost getting kilt.

I'm not thinking Dad likes me much anyways since he's a lot stricter with me than the boys, but he never got after me like that before. I can't say it hurt when he whooped me with that hat, because it didn't. It made me ashamed. I feel terrible bad about breaking the window, too. Now, Dad will have to board it up or cover it with screen, and what if I'd hit Allen or Doodles with that box of rocks?

I'm just bawling my eyes out and talking to the tree and the critters and anything in creation that will listen how poorly I feel. "I'm sorry," I say out loud, over and over. My belly and chest are having spasms from my agony. My nose is dripping like a pump, and I have no choice but to consider using elm leaves. I pick a handful and blow my nose clear off. The leaves are big and make a pretty good hankie rag.

Blowing my nose gets my head feeling better. I start yawning and lay myself down to stare into the branches. Watching the leaves jiggle in the breeze soothes me. I allow trees know lots of languages—wind language, storm language, bird language. Maybe even people language since they've been living around human beings so long. Allen says they whisper secrets to one another, and I don't doubt it at all.

I take a deep breath and my chest jerks from all my bawling. I flip over on my belly and before I know it, I'm waking up from a sleep.

You could have fallen out of the tree and broke your goofy neck, I'm saying in my head.

Soon's I blink hard enough to wake up, I see a folded piece of paper laying right beside my face. I sit up and unfold it. The ragged edge means it was torn out of a catalog or magazine. It's sort of like an ink drawing of a fancy farm house. There's a large upstairs with four more bedrooms, not just a little bitty upstairs with one bedroom like our yellow house. It's even bigger than Evelyn's house in Arkansas.

A little girl is outside watching a herd of sheep eat grass. Two men are in a nice car driving up to that fine house. At the bottom of the page is a line, and underneath the line it says,

SEARS ROEBUCK AND CO.,

CHICAGO, ILLINOIS.

The price of the house is one thousand and six hundred and forty-nine dollars and no cents. I whistle at so much money, and I'm glad Dad didn't hear me. He doesn't take to women whistling. It's not fair, because the boys can whistle their lips off, but I'm not allowed to.

"Who gave me this?" I say out loud, and then I think it has to be Calvin since he's the only one who said he wants a fancy house and a car and all that. I fold it up and stick it in my overalls pocket.

I'm still bothered in my soul about what happened with my dad and that hat-whooping, so I don't take to going home yet. I climb down and mosey along the water till I come to the two persimmon trees growing by the bank of the creek. Small whitish green flowers with their petals curling backward grow like little bells along the skinny part of the branches of one tree. I'm fond of how the tree looks altogether, mostly how its branches reach over the creek like it's checking for tadpoles. There's a second persimmon tree right beside it, and it never gets a flower one. I hug the rough, dark bark and take a deep whiff under the blossoms. Smells a little sweet.

One time, Carl and Tommy tricked me into biting a green persimmon. "Take a big bite so you get all the juice," Tommy said. Dang if that green thing didn't suck the spit right out of my mouth and turn it inside out. It puckered me up similar to the top of Tommy's drawstring tobacco sack. I swear I would've drunk water out of an old boot if I had to. As it was, I dropped to my belly and drank half of Hoot creek, and those two mule brothers of mine rolled around laughing the rest of the day. So did everybody else when they heard about it.

Birds are jabbering all around me, and I particularly make out a mockingbird who thinks he knows everything, like Cal, and he sure might. He trills and sings in so many bird tongues, I start missing Charley. That makes me think hard about Mr. Leroy's plight, and I'm glad I don't have any tears left in my eyeballs.

I cross the old beat-up bridge into the woods, not one bit worried it will fall through to the water, and plop down to do some thinking. My hair blows in my face and I sure wish I could get me a permanent. I think about maybe going to meet Mr. Leroy's sister. Maybe she has some good news about Mr. Leroy on account of Calvin giving the sheriff that cufflink. I lick my dry lips. I haven't heard of any wild dogs around here lately, and our dogs haven't had any barking fits at night. I guess I'm sitting right here talking myself into going to Mr. Leroy's shack to meet Miz Abernathy.

Soon's I get into the huckleberry trees and some of those cedars of Lebanon and oaks where they thicken up and have bushes along the ground, I start noticing something strange. I pull a handful of wild grass and work it in my hand like I don't have a care in the world. I walk and stop. It's kind of like a deer is shuffling alongside me just out of sight. I walk. It does too. I stop. It stops. Leaves and branches wiggle from where I hear the sounds, then they settle down.

Now, I got better sense than to think a deer would walk alongside me like that. What if it's a panther waiting to pounce? I thought they came out at night. Do mad dogs stalk folks before they attack?

I'm starting to get plumb lightheaded with frightfulness. I turn around real easy and aim towards the house. Clouds are starting to cover the sun, making the woods darker than they ought to be this time of day. The wind goes to worrying the treetops and twisting them around. I'm guessing it's going to storm, and I sure don't want to be in the woods when it does.

My steps get bigger. Birds flap wild over my head. A cross between a howl and a song—sad, beautiful, and terrible at the same time—fills the woods. My hair 'bout stands up on its roots.

The Wood Ghost!

Can't man nor haint stop me now from racing to the

creek and following it till I come to the shallow part. I jump in the water and don't bother to roll up my overalls or bloomers. That ghost sound fills my ears, and the funny thing is, I love it and hate it at the same time.

Tornado!

Wind grabs my hair and tries to yank it out while I'm climbing up out of Hoot Creek. I see Dad's two work-and-wagon horses and Old Blue the mule galloping around inside the pasture. The cows are all huddled together under a tree. Then there's Sammy running toward me and hollering. I can't make out a single word till he gets closer.

"Hurry, Biddy, tornado's coming! I been trying to find you. Dad says we have to get in the gopher hole."

I try to run with Sammy to the house, but I'm as slow as a land turtle on account of my bloomers and overall legs being soggy wet. The wind feels like a flat door pushing me back. The sky has turned dark gray and green. I can't hardly get up the little hill to our front porch.

"Come on, sis!"

Sammy grabs my arm and pulls me the rest of the way. Rain is blowing sideways now, and the wind sounds like a cow bellering. Mama and Tommy are gathering the washing off the line and fence and ground, and Dad is hammering wood over the window I broke. Their hair is near blowing off their heads in ripples. I laugh out loud but no one could ever hear it in this racket. Chickens and geese are running stupid everywhere, and Dad's making hand signals for Sammy to help him pen them up in the henhouse.

Calvin sticks his head out the front door and yells, but I can't hear him. He motions for me to get in the house. I climb the porch steps and stagger through the house to get myself a drink from the water bucket dipper. My hands are shaking, and Calvin sees them doing it. I get another dipper of water and drink it all down.

"Come on, Bid. I've got Mama's chair off the porch and the upstairs windows are closed except for one is cracked about two inches like it's supposed to be. Let's get in the cellar. Doodles is whining for you."

"Where's Allen?"

"Tucked into the gopher hole bed."

"Wait, I have to get Charley."

I take the steps as fast as my legs will let me. I feel like rocks are tied around my waist holding me down. Charley is all aflutter and scared. I put his tea towel over him and carry him down to the gopher hole. There's Allen in the bed smiling all lopsided with War and Snipe sitting on the floor right next to him. Jay Bird is beside Doodles on the floor. She runs to me. I set Charley out of the way and hug her. I plop her on the end of the bed and wipe tears off her cheeks.

"I'm okay, Doodle Bug. You take good care of Allen now, okay?"

Mama, Sammy, Tommy, and Dad slam through the door looking wind haggard and excited. Dad bolts the door, and everyone finds places to hunker down on the floor alongside the wall. I settle in by Charley's cage. I sneak a peek at Dad. He sees me do it, and I don't see any mad in his face.

The gopher hole isn't really a cellar, but it's half as deep as one and built into the side of a small hill that runs alongside the house. Mama says it's the safest place for us in a storm, and now here we all are looking at each other and wondering what the wind will take with it, maybe even us. We hear it whistling and moaning outside the tiny window up high by the ceiling. It's almost as dark as night but light enough to see scared eyes rolling around.

Dad lights a kerosene lamp and puts it on the little travel trunk standing on its end at the side of the bed. "If the wind comes in here, whoever's closest, douse that flame or we'll all burn down," he says, and everyone looks around with fearful eyes. He takes a case off the top of the shelves where Mama keeps her canning, snaps it open, and takes out his banjo. Tommy pulls his guitar out from under the bed. It's wrapped in an old sheet with holes, but good enough if wrapped a couple of times to keep the dust and bugs out.

"Jump up, button, so's I can sit down and tune this jobber up," Tommy says, and Doodles comes to sit by me.

Before long, the gopher hole is full of *When the Roll is Called Up Yonder*, and *At the Cross*, and finally *Bingaman*, a strange song Dad sings to all the kids when they're little.

Bingaman drew his wooden knife,
Fiddle Aye Day Doh.
Bingaman drew his wooden knife,
Fiddle Aye Day Doh.
Bingaman drew his wooden knife,
Swore he'd take the Mad Dog's life,
Fiddle Aye Day…
Fiddle Aye Dee…
Koh-whim!

We don't understand it, but we like it and we're tapping our toes and Mama's humming. Most of us kids don't like to sing out loud, but Mama does when she plays her pipe organ. Dad too. Tommy sings all the time and doesn't have a bashful bone in his body.

"Hey, kids, I heard this one on the radio over at Stanfill's Grocery a while back," Tommy says. "You know how they leave that radio on all day long? Well, I sneaked myself back there behind the onions one time and wrote the words to this song on my arm so's I could write them down when I got home."

Mama laughs, and Tommy reaches into a fat-mouthed jar in the corner where he keeps his songs. "Let's see here…" He looks at the paper for a minute. "Yeah. See if you like it. It's called *Old Pal of My Heart* by Jimmie Rodgers." He strums the guitar strings a few times and turns knobs on the end of the arm. "Y'all ready?"

We sure are, and Tommy goes to singing so sad and pretty I'm nigh to crying in no time. Mama is too.

The shadows of twilight are falling,
On a heart so lonesome and blue,
I can hear a voice sweetly calling,
And it brings back memories of you.
Old pal of my heart, are you lonesome?
Old pal of my dreams, are you blue?
It's been many days since we parted,
My thoughts are forever of you.
Life is so empty without you,
I long for you forever it seems.
For I know you'll always be the same sweetheart to me,
When I come back to you in my dreams.
And oh how I long for you darling,
To hold you again tenderly,
And hear you say that you always will be,

Just the same old sweet pal to me.

Tommy breaks out yodeling, and all of us stare at him on account of we didn't know he could yodel. He gets done and sits the guitar down and grins bigger than a toad sitting on the creek bank.

"Why, Tommy, you learned to yodel," Mama says.

"Lots of time to practice in the cornfield, Ma," he says, looking at Dad.

Jay Bird says, "Do it again, Tommy."

Dad says, "Hang on now. Sounds like the storm's passed over." He opens the door to the kitchen real slow and pokes his head out. "House is still here."

We go out one at a time, except for Allen, who stays put like Mama told him to. We still got a house, that's for true, but one of our trees is laying down outside the kitchen door.

"Just missed the cistern and this side of the house," Mama says.

Leaves and branches are everywhere like someone beat the trees up and left their innards all around. Dad pushes out the kitchen door and says, "Smokehouse and shed still on the ground. Part of the shed roof's missing. Tommy, you and Sammy go hammer that up. Check and see if the grain got wet. If it's just the corn, bring it in and we'll dry it out. If it's the feed, we might lose it."

"Look at those hogs, Doobie. They're bunched up tighter than a jar of pickles," Mama says to Dad.

"War, you and Snipe go throw out their bedding hay and put some dry down. I'm going to go check on the livestock," Dad says. "Calvin, you and Biddy gather the twigs and branches and put them in the kindling box. Save all those leaves for the compost."

"Okay, Dad," Calvin says, but he's got ahold of my overall strap. He pulls me over to the side out of Mama's hearing. "Where'd you go?"

"You know where. You gave me this." I pull the folded page out of my overalls pocket. "Why'd you give me this picture, on account of you want a house like it someday? I thought you wanted to live in the city."

Calvin unfolds the picture and takes a long gander at it. "I never saw this thing before in my life."

"Stop trying to fool me. You know you did."

"Nope."

"Well, Sammy did it, then."

"No, he didn't. He never left here because Mama made him and the twins clean out the chicken house after Mrs. Russell and Rebecca left."

I look at Calvin with squinty eyes since I don't believe him. "What are you trying to pull?"

"Listen, I walked down the road a piece with Rebecca and brought her back here. When her and her mom left, I helped Mama pick tomatoes to can. Ask her if you don't believe me."

Now I don't know what to think. If the boys didn't give me the picture of the country house with everybody so danged rich in it, who did? And why?

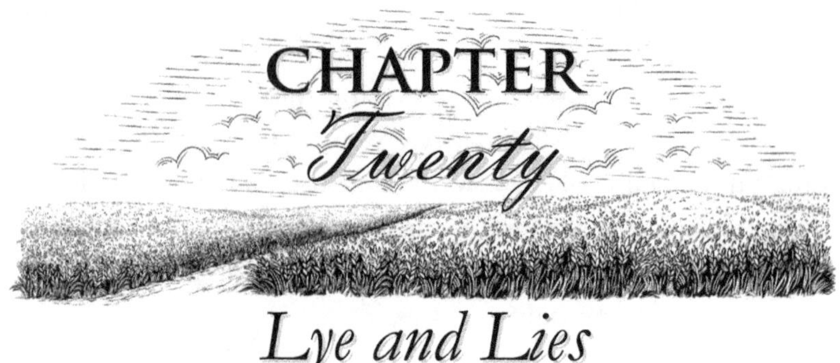

Lye and Lies

Tornado mess or not, next morning I get an inkling sort of like an itch I can't scratch about Mr. MacGregor's cabin. That inkling skirts around the sides of my mind like a cloud looking to land. I don't get to consider it deep 'cause Mama gets it in her head to make some lye soap. I don't understand growed-up women and why they get such notions. Mama usually makes her soap at hog-killing time or in the Spring, but here it is today and her mind is set. I sure can't sneak out to pay Miz Abernathy a visit if that's what I'd planned.

Mama sends me running here and there to fetch cans of pork fat and some of Dad's sassafras branches stored in the gopher hole. Then I have to run to the pasture and chip off a piece of clean cow salt lick.

While she's draining the potash out of the barrels, she sends me inside to wash the breakfast dishes and sweep the floors. Doodles helps me with her little broom Dad made her from an old ax handle and bundled straw. When I go back outside, Mama has the fire lit under our biggest iron kettle hanging from a wood stand by the smokehouse. Oh, law, I don't want to spend all day making lye soap. If I wanted to do something else, like satisfy those thoughts I was having before, it wouldn't matter now because what Mama says is what happens.

She pours fat and lye in the kettle and throws in the salt to make the soap harder. "Get yourself a jar of drinking water, Bid. It's going to be a hot one, and you'll be out here a long time."

So here I am under the trees madder than a bee with three bent stingers because I'm a girl and the boys don't have to help make soap. I stir and stir with the sassafras sticks since it's supposed to make the soap smell better. Dad says it keeps mosquitoes, flies, ticks, and everything else away too. I wish somebody would swat me with a sassafras stick so maybe I could stay away from that dumb soap. See, that's the way I'm thinking right now.

War comes and throws hisself on the ground under the shade. I know he has something up his sleeve, and I'm sure not going to tell him I'm near glad for his company since I'm so tired of stirring. He says, "I get to quit chores and go swimming once I get my hoeing done and sweep out the smoke house."

"So what?" I say, staring into the kettle.

"You'll be out here all day, and I'll be swimming and laying in the sun like a hound dog. Snipe, too."

"Yeah, well this is more fun than anything, mostly since I don't have to look at you all day."

"It is not fun. You hate it. You said so."

"I was just fooling. It's funner than swimming, and it smells so good from the sassafras stick. I'm glad I'm the only one who gets to do it." I take a deep whiff of the soap and close my eyes.

"Can I try?"

"No, it's my job."

"Don't you have to go to the outhouse?"

"Maybe."

"Let me stir and you go on."

"Well… if you promise not to tell anyone," I say.

"I promise!"

"Don't stop stirring or it'll be ruined and Mama will tan your hide."

"I won't."

I hand him the sassafras stick and go use the outhouse. I come back and sit down on the other side of the huckleberry tree so he can't see me. I'm thinking hard about this summer and why they haven't found out who kilt our Mr. MacGregor and why Mr. Leroy has to be locked up when he's innocent. I do a few cartwheels and run around the tree a couple of times. I ignore War trying to tell me something while I drain my quart jar of water empty. He throws the stick down on the grass and runs off. I guess he figured out it wasn't fun anyways to stand over a burning-hot kettle and stir up a batch of lye soap.

Mama brings me a fresh jar of well water and peeks in the kettle. She's holding Doodles' hand tight since she's squirming to get to me. "No, baby girl. That kettle will burn the hide right off your bones. It's looking pretty good, Bid. Keep stirring."

I'm wishing I could fly away like an old lazy crow, but it doesn't do me any good to wish it. When it's nigh to evening and the sky gets streaked with gold and pink, Sammy and Jay Bird bring the cows in from the pasture. Jay Bird is holding Granny's tail with his feet flat against her haunches while she walks to the shed. If Mama or Dad sees him, he'll get his britches tanned for sure.

I let out a big tired sigh like I'm about to die when all of sudden, a miracle happens—the soap turns into a thick, foamy mess. I run to get Mama. I've never been so happy to see foam in all my life. Mama takes a big wooden spoon and puts a few drops on her tongue.

"No bite to it. It's ready. In the morning, we'll have lots of nice soap, Biddy."

Mama seems happy she has new lye soap. I'm so tuckered out my tongue is 'bout hanging out while we have supper. Those cabin and cloud ideas circling my noggin today come to land while I'm washing the dishes. Here's what I come up with… I aim to sneak out first thing in the morning before anyone sees me. I can't rightly say why I'm thinking this way, but it burns inside me to do so.

Next morning while Dad and Tommy are milking the cows and Mama's boiling coffee grounds, that's exactly what I do. I stick a pan in the grocery sack Mr. Leroy gave me. Before anyone can say Jack's lantern, I'm trotting down Blackberry Road hoping no one sees me. It doesn't take long to get to the gravel road and the Y-spring. I get myself a cool drink from the spring. I'm pretty jumpy, but my curiosity keeps me going.

At the bob-wire fence, the white enameled bowl with the dewberries is gone, and I reckoned as much. Barefoot tracks, fresh ones, are everywhere. All the dewberries, save a few scraggly ones, are over for the season. The blackberries are just right for picking today and the next few days, and part of one whole vine has been picked clean. I pick off a handful and throw them in my mouth. I'm about to plop another juicy one in my mouth when I see a brown bug with long sticky legs and antennas staring straight in my eyes.

A stinkbug!

"Bleeeh!" I throw it to the ground and dance around in the dirt a little sick about almost eating a bug. "Okay, Biddy, get a move on," I say out loud, mostly to forget about that stinkbug.

I walk over a hill and there's Mr. MacGregor's cabin tucked up into the edge of the woods and close to Wayne's Road. My breath sounds ragged all of a sudden, and I think I might start crying. I remember how I'm stubborn, and how that ain't bad, so I run right up to that cabin and turn the door knob. It's locked. I walk around to the cabin side closest to the road and try the windows. They're locked. There's a locked door in the back. I walk along the woods side of the cabin that's almost hidden in trees, and dang if I don't find a window open about an inch.

I find me a big ax stump by the woodpile and haul it over by the window. I use it to climb up and reach the window. The window slides up easy like, and I find myself climbing through it like I got good sense. I stand inside and roll my eyes around Mr. MacGregor's cabin and go to shaking. What am I doing in a dead man's cabin? Who might be using it now that he's gone? Killers? Ghosts?

My eyes roll around looking everywhere, and I think I never saw nicer things than Mr. MacGregor has in that cabin. Leather-skinned furniture with wood arms. A wood plank floor shining like a mirror. An inside sink and faucets like my cousin Evelyn had in her house in Siloam Springs. A glass window with a dragonfly design made with green and red and blue glass is over the door where clear glass usually is. A bookcase stuffed with books and do-dads covers a whole wall.

That cabin is sure bigger than it looks like from outside. A bed twice as wide as Mama's bed is covered in a beautiful quilt in the big room, and I see two more bedrooms and a little inside toilet room down a short hall. On a desk sort of like a teacher's desk but smaller and fancier, I see a picture in a frame. It's Mr. MacGregor with dark hair instead of gray, a pretty woman who must be his wife, and a girl about my age. *April 30, 1919* is written in fancy black writing across a corner of the picture.

Now I'm walking all around touching things since they look so pretty. In the kitchen, I stop and take a fast breath because the white enamel bowl I saw when Ruby and I picked dewberries is clean and sitting on a shelf over the sink.

That lights a fire under my feet all the way back to the window. My heart is beating hard while I climb out. I close the window back the way I found it, with just a small crack at the bottom. I drag the ax stump back to the woodpile and I'm feeling like I did something terrible bad. Did I? Why did I do it? I don't know. *I don't know.*

I hightail it back over the hills to the blackberry vines. I pick the pan I brought in my brown sack full, not mindful of the scratches on my arms and hands on account of I'm picking so fast and I'm scared by what I did. Why I didn't get a chigger, I don't know. Maybe I was moving too fast for those red devils to latch on me. Soon's my pan is full, I run home.

In sight of our yellow house, I slow down and act like I'm having fun walking home with a pan of blackberries. War and Snipe come galloping from the porch to see what I have. I let them have one berry apiece before I go on in the house.

"Here's some blackberries for you, Mama. We better get down there and pick the rest today or tomorrow or they'll be eaten by the birds."

Or by someone else.

"You picked them this morning?" Mama asks. "What got into you to do that?"

"Oh, nothing. I just wanted to get us some so we could sprinkle a little bit of Jane's sugar on them. They don't need much they're so sweet."

Just like that, I lied.

Mama doesn't put up with lying, and she'll switch us good and proper if she catches us doing it. I'm doing it now, and I know I'll do it again if I want to go back to that cabin.

I don't know much about religion like Ruby does, but I'm pretty sure I'm headed to hell.

CHAPTER Twenty One

Something's Out There

I have to make up for my sins, especially since I know I'll be lying some more before curiosity stops eating me up. I help Mama all the rest of the day before she asks me to. I go down and cut her new soap into squares and save the brown stuff underneath it in jars to use outside for the big wash-ups the men do after plowing or pulling stumps.

I cook dinner and supper and do the dishes with not even a frown. I grab a hoe before sundown and hoe weeds around the squash and okra. In the outhouse, I knock all the spiders off the walls with a broom and sweep them outside. When I go to bed that night, I hope God's not as mad at me now since I been so good all day.

Next morning early, I jump in the dishpan while the boys are still eating and scrub the gravy skillet and the biscuit pan. As soon as someone finishes a plate, I take it, wash it, wrench it, dry it, and put it away.

"What's ailing you, Bid?"

"Nothing, Dad. Are you finished with your plate?"

He hands it to me, and I clean it and put it up before he leaves the table. Mama is looking at me strange like, and

Tommy says, "Gaw, Biddy, you taking some of Mama's Herb Whiz?"

"No, I'm not. Hand me that bowl and platter, Tommy." I wash them quick and grab up the other plates and silverware. Dad gives orders to all the boys for the day, and Calvin's supposed to help Tommy do something or other.

"Okay if I gather more blackberries after I finish the dishes and make the beds? They'll go to waste if we dillydally." I say all that, but I know the real truth is I want to be near that cabin again.

"Is there a good mess of them?" Mama asks.

"Sure is. Plenty to eat, some for canning, and maybe a cobbler."

"Doobie, can we let the younger boys off to do a little picking today?"

Dad nods his head like I knew he would. He cherishes blackberries near as much as he loves that fiddle and banjo of his.

Mama stands up giving orders. "Cal, take Sammy, War, and Snipe to help your sister with the picking today. All of you put your old shoes on. I don't care if they're too small—put them on anyways. Pull your socks up over the bottom of your overalls and tuck them in tight.

"Soon's you get your shoes and socks on, come to the shed. I'll soak your socks and arms with coal oil. Don't want you turning into one hot chigger bite like you did last summer. You'll still get some, but not as bad. Keep your eyeballs peeled for snakes, especially right in the middle of those bushes. Take Moolie. He'll let you know if there's a snake anywhere."

We shuffle off to the blackberry vines with Moolie running circles around us and yapping at squirrels and barking at whoever knows what. We got us two milk buckets, three lard cans with skinny wire handles, and a bean pot to carry our berries home. Snipe has to carry the water jar, and I tell him to quit sipping out of it. He makes a face and looks at War. War thumps him on the head, but not as hard as he usually does.

"Stop drinking all our water, stupid," he mumbles.

I don't know what to think of War right now. He hasn't been in any trouble since Allen's accident, but I know he's got a secret. I feel it in my bones. To be honest, I don't trust him.

Allen bossed us to hurry back with those blackberries so Mama can make him a cobbler. "I'm the only lucky fella who gets to eat it," he said before he busted out laughing at how all the kids looked like they were going to blubber over not getting any cobbler. He's out of the bed now and gets to walk around inside the house and eat whatever he wants. He's teasing us something terrible again, so I figure he's sure enough getting over that head kicking.

John is supposed to come in a few days to see if Mama has been taking proper care of Allen's wounds. I figure he might give her a prize she's done so good.

Before the sun is high in the sky, our buckets and pan are about full, and I'm itching to take off over the hill to the MacGregor cabin. I'm also itching from chiggers eating my arms, but I don't give them any attention. What would Calvin do if I told him what I did yesterday morning?

It takes us longer going home with our heavy load and we're stopping to claw ourselves every little bit. Snipe has the worst case of chiggers, and he's miserable. Soon's we get home, Mama puts on kettles of water to heat so we can take a baking soda bath. On the table are cold biscuits with cow butter and sorghum. We eat it up like pigs on account of we're near starving to death.

"I never saw any prettier berries, kids," Mama tells us,

and she's smiling.

Water heated, Mama wants me to get my bath over with first, so everyone is shooed out of the kitchen. We have to undress outside and give her our clothes to boil. I won't do it till she sends the boys to the field so I can have privacy. Not even when she promises to stand in front of me like a curtain, no sir. We get a bath every week, and we always go through a bunch of my shenanigans. I can't help it. I'm stubborn.

I'm cleaned up and my chigger bites are doctored. Mama says, "I didn't get to make that dewberry cobbler with Allen getting hurt, so I intend to make us a blackberry cobbler right now. I'm cooking supper, too. I know you're tired and sunburnt, so go sit on the porch and rest till it's time to do the supper dishes."

Those dadgummed dishes. If I was an inch from meeting my Maker, I'd still have to do dishes. Still yet, it felt good to have Mama tell me to rest. I don't remember her ever doing that before.

Calvin comes out to the porch all clean and his hair slicked up with a part on the side. "How'd you beat out those younger ones for the tub?"

"Told Mama my leg was bothering me."

"Is it?"

"Nah."

"Calvin William Woods, you've gone to lying same as me, and you can bet we're going to be sorry."

He laughs, and I say, "Want to take a walk down the road? I might have a few secrets to share." Nothing gets Cal more excited than a secret.

"Yeah, maybe. Right now?"

I nod. I'm getting my nerve up to tell him I went to Mr. MacGregor's cabin and see what he says. I'm thinking I can talk him into going to see it for hisself. We don't see a living soul, so we take off towards the road. Calvin can't go as fast as me, so I hold back with him. I'm hoping some of the kids won't see us and try to follow, but soon we're out of sight on the real road. We don't go too far before we hear a beautiful and frightening sound coming from the woods. Calvin stops in his tracks. "Lordy-lord, that's a terrible sound," he says, his eyes rolling around every which way to see where it's coming from.

"I kind of like it now."

"You had too much sun today. Maybe we should go back."

"Nah, it's fine."

"Well, something's out there, that's for true," Calvin whispers, still looking around.

He's right, and I'm sure thinking hard about what Mr. Leroy said when the sheriff arrested him.

CHAPTER Twenty Two

A Concerned Citizen

Dang and double dang, but who should come down that road right before we cut off to head to the Y-spring but Sheriff Murphy. Cal and I go to looking like we're innocent as newborn calves when the sheriff stops his prisoner truck in the caliche gravel. White road dust floats up and coats the outside of his sunglasses and the front of his truck. He's not saying one word to no one, just stares at us through the open window with his arm leaning out of it and a lit cigarette in his fingers. What should happen next but Jean's head pokes from around the sheriff's shoulder. She's wearing sunglasses too.

"Jean, what in tarnation are you doing with the sheriff? You ain't arrested, are you?" I ask, leaning close to the man I can't abide.

"Of course not, and don't say 'ain't,' sis. I'm coming home for a while, kids, that's all. Anyway, where are you two headed?"

"Nowhere. Just taking a walk," Calvin says.

Nobody says nothing, and I start thinking the sheriff knows we're up to something. My stomach gets to squeezing tight. He says, "Jump in the back, and I'll take you home."

Now this is a predicament. If we don't go back home, Jean will tell Mama she saw us on the road. Mama will say, "What road?" and Jean will tell her it's the one going into town. She'll go to puzzling why Calvin and I are walking around when we're supposed to be home helping with the berries or something else. I know for a fact I'm supposed to be watching Doodles when Mama starts supper. We'd be in for it.

We know we're licked. Calvin lifts the metal latch on one of the prisoner cages for us to crawl inside. He pulls the door shut behind us, and we slouch against the sides like two jail birds getting hauled off to jail. Calvin says, "That no-good for nothing…"

"You talking about the sheriff?"

"Naw, Jack. He's got rough with Jean again, and that's why she's coming home for a while like she said."

"You don't mean it."

"I sure do. Why do you think she's wearing those sunglasses? Probably has a shiner under there. And she's wearing that hot sweater to cover up her arms. That son-of-a—"

"If he's hurt her, I'll beat him till he bleeds to death. You can write home about that." I'm talking tough, but my insides are quivering.

We don't talk no more because we got ourselves so worked up about Jack. Soon enough, all our six dogs are yelping and baying like they treed something and want one of the boys to come a running with a slingshot. Old gander comes hurrying up to bite my legs. I kick at him till he leaves me alone. Me and Calvin roll out of the cage and stand there watching the family showing up from every direction on account of the men got finished in the fields early today. When they see the sheriff and Jean step out, it makes a stir.

Snipe and War come around the corner of the house and stop dead in their tracks. Next thing you see are their backsides running off to somewhere. A rattley truck with tall wooden sides on the backend parks alongside Sheriff Murphy's truck.

A man I never laid eyes on before gets out. "Afternoon, Tate," he says, touching the side of his cap and eying the sheriff. He looks at Dad. "Came to yap at you about that young mule you have for sale, Mr. Woodson. Saw your handbill at Stanfill's."

Dad nods and raises up one hand like he wants the man in the cap to wait a minute. "Can I be of help to you, sheriff?" he says.

"Just bringing a few of your children home, Mr. Woodson." He smiles at Jean. "Well, I'll be heading back to town now. If I can be of any more service to you, Mrs. Logan, just let me know," he says, looking at my sister longer than I think is civil.

"Thank you, Tate." Jean answers, and I'm wondering how she can bear to talk to him so nice like that. The sheriff puts one long leg after another in his truck and shuts the door. I can't tell you why, but all of a sudden, I'm madder than a turkey in a rain storm. I walk up to the side of the sheriff's truck and stare him down through the open window. My mouth goes to rattling, and I can't stop it.

"Why're you keeping Mr. Leroy in that jail? You know he didn't hurt no one. You got yourself that big clue thing from Calvin now, so why you still pressing in on Mr. Leroy so hard? He wouldn't hurt a fly."

The sheriff looks at me through those sunglasses so's I can't see his eyes. His knuckles turn red, then white, on the driving wheel.

"Rose, those are pretty big words." He looks past me at Dad with a smile I know is a faker from the way his lips curl around his teeth.

"Biddy, that's enough," Dad says, and his voice means I'm not being respectful of my elders and I'd better get to changing real fast.

"Aw, that's all right, Mr. Woodson. Miss Rose here's a concerned citizen. She seems to have taken an unusual partiality to Mr. Jones, and she wants to inquire about his welfare. Isn't that right, Miss Rose?"

I almost yell *damn right!* but I bite my tongue. No telling what would happen, and I'm sure not desiring to get my britches tanned in front of everyone, especially the sheriff. I nod my head.

Sheriff Tate says, "After a preliminary hearing before the court last week, Mr. Leroy Abraham Jones was remanded into custody because, Miss Rose, the judge finds ample reasons to hold this prisoner for trial. With all the hard evidence, Mr. Jones has been charged with first-degree murder."

He smiles that corny smile again, and for some reason, I think about the chalkboard at school. If I had one of those chalkboard erasers, I'd erase his grin off good and proper. His fancy words don't hide what he's blabbing about. Mr. Leroy is in big trouble, and the sheriff's glad.

I step closer to the truck window again so's no one can hear me and whisper, "I know what you're up to, and you won't get away with it." Then, before you can crack a knuckle, I tell him in a loud voice, "Why thank you for telling us all that news, sheriff. That's just fine, ain't it?" I plant a big fat smile on my face when I turn around. Faces stare and frown at me like maybe I'm touched in the head, and I don't care.

I march into the house and up to Charley-Bird. I wiggle my finger through the slats. He scoots along the little bar with his orange feet until he's close to my finger. He cocks his head one way, then the other. I make little smoochie sounds, and he answers back with noises I swear sound like someone blowing air through their lips.

"Yeah, that's what I think about that lawman, too, Charley. I don't trust him as far as I can throw him."

A long streak of lightning lights up the whole sky outside. Thunder sends the house frame into a rumbling shudder a few seconds later, rattling the thin piece of glass in the only window upstairs. Charley's feathers stand up like I've rubbed them backwards. He cheeps and flies from his roost to the top of his water catch-all and over to his food bin. I cover the cage with the dish towel, but Charley keeps flapping his wings and making a racket. I take his cage off the little table by the window and put it on the floor beside the wash stand. He makes a few more peeps and settles down.

I wish I could.

Lend a Hand?

Cal was right. Jean has a shiner, and Mama warned us to keep our traps shut about it. I may not like my brothers sometimes, but I like them plenty when they get off in a corner and say what they'd like to do to Jack Logan. I add my two-cents worth, too, and we're all in cahoots about our feelings towards that man we used to treat like family.

Later on, when everyone's gone to bed, Heaven and Jean cry their eyes out something pitiful. The loud thunder cracks shaking the earth and our house woke me up but not Doodles. I hear Jean crying in her pillow, and I stay still on the mattress beside the bed so she won't know I'm hearing her. Lord, I'm mad at that no-good husband of hers.

It keeps on raining all the next day, and we're about to wrestle each other to the floor we're so tired of being cooped up. Dad's been walking and spitting in his spit-can worrying about some of his new crops washing away. Jean and Mama sew on buttons and fix rips in our clothes, and the rest of us play or fight just out of earshot of anyone who might get a switch or belt after us.

"I don't think the rain's ever going to stop, Doob," Mama

says to Dad during our noon meal.

Late afternoon, Allen takes out his big book of *Grimm's Fairy Tales* and reads us cockeyed stories about trolls and princesses and things we never heard tell of except in that book. Law, who thinks up such things? Still yet, I like hearing them, especially the way Allen reads them to us with lots of big eyes and whispers and such.

We're about to sit down to a fine supper of roast pork, red-eye gravy, cornbread, cucumbers and sliced onion in vinegar, and a mess of snap beans with bacon when the dogs start barking. We have the big doors closed to keep the water from leaking inside, so we don't know it's Billy Mannicott from the Childers farm a few miles away till Sammy opens the door and there he stands outside the screen door.

"Come in and have some supper with us, Billy," Mama calls from the table.

"I'm about a drowned rat, ma'am. If it's all right, I'll stay out here. Uh, Mr. Woodson, Pa was wondering if Tommy might come and help us out some. We shore could use a hand."

Dad turns around to look at Billy with a hunk of meat on the end of his fork. "What's this about, son?"

"Well, sir, with the creek rising with all the rain and that wash out last night, we're getting in trouble. Old man Childers don't give us much of a house to live in, and it's done sunk in the ground about a foot. Now, the creek's rising higher than our house, and dadburned if it don't look like it might come rushing down and wash us and our livestock clean to Talala. We ain't letting no rain beat us out of house and home, so me and Pa and Dodson's making us a dam around the house on the creek side. We're using rocks, gunny sacks, and the timber we found stored in the shed when we come here last year."

Billy bends over coughing into his hand.

"You better get that cough tended to," Mama says. "You need some horehound?"

"No, ma'am. Ma will give me something when I get home. We been working since before daylight stacking rocks and stuffing everything not nailed down between them. Mr. Woodson, Pa's all wore out." Billy turns his face to cough.

"You think it'll work, Billy, the dam you're making?" Dad asks.

"Yessir, it's working pretty fair. Needs constant tending to keep the water from gaining on us. I've dug some side channels to run that creek off in another direction. If Tommy helps me and Dodson, I'm pretty shore we can keep things built up tonight and save us from flooding away. Ma and the little kids ain't much help with the heavy work."

Tommy's been scooping big forkfuls of food in his mouth and listening at the same time. Now, he hops up swinging a leg over the bench seat and grabbing two biscuits at the same time. "Let me fetch my slicker out in the shed and we'll take off, Billy."

"Wish I could come too, fellas," Allen says. Mama looks at him with a stormier look than the gray sky outside. Allen smiles a crooked smile back at her.

"Tom, use my tall rubber boots and get your coat, too," Dad says.

"I don't need a coat—"

"Yessir, you do," Dad says.

Tommy grabs his coat out of the old wardrobe in the front room and slings it over his shoulder. He pulls a cap on his head and pushes through the screen door handing Billy a biscuit. Billy nods at Dad before he turns to follow Tommy. We hear Billy coughing while they walk off.

We sit there not saying a word or nothing till Jean says, "Now, isn't this something? A table full of food and not a soul wants to eat it."

That's all it takes, and we're busy piling up our plates and savoring Jean and Mama's good cooking. Shoot, mine too, on account of I made the gravy. Dishes after supper aren't so bad with Jean helping. She always goes to the dishpan and lets me dry. Drying is the easiest of the two chores, and we usually jabber while we're working. She isn't too much to talk right now with her sad feelings about Jack jumping around in her head.

Dad and Calvin bundle up to go outside and make sure the pigs and cows are bedded down and the chickens haven't washed away to kingdom come. Dad comes back carrying Tommy's coat over his arm. He doesn't say anything, and I'm wondering if Tommy left it in the shed on purpose. Seems like he wants to be his own man with nobody bossing him since he's nineteen.

Next morning, the sun is shining and we have the solid doors open both in the kitchen and the front room. A nice breeze is mixing through the house, and it feels good after all that cooping up inside. Billy-Jack, our Rhode Island Red rooster, is crowing like he's the King of the Cow Patties or some such thing. He's Mama's favorite, so he gets away with everything, even chasing us down to spur our legs if he gets a mind to.

We're passing the breakfast food around the kitchen table when Tommy pulls the screen door open and stands halfway inside, dripping wet. I never saw Tommy looking so tuckered out or his dark hair so messed up. He's mighty particular about his hair usually, but not right now.

"My lands, Thomas, Jr., you look like you're dragging.

Come on in here and sit down. I'll fetch you a towel," Mama says, raising up from the table.

"Mama, I just soaked a mountain of mud off me and my clothes in the creek, and to tell you the truth, I'm nigh to freezing clear down to my bones."

Mama crosses the room and digs in one of the old trunks lining the same wall where the wardrobe sits and pulls out a pair of folded overalls, a shirt, and a pair of long underwear. She pulls a towel off the hook inside her bedroom and hands all of it to Tommy. The pair of long underwear falls to the floor, and War, Snipe, and Jay Bird snicker like goons.

Tommy says, "Say, can't a man have any privacy around here?" He winks at the kids and walks past us, stopping with his hand on the gopher hole door. His blue eyes are bloodshot marbles, and he looks tireder than a rat outrunning a broom.

He says, "I think I'll take a little snooze. Get me up in an hour, Dad, and we'll finish working the side field."

That's the last thing Tommy says to us before he dies of pneumonia two days later.

Medicine Tea

Before you go to blubbering about Tommy, let me tell you what happens with Old Sawbones. You're going to want to hear it, so just sit back and take it easy. There's time for bawling later on, if you still feel like it.

After Tommy came home so blessed tired, he slept and slept the whole rest of the day like he'd never wake up. I cooked dinner and made beds and watched over Doodles and Jay Bird, all the time not knowing how bad things were about to get around here. I warned you, that summer of 1934 was a bad one.

Allen spent the morning raking the sides of the garden and doing easy chores that wouldn't make Mama go crazy about him doing it. She went to work out in the muddy fields with Dad, Sammy, War, Jean, and Snipe, and she kept sending Snipe to tell me to check on Tommy and give her a report. Twice I told Snipe Tommy was still sleeping and that's all I knew about it. I didn't know why so much was being made about Tommy's condition since I figured he was just flat worn out from digging mud and carrying big rocks all night long at the Mannicott household.

Soon enough, Doodles tells me from her spot by the kitchen screen door that Calvin's washing up outside at the pump. All morning he's tied up garden vines for Mama and picked tomatoes and anything else ripe and needing to be brought in. About then, we hear Allen holler, "Looky there, a bunch of mud hens traipsing in from the field!"

Allen pumps water in buckets and throws it on everyone on account of they're covered in red Oklahoma mud. Everyone gets tickled about it since it's so foolish looking. First thing Mama does after getting into dry clothes is go to the gopher hole. She comes out declaring Tommy has a fever building.

You won't believe what she does next. She up and wrings a chicken's neck and fixes chicken and noodles especially for Tommy. She says it cures what's ailing you, and most times, it does. Not this time. Mama spoons a little of the broth into Tommy and quick as anything, he throws it back up.

I'll tell you this, none of the rest of us gets sick eating that pot of chicken noodles for supper, no sir. Especially with Jean's cornbread with cracklings and a pot of beans besides. After supper, Dad comes out of the gopher hole with jars of dried broom weed and mullein and a little brown bottle with a stopper.

"Hand me the honey, Biddy," he says and I dry my hands on a dish towel and get the honey from the cabinet over the sink. He sets the kettle on to boil and goes back in the hole to get one of Mama's empty quart jars. I wash the jar and dry it careful-like on account of I know Dad's going to use it for Tommy's medicine tea. Mama already canned some of Dad's medicine tea, and it's right on the shelf with her beets and sauerkraut.

"Why don't you use the medicine tea already canned up,

Dad?" I say.

"Tommy needs fresh and strong," he says. I'm thinking Tommy must really be ailing as I watch Dad crumble broom weed and mullein into a piece of dish towel rag he keeps in the drawer for making his medicine teas. He ties the piece of towel rag into a bundle and sets it in a crockery bowl. When the water boils, he pours it over the bundle all the way to the top of the bowl and puts a plate on the top of it.

I finish the dishes and prop the dishpan on its side to dry. Jay Bird, Doodles, Allen, and Calvin gather quiet like at the table to watch Dad finish making medicine. I sit on the bench and pull Doodles on my lap. Dad takes the plate off the crockery bowl and mashes the weed bundle with a spoon to get all the medicine stuff out. He hands the wet bundle to Jean just when she walks by. She shakes it into the garbage bucket.

Dad adds two big tablespoons of honey to the bowl and three droppers full of horehound syrup he takes from the dark bottle. He stirs it with a fork and uses the drinking bucket dipper to dip the hot mixture into a quart jar. There's just enough left in the bowl to fill a fat coffee mug about half full.

"I told him to wear his coat," he says staring into the mug. "Jean, fetch the Vicks VapoRub from the chest of drawers in my bedroom. Take it to Ma and have her rub his chest up good. I'll start getting this tea down his throat. I made enough to keep him sipping all night."

I catch the gopher-hole door behind Dad and slip inside the dark room that feels like sickness. Mama is in a chair beside the old bed, and Tommy lays there not moving nor saying a word. The door opens and Jean steps in with the blue jar of Vicks. Mama unbuttons Tommy's shirt and rubs his chest with it. He groans like it hurts when she touches his skin. I'm feeling a stomachache coming on like when Mr. MacGregor got kilt. Jean comes by and pats my shoulder. I look up in her face, but she's looking back at our brother.

Tommy is our fun brother, our handsome brother, our hard-working brother, our singing brother. The one the girls at school fight about on account of they all want to be his girlfriend. The one the men and kids all like. The one Squirrel tries to beat and never can. Him sick for the first time makes all of us scared, but we hide to do any bawling. Red eyes tell on us, but we don't talk about it. That's just how our family acts about private things.

We get sent to bed early and not one kid acts up. Jean and Mama take turns sitting with Tommy and helping him sip medicine tea. My stomachache curls me up in a ball, but I don't let on to Doodles. She goes sound to sleep, and I get up and talk to Charley-bird till I start yawning. I guess I fell asleep wrapped in a quilt, because here I am the next morning sprawled across the foot of the iron bed.

My eyes pop open and something's not right. I don't hear any *Hey-hoe, Hay-yah-gah,* or *Hoe-hey.* The cows are mooing to be milked in the pens outside, but no screen doors are opening and closing. No milk buckets are clanging against the gate when someone opens it. Jean hasn't been to bed. I clomp down the steps and see her rolling out biscuit dough.

"Where is everyone?"

"Morning, Bid. Calvin and Sammy went to milk the cows."

Calvin and Sammy milk the cows? Whoo-boy, that should be a good one.

"Where's Dad?"

"In the field. I fixed him an early breakfast."

"Is Tommy worse?"

"I'm afraid so. He's coughing really bad now."

That makes my heart jump right into my throat. I trot toward the gopher hole.

"No, Bid, don't go in there. We think Tommy has pneumonia, and you might catch it."

"What about Mama?"

"She's used to it. She stayed up with all of us no matter what sickness we had. How about washing up and making us some of your good gravy?" Jean smiles, but her eyes don't.

Soon's the food is ready and we're all at the table, Jean opens the gopher hole door and calls Mama. Calvin and Sammy put the foamy milk on the end of the counter and cover the buckets with dish towels to keep out everything that wants to fall in, like a fly or gnat. I'm feeling a mite poorly, but I go ahead and eat and watch Mama at the same time. She takes a biscuit and puts a piece of bacon in it. She takes a nibble or two and puts it down. She gets up and goes to her bedroom. She doesn't fool any of us. We know she's crying and worried sick.

By noon time, we know Tommy's in real bad trouble. We hear him coughing to high heaven when the door opens. We aren't allowed to go look at him. Calvin hitches up the horses and Dad leaves out in the wagon with the horses hurrying along to get the doctor.

I need to tell you about this. When my dad gets mad, he talks to hisself. You can't make out what he's saying, only some of the words. Soon's he got back from town, that's what he's doing. He puts the horses up and comes inside to get him a drink out of the dipper. He crams a big wad of Beechnut in his mouth and mumbles all the way out of the house. He doesn't act like he sees us staring at him and wondering what happened in town.

Like usual when he has this affliction, he gets busy hammering around outside and messing with this and that. None of us kids bother him. Except Jean. She'll kind of mosey along and take him a glass of sweet tea and follow him around helping him with whatever he's doing till he gets okay. She has a soothing way with him, that's for true. When we told her how he was acting, she went outside to find him.

Me and Calvin and Sammy don't know what to do with ourselves. We're sitting on the boards covering the cistern waiting for someone to make us do something. Mama is with Tommy, and Allen's curled up kind of sideways in the front room reading another book. Dad's mad. Jean's with him letting him carry on, and the other kids are messing around here and there.

"What you think happened in town, Calvin?"

"Don't know. We'll find out soon as Jean comes back around."

Pretty soon, Jean comes and sits right down in the middle of us.

"Ain't you tired, sis?" Sammy says. "You shore look it."

Jean sits up straight and brushes the hair off her forehead. "Why, thank you ever so kindly, little brother."

"Huh?" Sammy says.

Jean laughs and leans back against the water pump. "Never mind, Sam. I am tired, and that's a fact."

"What's Dad so upset for?" Calvin says.

Jean shakes her head. "My, my, that man sure doesn't know how to get along with the folks around these parts."

"Dad?" asks Sammy.

"No, the new doctor. Doc Silvers. He argued with Dad that Tommy can't possibly have pneumonia since it came on so fast. Dad told him otherwise, and that he's seen that kind of pneumonia before and it comes on just like Tommy's did with fever, stomach ailings, then the body aches and cough. The doctor asked Dad if he'd given any medicines to Tommy, and Dad told him about his medicine herb tea."

Jean starts up laughing. First, it's a little rumble, then she's holding her arms and rocking back and forth with laugh tears dropping down her cheeks.

"What's so blamed funny, Jean?" I say.

"Well… Old Sawbones told Dad, 'That's the trouble with your kind. You think you're medical doctors with all your herbs and roots and leaves, and truth is, you're a bunch of barbaric medicine men no better than the savages!'"

Us kids stare at Jean like we can't believe our ears, and we can't. We never heard anyone say such a terrible thing to our dad. He learned his healing secrets from the Choctaws and the Cherokees and other Natives, and that settles it for us. When he says we need to drink sassafras tea every Spring to thin our blood and keep us strong, we drink sassafras tea. When people come from miles around for his herb medicines, they lift him high to all who'll listen. To hear him spoken to mean makes us downright bewildered.

"Dad said he would have thrashed that big-mouth doctor if John hadn't been there. He put his arm on Dad's shoulder and conversed with him while he walked him outside. He promised to get the doctor here first thing in the morning to look at Tommy. He shook Dad's hand and told him he believed in the medicine and ways of the old timers and the Natives. That young doctor must be quite the smart young man, I'm thinking."

An idea that seems so bright it would hurt your eyes if you were looking at it pops into my head. It's about Jean and John and some big maybes, but first, you have to settle in and hear what happens when Tommy dies.

CHAPTER
Twenty Five
It Don't Make No Sense

It's funny who's the biggest comfort when things go wrong. This time, it's Snipe. First off, he begs and pleads for Mama to allow him to bring things to her in the gopher hole so's he can see Tommy. She won't do it. She said he'd turn up sick, shore as the world. I expect Snipe to get mad and act up like usual, but he doesn't. He picks up a broom and sweeps the whole house and the front porch, too. He tells me he'll help me with the supper dishes later, and I near fall over from hearing it. Next thing I know, he sidles up to me and says he's got something to tell me but don't say a word of it to War.

"What's it about?" I ask him.

"You double, double dog promise not to tell?"

"Sure, I do."

"Swear on your own grave?"

"Yeah."

"Swear your eyeballs will catch on fire if you tell?"

"I guess so."

"Naw, I can't. War'll thrash me to death."

"I won't let him."

He looks all around and whispers, "It's about something we found." He takes off running out of the house and I look out the door and see him hurrying in the direction of Hoot Creek. I'm halfway on his trail when geese and guineas start up a terrible racket. The dogs whine and bark at Doc Silver's black car bobbing up Blackberry Road to our house. I holler upstairs to tell Jean so she can let Mama know. Jean says Mama's orders are for Dad to stay in the fields today so's not to get that doctor riled up no more.

All the kids come running inside, and I tell them to stay put in the front room and be quiet. Allen says, "According to Old Sawbones, I'm supposed to be dead already. I think I'm the one, being in the grave and all, to go out and say howdy-do and bring him in the house."

That makes us snicker and feel better. Law, we need it. We're a scraggly bunch around here worrying about Tommy. Our whole world has stopped, it seems like. Tommy's worse than ever, no matter how hard Mama and Dad and Jean fuss over him.

The doctor walks in the front door with Allen leading him in. Allen's crossing his eyes and sticking out his tongue. His head is dented in over his eyebrow from where he was kicked and the doctor took out the crushed bones. He looks so funny making a face at us, we ball up in giggles. The doctor stares at us sitting against the wall on the rolled-up straw mattresses in the front room barefooted and messy hair-ed since Mama nor Jean has said a word about us taking a comb to it. He sweeps across us with his eyes and sticks his nose up so high he'd drown in a rainstorm. That makes us laugh harder, and soon we're hooting like folks who never did have good sense.

"If you'll be so kind as to show me where the patient

is…" Doc Silvers says, and Allen sweeps his arm all fancy in a half-circle aimed at the gopher hole.

"Right this way, sir," he says, and that throws us into another cackling fit. He opens the gopher hole door for the doctor and comes back slapping his leg and laughing to high heaven.

Snipe slips through the front door and sits down against the wall away from War.

"What's so funny?" he says, and that makes us take off on another row of laughing. Doodles doesn't know what we're laughing about so she rolls on the floor acting silly and jumping from one rolled up mattress to the next.

"I'm going to go spy on Old Sawbones and see what he says," I say.

"Why can't I do it?" says Snipe.

"Cause women are better at spying than men. More sneaky," Allen says, grinning at me. I tiptoe to the gopher hole and pull the door open real quiet-like.

"What are you doing, Biddy?" says Jean from behind me. It gives me a start, and I holler a little. "You just as well come on in with me. You're a big girl now," she says. I look back at the boys and raise my shoulders. They look kind of jealous about me getting to go in when they can't.

Mama is standing at the foot of the bed holding her hands tight together while Doc Silvers listens to Tommy's chest with his stethoscope. I know it's called that because Calvin told me it's the one thing I should know about doctors' stuff or folks would call me dumb. I sure don't want that to happen, so I memorized the name of it. The doctor feels Tommy's head and takes hold of his wrist. He shakes his head and takes his stethoscope off and drops it in his black bag. He stands looking at Mama and Tommy with his lips all puckered up.

A loud knock on the gopher hole door startles us. It opens wide and a colored woman with the friendliest face and biggest yellow hat I ever did see sticks her head through the door.

"Good after-the-noon, y'alls. I'm Miz Abernathy, Leroy's sister from Selma? I come calling this day to invite you to our revival at the First Calvary Hope Church in Nowata this week. We's got a big tent all set up to bring the word of God to y'alls starting Thursday and going to Sunday morn.

"My Leroy speaks so highly of you good folks. I wondered would y'alls come to hear our 'vangelist, Mr. Noah T. Brown. Mm-mm, that man can preach the socks off a rooster, he can! I'm an 'vangelist too, don't you know, and I'll be preaching a mite afore Mr. Brown each evening. We'll have lemonade and cakes and pies after the meeting each and every night, so I shore do want y'alls to come and bring the whole family with you."

I can't stop staring at Miz Abernathy's bright yellow dress and hat and the way her eyes spark like two battery plugs rubbed together. For two cents, I'd get up and go home with her right now, that's how happy she makes me feel.

Just like that, Miz Abernathy's shining-sun face changes to a worried frown. "Your chil'ren out there tells me there's a real sick boy in here, and I'm wondering if I can come in and pray with y'alls? I'd be most honored to do so."

"Mrs. Woodson, these are the last moments of your boy's life. I insist you remove this woman immediately." Doc Silvers's face turns bright red over his cheeks and nose while he's blabbing at Mama. His blue eyes go bloodshot, and when he gets through talking, his lips are creased tighter than mouse lips.

Mama cries out hearing that it's Tommy's last moments of life. She drops to her knees by Tommy's head and lays her chin on the edge of the bed. "Don't leave us, Tommy," she says with the saddest voice I ever did hear. Strange wails sound like they're coming from her stomach but can't make it out of her mouth.

Me and Jean grab hands and sink to the floor bawling our eyes out. Miz Abernathy steps around us and the doctor and goes to stand behind Mama. She raises her hands. "My God, my God. I'm calling on Thee right here, right now. We're a'humbling ourselves and seeking Thy face. We fears You, Lord, and tries hard to leave behind the evil things of this here world, so's we be looking for that health to the flesh and strength to the bones for this young man."

"Have some respect, woman!" the doctor hisses at Miz Abernathy, but she doesn't act like she hears him. I'm watching her and feeling tears roll off my face like they been greased. She paces up and down behind Mama the length of the bed twirling her hands in a circle. Her eyes are shut, and I don't see how she's not running into Mama or the doctor, but she isn't.

"Rain the mercy of Thy Son and His resurrected Self down on us now, precious Lord. We're your servants a-calling on Thee. Heal this boy in Thy Son Jesus's name. We're waiting for Your spirit to fill this here room and this here boy's chest. He is weak, and his bones is troubled. Shine down Thy grace on him 'cause he's your chile."

Me and Jean are staring at Mr. Leroy's sister with our mouths open. Jean catches my eye and nods toward the doctor. His face is a mess, like a wind storm whipping up red dirt and blowing it on fresh-washed clothes. He reaches around Mama and bends over our brother. We stretch our necks so we can see. He's feeling Tommy's neck with three fingers. He bustles Mama aside and puts his ear to Tommy's chest. "If you will excuse me…" he turns and says all mean-like at Mama. With his cross-looking scowl and his glasses sliding down his nose, he looks like a hooty owl hunting for supper.

Miz Abernathy talks and hollers to God with more of those Bible words, and I'm thinking she sure is a good friend of the Almighty to talk to Him like that. The doctor dips in his bag and pulls out a small mirror. He sticks it in front of Tommy's mouth and nose, then lays it on the bed. He picks up Tommy's wrist and presses two fingers into it. He puts our brother's wrist back on the bed and looks at a watch on the end of a chain he pulls from his pocket.

Jean and I are shaking so bad our bones are nigh to rattling. Mama's cries have gone high and pitiful like a trapped rabbit.

"Lord, You be the Lord who heals us. We're waiting for Thee to works a miracle here in this room. Won't You raise him up, O Rose of Sharon?"

"You should be ashamed making light of this family's grief," the doctor spits out at Miz Abernathy, but she's looking up at the ceiling with tears running down her face in streams. The doctor pulls the sheet over my brother's face. Mama shrieks and bends all the way over to the floor.

"I demand that you stop this! This young man is dead, and you, madam, are a heathen."

"Lion of Judah, heal this boy," Miz Abernathy says to the ceiling.

The doctor pushes past her and stumbles over me and Jean. He grabs the wall to keep from falling down. He turns and stares at us like it's our fault he tripped. He's shaking from head to toe when he grabs hold of his doctor bag. He says,

"I've never seen anything like this backwoods place of witchcraft. Good day, Mrs. Woodson. I shall record the time of your son's death on this day as 1:30 p.m. I'm sorry for your—"

Tommy sits straight up in the bed with the sheet over his head.

"I'm hungry, Mama," he says.

I scream. Jean screams. Mama jumps off the floor and gawks at Tommy like he's a ghost—and maybe he is.

"Oh, Blest Assurance, thank you! You done brought this dead boy back to his family!" Miz Abernathy claps her hands and looks up like she's seeing things our eyes don't see and never will.

Doc Silvers's face is horrible mad. His lips move, but no words come out. He grabs at the leather door-pull and misses, near falling down. "Humph!" he growls, scrambling up and near yanking the door off its hinges to escape our gopher hole.

"Mama?" Tommy says, the sheet tumbling off his head.

Mama bends over Tommy and smooths the hair off his face. "Son, it don't make no sense, none at all, but you're not dead, and I'm going to make you the best supper of your life."

Roastnears

All the boys are at the Henson's place with Dad, Mr. Henson, and the Henson family hammering up more pens to have a rodeo this Saturday. Even Jay Bird got to go since he gets to play with Mr. Henson's son Benny, who's the same age as him. Mama sent them off with cold sausage patties and biscuits and our biggest jars full of well water. She pointed me to the heap of dirty clothes she'd gathered from everywhere in tarnation.

Oh, law, did I ever cuss in my own head about that. All that good revival preaching and singing we attended after Tommy came back to life, and I'm still cussing. Whoever said it was women's work to do the cooking and the dishes and the washing? Why can't I do what the boys do? It ain't fair, and it never will be. It boils my blood and out comes those cuss words.

Talk about boiling, I'm boiling my third tub full of bloomers and long handles. My knuckles are sorely raw from scrubbing on the washboard all morning, even with Mama and Jean taking turns with me. Jean boiled some thick clothes' starch made with flour and water and we dunked the best overalls and shirts in it before hanging them on the clothes line. Doodles handed me the clothespins, so I guess she'll start helping out around here. Thinking of that kind of makes me sad for my little sis.

I'm taking the empty clothes basket to the house and Jean meets me with a measure tape and loops it around my waist. "Jean, do you have to do that right now?"

"Hold still. You want pretty clothes when school starts don't you?"

I do want nice dresses, but I can't stand all the fussing before they get made. All that measuring and pinning and snipping with scissors makes me want to run to the woods. I let out a big groan so's Jean knows I hate it, but I go ahead and allow her to tape measure me for about the hundredth time. Jean and Mama have been so dead set on measuring me lately you'd think I was a dressed scarecrow about to be stuck on a pole in the kafir corn.

Jean's got it in her head they need to order the material for my school-term dresses and make my new winter underwear at the same time. I don't like any talk whatsoever about underwear, but they don't care anything about my modesty. I ask you, would you like it if your mama and sister cut strips of innertube rubber to hold up the legs and waist of your bloomers they're sewing, and they did it in front of everyone? 'Course you wouldn't, and I don't like it, neither. Besides, if I'm growing like a weed like they say, who says I won't grow out of the new underwear and those new dresses they're going to make before September?

I know the problem is Jean's just restless, 'bout as much as Calvin. I don't want her going back to Jack ever again, but she's scrubbed every inch of this house and all of us and canned everything that can go in a jar from the garden and now she's starting in on me in particular. Makes my life miserable, I'm telling you that.

Mama comes outside smoothing her hands over her hair from her forehead all the way to the hair knot at the back of her head. "Girls, I think we about got this done," she says. "Come inside and eat a bite of dinner, and we'll go gather that corn for tonight."

Jean wipes her hands on the towel around her waist, and we drift inside to the smell of boiling beans. Mama drops little pieces of dough in the top of the bean pot, and she's made us some sweet tea. I reckon it isn't so bad to be home today and get Mama's hot bean dumplings and tea, and the boys don't get any.

While I'm eating, I'm thinking that harvesting all that field corn by hand is going to be hot work. I guess I don't mind since the Woodson family sure does love it's roastnears. When the first mess of corn comes ripe every summer, we take it to the creek and boil it up in pots over an open fire for supper. If you want cow butter smeared on it or salt and pepper, you're welcome to it, but most of us slick it down our throats with just a shake of salt. We eat till we're ready to pop. If we have any left over, Mama bakes it slow the next day into parched corn. She throws it up on the cook stove when it's finished. In no time at all, it disappears.

"Let's just scrape our plates and leave them on the counter. That sun isn't going to be friendly as it is," Mama declares when we finish eating. We put on our bonnets and long-sleeve shirts and head for the cornfield in the heat of the day. Mama says she isn't taking any chances about snakes, even with Moolie around to sniff them out, so she puts Doodles under a tree and tells her not to get off the old blanket she spread out. I give her some buttons to pretend she's sewing them on the blanket with a stick for a needle. Now, here we are, twisting off those ears of corn from the stalks and throwing them in bushel baskets and everyone's sweating except for Doodles.

Grouchy Pants, our billy goat, is hitched to our smallest carry wagon, and we've almost filled the empty hull with corn. Mama fixed it where he can't move his head but a little ways in ever direction so's he doesn't eat up our corn. He'll eat anything, and I'm not kidding. I've seen him bite out chunks of old innertubes and swallow them. He'll gobble a nail, or bite through wood, or anything else. That's goats for you, and I think they stink.

"Ain't this enough yet?" I whine, since I sure do want to be done to get out of the sun.

"Don't say 'ain't', Bid," Jean says before the words barely drop out of my mouth. "You're doing a good job breaking yourself of that habit. Wish Sammy and the twins would try harder."

"Oh, Jean, I have to say it because I'm so hot and tired."

"One more bushel, and we'll have enough. Roll your britches legs up. That'll cool you down."

I pull my half-filled basket down to the end of the row we're working on and slip into the next row so's I can't be seen. I roll up my overall legs and lay back in the furrow between the rows. It's sort of shady, and a little breeze makes the corn leaves wave soft in the air and the yellow tassels at the top tip back and forth. I start a big yawn and shut my mouth in the middle of it. You might be wondering why, and I'll tell you. It's because I heard something moving through the corn stalks, and then it stopped.

At first, I think it might be a snake. I jump up and check all around on the ground. I stay still and listen. Something rustles a few feet away but not so's I can see anything. From the far end of the field where Doodles is, Moolie starts to bark.

The strange noise swishes through the leaves faster and faster until I can't hear it no more. Something was in that corn with me, and I'm sure wondering who or what it was.

Naked corncobs are all over the ground. Dad's fiddling, and I'm dancing my feet off. The sky is a dark blue, almost night-colored. Everyone sits in a jagged circle on the ground or on a stump they drug down from the house. I look up. The stars are lighting up and tiny embers from the fire float over our heads. Dad plays faster, and I feel near crazy in my feet as they clip and clop and move to the rhythm. My brothers are clapping in time, and law, I feel good. Dad finishes his song and hollers out, "Oo-weee!"

I fall on the ground beside Cal and Sammy, feeling happy as anything.

"You dance real good, sis," Sammy says.

"Why don't you dance with me sometimes?"

Sammy drops his head. "Pashaw, don't ask me to."

I grin and go pick another roastnear from the pot. I shake our metal salt shaker a few times over the kernels and sit down cross-legged to eat. In a few minutes, Snipe says, "Hey, down by the creek—you hear that? Sounds like a harmonica stuck on a low key."

"A bullfrog," Cal says.

"Let's go see if we can catch him," I whisper in Sammy's ear just as Tommy starts strumming his guitar. We crawl out of the campfire light on our hands and knees. "Okay, come on," I whisper, standing up and running toward the creek. My eyes can't see nothing after the light of the fire. Almost to the water, I trip and fall.

Something wiggles and grunts underneath me.

I roll around hollering. "Aghhh! Sammy, help me!"

"Bid, where are you?"

"Right here! Someone's got me!"

"Someone? Who? Where?"

"Listen!" I hiss.

Padded sounding footsteps run away. Loud splashes through the creek water, then cricket chirps and katydid buzzes fill up the air.

Sammy's voice is scared. "Bid, what happened?"

"Somebody," I breathe out in a scratchy whisper.

"Somebody? Did they grab you?"

"No, it wasn't like that. More like we got tangled up at the same time."

"Think it's a killer?"

"Too small."

"Who then?"

I don't answer, but my noggin is calculating hard about it.

CHAPTER Twenty Seven

Mule Rodeo

We run back to everyone like we got lit matches between our toes and sprawl on our bellies breathing hard. No one but Calvin pays us any mind. "Where'd you guys go?" he asks.

I take hold of Sammy's arm and shake my head. "Not here, Sam."

That sets Cal on a trigger to find out since he's so restless in his innards. I'm not going to tell him nothing with so many ears leaning in close, and by that, I mean War and Snipe and Jay Bird.

By the time we pick all the corncobs up and put them in a gunnysack, we're yawning like tuckered out raccoon dogs off the hunt. Dad sends Tommy to fetch a bucket of creek water to douse the campfire. The moon is covered over by clouds as we single file back to the house kind of stumbling along in the dark. My sleepy mind tries putting some horse sense on everything, but it can't. All I can rightly think of is my little mattress on the floor and falling into it and a little bit about Tommy.

He's been so well since Miz Abernathy came calling that day, he's doing everything he did before, and sometimes more.

His pneumonia just melted away, and he ate everything in sight for three whole days after he got up out of bed. We just shake our heads because, like Mama said right off, it doesn't make sense. Mama told Tommy more than once he's owing a bunch to the Almighty from here on out.

"You got that right, little Mama," he says back at her with his wide grin. She likes it when he calls her that, and nobody else does it but him.

Next morning, my eyes pop open to Dad's *Hey-hoe. Hoe-hey.* Cows are mooing low and long for milkers to hurry up and ease their burden. Next, I hear the screen door open and close a couple of times, and I accidentally fall back asleep. I wake back up and be real quiet while I dress so's I don't wake up Jean and Doodles. My plan, which I kind of dreamed about in a way, is I tell Calvin everything I think I know about the Wood Ghost, which was the secret I was referring to when that ol' lawman came along with Jean. Then we sneak off to Mr. MacGregor's cabin before everyone gets up and see what we see.

Calvin gets up with Allen and Tommy lately to help with straining the milk and even milking. I suppose he had to take that up since both our older brothers just about got dead this summer.

I tiptoe downstairs and here's Mama already starting breakfast earlier than ever. "Wash up, Biddy, and help me. Let's let Jean sleep in a bit this morn."

Heck fire and tarnation! Now I have to change my plan about going to the cabin this morning. I make a deal with myself—nothing in this world is stopping me from going tomorrow, or from telling Cal about my other suspicions.

I don't say nothing to Mama, just push the screen open to go use the outhouse. I see Tommy closing the gate on Dad's four young, unbroke mules he's taking to the mule rodeo today. Snip and Brownie are outside the pen with their tongues near to the ground panting with big silly smiles on their faces on account of they got to help bring the mules in from the pasture.

The cows are haltered to the smoke house for milking since their pen is full of mules, and that's what Cal and Allen are doing is milking. I know one thing, none of us will allow Allen anywhere near those ornery mules. Right now, those cusses are raising a ruckus, bucking and kicking each other and making hee-haw sounds. I'm thinking almost nobody can ride an unbroke mule, not even the best cowboy. I'm wondering why they're hankering to try. Tommy told me last night there's more going on than riding mules at the rodeo and I have to wait and see what it is. I know Dad's glad because he's about to make a little cash, and that's never bad.

Anyways, Dad is bringing mules to the rodeo, so he and Mr. Henson and one more fella—a rancher bringing livestock—are sharing the money they take in. Allen said it won't matter if it's a car with two people or a wagon with ten people or a man on a horse by hisself, it costs a dollar a load to come in.

Dad said he can't sell any corn liquor at this rodeo, but he sure can and rightly will at the one over in Washington County next week. That one's a real rodeo with cowboys and bucking horses and such, and they like a quick snort before and after they ride, especially when they take on the wild bulls. That's what he said to Mama on a private nature, but I heard him since I've been kind of big-eared lately.

I know you're thinking it's not right to sneak around and hear growed-up talk, and I don't think so, neither. Thing is, there's so blamed much going on that I don't understand, I just keep on keeping my ears wide open. It sure is interesting what you hear when you do that.

Anyways, Mama, Jean, and Doodles aren't going, and Mama said she's in no mood to see somebody get kicked by a mule when they try to ride one. Her and Jean are canning up a storm today, and I thank my lucky stars I got out of that chore. I think it was Jean's doing because Mama never thinks I should get out of work.

We've never been to a rodeo, so you know our eyes are big as cantaloupes when the wagon full of us pulls up to Mr. Henson's place and we see all kinds of pretty saddle horses tied up to a hitching post like the ones they have in town in front of the mercantile and bank. Booted kids are running around half-silly, and two ladies, one of them being Mrs. Henson, are selling some kind of orange-colored juice drink in pint jars. My mouth goes to watering when I see them putting ice chunks in the jars before pouring the drink on top. A little sign sitting on the table next to the jars says the drinks are five cents.

Law, I wish I had me a nickel right now. I have three hidden in a hole in the wall behind the iron bed upstairs, and I got them as a reward for reading three books and giving book reports to Mr. MacGregor. With him kilt, I'll maybe be old before I earn any nickels again unless I start taking in ironing. Jean gets a whole dime for ironing a basket of clothes.

Mr. Henson shows up out of nowhere and tells the boys where to pen the mules. Tommy and Sam herded them the four miles from our place to the Henson place behind Dad's work mule he tied to the back of our wagon. I have to tell you, this particular mule, Old Blue, isn't nothing like most mules. He and my Dad are close as sugar peas. Old Blue, he loves a chaw of tobacco now and then, and he'll sit on a step beside

Dad and look around like he's a man. Nobody can believe it when they see it, but Dad has a special way of training animals and settling bees and growing anything out of the most stubborn Oklahoma dirt. Mama says it's his Indian ways, and I don't doubt it none, no sir.

Dad jumps down from the buckboard seat, and Mr. Henson shakes his hand for a long time. He's wearing cowboy boots with his britches tucked into the tops of them, a white shirt, and a skinny little black ribbon thing tied into a bow underneath his shirt collar. He sure looks happy, that's a fact.

The rest of us hop out of the wagon and kind of stand around shy and all. Pretty soon, little Benny Henson runs up and grabs Jay Bird by the arm to go play. Dad and Tommy unhitch the mules and take them somewhere. War and Snipe take off in two opposite directions to who knows where, and Allen tells Cal the young lady with Mrs. Henson is seventeen-year-old Martha Henson. Allen jokes that since she's so pretty, the two of them ought to go "get acquainted and maybe Cal could get hitched since he's fifteen years old now."

Allen's forehead isn't as swollen now, just purple-red, scarred, and it dips in where the hoof broke the bones and the doctor took them out but didn't put anything back in. It's not as bad as we all thought it would be, and he's still Allen—funny, loves to read his books, and a big tease. Girls always take to him, that's for sure. Mama keeps one of his head bones in an empty snuff can with a lid in her sewing stuff, and I don't know why. I reckon I'll never understand growed-up women.

Everybody's gone now and that leaves me standing here by myself with my droopy hair needing a permanent so bad and my hands in my pockets wondering if I look like a hillbilly. I got Jean's shoes on with the Sears and Roebuck catalog pages in the toes, and I was careful my face and hands were clean so maybe I look like everyone else. I don't see any boys or girls from our Armstrong school, just kids belonging to the rancher cowboys.

I mosey around trying not to get in the way with all the clamor of men and horses and a few steers some boys about my age are pulling by ropes into a pen with a chute. I walk down a shady lane wide enough for a wagon or a car and find myself standing in front of the Henson house. It's pretty big with an upstairs and a nice porch that goes all along the front. All the windows have glass, and I don't see a single patch on any of the screens. Big shade trees around the house look like someone planned where they'd be and not where some tree decided to shoot up wherever it wanted like at all the places we lived in.

Why did Mr. Henson want to have an old mule rodeo here anyway? Looks like he's pretty rich, but maybe it's because people say he grew up in Nowata dirt poor like the rest of us. Mama says you can't outrun your roots, even if you sprout up to the clouds. I don't know what she means by that, but I heard Mr. Henson was so smart when he was a young'un, someone up and sent him to a college in Oklahoma City. He was gone for years and years and one day he comes back here with his family and starts working in the bank and being friendly to all his neighbors, like us. I mean going out-of-his-way kind of friendly.

Dad mentioned to him about the mule rodeo since he already had a few pens built at his house, and right away, Mr. Henson wanted to have one. His daughters are already out of school and one married. They say Mrs. Henson teaches Benny his schooling at home, and Ruby says the Hensons are connected to some Indian school in Oklahoma. She said her church goes there to take Christmas presents to the kids and such, and the Hensons, Mr. Henson formerly of Nowata, are big givers and do things like take the kids on camping and fishing trips in the summer.

"Would you like a drink?" someone behind me says. I spin around and there's Martha Henson holding a pint jar full of orange drink and chipped ice out to me. I can't find my tongue on account of Martha's even prettier than Rebecca, and her blond hair is soft curled with a piece of blue material holding it back from her face. She's wearing the nicest blue britches I've ever seen in my life with an ironed blue and white checked shirt tucked into her waistband. I know I must look ugly as sin in my boy overalls and old shirt.

I can't help it. My chin drops down kind of shameful like and I can't hardly speak. "N-n-no… that's all right," I say.

"Are you sure? I have an extra one just for you," Martha says.

I look up and she smiles so nice I decide I'm not ashamed no more. I take the drink and sip it. Lordy-lord I want to swig it down all at once, but I don't because I think that might be what a hillbilly does. I'll tell you right now, it's the best thing I ever tasted that wasn't cake or hard candy.

"You're Tommy's sister, aren't you?"

"I am."

"I thought so. You want to go sit on the chairs we fixed under the shade and watch the rodeo with me? They're starting with steer roping. Daddy's bought a megaphone so he can announce and everyone can hear him."

I never heard of a megaphone before, but I smile and act like I know what she's talking about. I'm thinking I'm mighty lucky, and here I go with Martha to the shade and she seems so friendly, but then I figure out what she's after when she says, "Say, why don't you go invite Tommy to sit with us, too? I'll bet he's hot and tired from his busy morning. I'll give him one of Mother's orange drinks."

She gets that dopey look in her eyes I'm used to. I take my pint jar and go find Tommy. He's standing on the boards of the pens watching boys practicing roping the steers. "You got a new girlfriend, Tommy," I say, pointing over toward Martha Henson. A big grin breaks out on his face showing me all his nice teeth. He jumps down and heads in Martha's direction.

I drain my drink dry, hillbilly-like or not, and go back to our wagon where it's safe from swooning girls. Soon's I find Cal, I'll load up his ears with my suspicions and what we might could do about them.

Secrets

I'm sucking on my chunk of ice and explaining to Old Blue how ignorant all that mushy stuff is with girls chasing after Tommy and acting plumb dumb. He cocks an eye on me, and I'm thinking he understands what I'm telling him. I pour him a drink in his water pan from one of our water jugs and he sucks it up and kind of smiles at me.

Cal walks over to pat Old Blue's neck. "What happened last night, Bid? You and Sammy looked scared as all get out when you came back to the fire."

I check to see none of our big-eared brothers are hanging around under the wagon, and they aren't. I take my time considering what to say to my brother since I need to do it just right.

"You going to talk or aren't you?"

"Cal, hold your taters. I'm thinking."

He eyes my empty pint jar. "Where'd you get a nickel for that drink?"

"Martha Henson gave it to me so I'd fix her up with Tommy."

"Damn, that guy gets all the best girls."

"I didn't know you were so interested in girls."

"I'm not, but it just doesn't seem fair."

"Fair or not, it ain't Tommy's fault. Those gals go for him no matter what."

Calvin digs his shoe in the dirt and looks perturbed. I lean against the side of the wagon.

"This is a big one, Cal, so it's just between us, no one else. It's part way that secret I was going to tell you when we went up the road and the sheriff brought us back home. Truth is, there's lots of strange things going on this summer, and you know it's so.

"It started with Mr. MacGregor getting kilt, and who but a devil would ever harm that kind man? Mr. Leroy's rabbit foot being in that pump house is still a perplexing thing since you didn't get to hear all of Mr. Leroy's story in the jail house. But we know it wasn't Mr. Leroy who left it there because he said so. And what about that danged *calf link* thing?"

"Calf link? It's called a cufflink."

"So what? I don't care what it's called. It didn't come from around here, so it must be the killer's no matter the name of it."

"Maybe."

I blow out a big breath of air. "Guess what? You know that sound we hear in the woods—the Wood Ghost?"

"Yeah, if that's what you want to call it. What of it?"

"I heard it again. By myself."

"So?"

"Listen to this… when me and Ruby were dewberry picking, we came across a bowl full of dewberries shoved into the thorns and vines just out of sight. Fresh picked and sitting there pretty as you please. The sandy dirt around the fence was covered in barefooted tracks, and they weren't no man's feet neither. Too small. About Sammy's size."

"That's not a big deal," Calvin says, but I see his eyes getting that certain look in them.

"Maybe not, but who else could have put that torn-out catalog page up on the boards when I fell asleep in the tree after Dad whooped me? I mean, well, you swear you didn't do it?"

"I swear. What're you getting at?"

His eyes are narrowed down, and he looks suspicious and curious at the same time. I climb up in the wagon bed and sit down cross-legged. "Can you come sit in the wagon so I don't have to talk loud?"

He rolls his eyes and comes into the wagon. "This better be good."

"Listen, I was right there on the spot when Mr. Leroy found out Mr. MacGregor was murdered. He went to bawling and talking so sad and pitiful. He said something about a poor little thing and who would take care of him now. He didn't say who he was meaning by that on account of he was blubbering so hard, but it seemed like he was talking about a person for sure."

I let that soak in. Cal's thinking hard, I can tell. I keep talking on account of it feels good to be telling him this instead of thinking it in my head all the time.

"I don't know exactly who, but I know somebody was walking with me in the woods right before the twister came. It was someone right behind the trees and bushes so's I couldn't see who it was."

"Biddy, you know better than that. If someone was following you, you should have come home and told us boys. We would have taken out looking for him. What if it was the killer? What if it was somebody else who isn't right in the head?

"Besides, we've had a string of things going missing from folks' houses and barns around here, lately. Maybe a robber was following you."

"Well, I didn't tell no one, so there it is. Here's something else. He or it or whatever it is was in the cornfield with us yesterday. Moolie barked, and it ran away. Then when me and Sammy were looking to find the bullfrog last night, I tripped over someone who wasn't expecting me. We rassled in the dark to get away from one another, and he ran off. Heard him splashing when he crossed over the grass and through the creek. Scared me and Sammy, but mostly me since I was the one all tangled up with him."

"I ain't believing you didn't tell me this!" Cal never says "ain't" unless he's mad. "Who do you suppose it was?"

"I don't know, but I aim to find out." I gather my courage and say, "You need to know something else. I went inside Mr. MacGregor's cabin."

"Are you touched in the head? What in the Sam Hill made you do such a stupid thing?"

"I had to. My curiosity was driving me to it. Now, I want to ask you something."

Cal puts his head back and looks up at the sky. "What now?"

"Will you cover for me while I go check it one more time? I want to do it in the morning on account of I can't wait no longer to find out who the Wood Ghost is and besides, I think he's using Mr. MacGregor's cabin."

"No, and *hell* no. Not now or never, you corn brain!"

My face burns hot and I jump to my feet. "Let's arm rassle. If I win, I go. If I lose, I'll forget about it." I'm saying this, but I already know I'm lying again because I'm not going to forget about it, no sir.

Cal's careful about his leg while he makes his way off the side of the wagon. "If you aren't the most stubborn thing I've ever seen. Keep this up and you'll never amount to anything but a… a mule's hind end, Biddy," he says, pointing at Old Blue's rear.

I can't take no more. I jump off the wagon with my fists under my chin. "Take it back or I'll whoop you. I mean it."

He stares in my eyes. "Dang if you don't think you're big enough to do it. Sheesh. One of these days, Bid… someone's going to show you how it really is." He shakes his head and looks at me like I'm the biggest bunch of trouble who ever walked on the earth.

"I reckon I got no choice but to go with you to that cabin, you no longer being of sound mind."

That puts a grin on my face. "You intended to go all along, didn't you?"

"Someone has to look after your foolish self if you're going to live to be a day or two older."

It's a deal, and I'll take it.

"How will we swing it?" I ask.

He picks up a stone and throws it toward a tree. He doesn't talk for so long I feel like I'm about to bust like the watermelon we rolled off the smoke house roof last summer.

"I still say it's stupid," he says.

"Yeah, but how will we swing it?"

"I'll ask Sammy to do the milking chores with Tommy in the morning. When no one's looking, we'll take off. It'll have to be quick, and we'll have to make up a story when we get home. I'm telling you, this isn't going to end up good. If anything happens, I'm the one who'll lose his hide."

"It'll be all right, brother. I have a feeling about it."

"Ha! That doesn't mean a thing, and you know it."

I don't say another word.

I got my way, and that's when I know to shut up.

Missing

Watching the cowboys take turns trying to mount our young mules had everyone busting a gut. I don't think most of those guys ever met their match before, but now they did. Sure did look like some feelings were bruised, but they got over it soon enough. First the younger men and boys tried it, all trying to win the five dollars offered by Mr. Henson to stay on the mule at least ten seconds. Nobody stayed one second as far as I could see. Next, the experienced cowboys gave it a try, and it was the same thing. Then Mr. Henson announced he'd pay three dollars if anyone could mount any mule and stay on any time at all, even two seconds.

I never did stop laughing until the steer roping thing started, and that scared me, since those critters have horns. The way the cowboys swung their ropes and took down the steers was the finest thing I ever saw. Once, I saw War and Snipe helping the rancher boys get the steers lined up for the cowboys and it kind of made me proud since they weren't getting in any trouble.

When it was over, Mr. Henson said he was going to let

those cowboys go home and practice and we'd have another rodeo in the fall time. Everybody laughed. Then, he said he had a surprise for us before folks headed home.

"Direct from his performances at the Austin-Doolittle Rodeos in the big state of Texas, we have a young performer with us today. Lightning, take it away." A boy about Snipe and War's age, maybe younger, climbed up on a box in the middle of the main pen. Mr. Henson handed him the megaphone and the boy started making sounds like birds, cows, chickens, mules, horses, and even crickets. Now, some of my brothers can make good critter noises, but just two or three things each. This little cuss did all of them, and it was a sight to see. We talked about that Lightning kid all the way home.

We were all tired and hungry, and thankfully, supper was almost on the table when we get home. Right in the middle of eating, Mama says, "Daniel Frost stopped by today. Said his missus has been up in Lawton tending to her sick ma. Oh, and Mr. Leroy is missing."

My fork just falls out of my hand.

"What do you mean, Mama? Where did he go?" I say.

"Don't know. All Mr. Frost said was he's missing, and no one seems to know what happened."

I started bawling right then and there, and that's a new one 'cause I never do such a thing in front of my brothers since it makes me look weak. Right now, I don't care.

"Biddy, take it easy, okay? Let's find out the facts before you take it so hard," Jean says. "Maybe it's not true."

"Oh, it's true all right. Daniel said the whole county's talking about it," Mama says.

"So they just up and lost a man as big as Mr. Leroy?" Calvin asks.

Now, Doodles is sniffing because she isn't used to seeing

me cry. That makes Jay Bird start up, and Mama says, "For heaven sakes, kids. I'll see what I can find out tomorrow. Eat your supper and stop your fussing."

"Ma, are you sure Mr. Frost didn't explain anything more about it?" Allen says.

"Not another thing."

Everybody mostly shuts up after that, and Jean tells me she and Snipe and Jay Bird are doing the dishes and to go get my tired self to bed. I sure do appreciate Jean for that, and I do what she says and drag myself up the stairs.

"What happened to Mr. MacGregor, Mama?"

"He's dead."

"Why?"

"I don't rightly know."

Where's his body, Mama?"

"They buried him beside his wife and daughter in Bartlesville."

"Why?"

"Do you want to be all alone when you die?"

I sit straight up in the bed breathing like I been running all the way from Hoot Creek to Sweet Creek more than once. What kind of a dream was that? I shake my head to clear it out. Doodles and Jean are snoozing away, and I wrap Grandma Massy's crocheted lap blanket around my shoulders and go sit by the open window. The night air feels good, but I don't.

The way I see it, Mr. Leroy's been suffering all this time in that Nowata jail like they up and forgot about him for weeks and weeks. They were supposed to bring in a judge for trial, but what happened? Nothing. Miz Abernathy came to sort it out, but maybe Sheriff Murphy treated her like he did

Mr. Leroy. Maybe she couldn't make any headway at all.

I went with Mama three times to that revival, and I never did get alone to talk to Miz Abernathy about none of this. Those revival folks sure do know how to bake up some cakes and pies, but that doesn't tell us where Mr. Leroy is.

I sniffled so much at the table last night Mama said maybe she'd go see Miz Abernathy in a day or two. I cried harder to go with her, and she said, "Lord, child, you're wearing me down to a nub."

I put my head on the bumpy window sill and listen to the katydids outside. It's a soothing sound and I wonder who or what that Wood Ghost is and why it keeps coming around. Does it want something? One thing's for true… he ain't very big. I know since I fell right on top of him and scuffled my way out of the tangle. Maybe he's one of those pixies or elves Allen tells us about from that *Grimm* book of his.

I kind of smile about that, and the next thing I know, Jean is bending over me staring into my face with her eyebrows all wrinkled together. She's still in her nightgown, so I reckon I fell asleep sometime or other, and here it is getting light outside. How I rolled across the floor by the door, I can't imagine.

"Biddy? What're you doing down there?"

"I got hot," is all I can think of.

"Hmm. Well, guess what?" she says, stepping behind the dressing curtain to change into her day clothes. "I may go to the Summer Festival in Nowata with Sheriff Murphy."

I come off the floor and stand outside the dressing curtain with my head dizzy.

"Y-y-you don't mean it, Jean. You just can't!"

She pokes her head out. "Why not? Mom and Dad and everyone else keeps saying I should start looking ahead to a different life now that Jack's, uh… he's not himself anymore. Besides, the dance is still a little ways off. You'll get more used to it by then. I haven't said yes yet."

I can't do nothing but stand in one spot and be mad.

"Listen, Bood, Sheriff Murphy—Tate—found a lawyer for me for free. Now, wasn't that nice? You just have to get to know him." Jean steps out of the curtains and runs a brush through her hair. "I'm not an old lady yet, you know." She smiles and squeezes my arm with her hand. "Come down and eat something. You don't look so good."

When Jean goes downstairs, Doodles sits up on the mattress and smiles at me. I can't smile. I can't nothing. Jean with that law man? He's mean. He's too old. He hates Mr. Leroy. He looks down on sharecroppers. He never shows his eyes. He… he…

"Don't worry, Biddy. Jean will be all right," Doodles says, taking my hand.

"Huh? You can't talk like that, can you?"

Doodles is grinning, and I stand there just flat amazed. When did she grow up so much?

Hide!

Me and Calvin are about to find out something that's going to make your lips drop clear to the ground, but I'm getting ahead of my own self again. I'd better scoot back and tell you the whole story. It starts with us sneaking away from the house when Sammy, Allen, and Tommy head off to the shed clanging their milk buckets. Just like that, Calvin and I meet on the front porch and take off.

"What'd you tell Sammy last night?"

"That I wanted to be alone a while to think some things over. Now he won't try looking me up when the milking's over," Calvin says.

We barely get off Blackberry Road and head down the gravel road when we see a dusty truck dipping into the bottom of the hill we're on top of. We just have time to hit the ditch. The truck rattles by fast and who should have his arm out the window but Deputy Floyd.

"Dang almighty, Cal. Where you suppose he's going in such a rush?"

"No telling, but leastways he isn't headed in our direction."

"Think he saw us?"

"Naw, he looked like he had something on his mind."

It makes me so mad to lay eyes on that man I have to stop to growl and tear a few weeds out of the ground. When I get through with my fit, we pass the Y-spring and climb the shallow hills to the bob wire fence. We climb the last hill, and here we are looking at Mr. MacGregor's cabin below us in the edge of the woods. We keep watch for a bit to see if anyone's coming or going around the cabin. No one that we can see. We run down the hill so fast our legs can't barely keep up with our bodies. Well, I do, anyways. Calvin hurries his best.

Hunkering down, I take Cal around to the window that wasn't locked the last time I paid a visit to that cabin. It still isn't. The tree shade's so thick on this side of the cabin, it makes everything dark. The ground is mossy and feels like a cushion. Calvin locks his hands for me to step on to reach the window sill. I don't see nobody inside, so I raise the window all the way and climb through it.

Law, it's quiet in here. Kind of pleasant dim from all the trees shading the windows, and it's clean as a whistle. Calvin comes through the window and closes it back like it was to a crack. It feels like we're stealing or doing something bad, but we aren't. Or are we?

My brother gawks at all the fine things in that cabin and it seems like he's looking at a table full of food. He whistles under his breath. "Look at the leather-skin furniture… and these shiny floors and all those books," he mumbles, looking up and down at the book shelves that cover up a whole wall. I can't answer him about those books because my eyeballs have hooked onto something else—the chipped bowl sitting on the table filled to the brim with pork cracklins.

"Look," I whisper in a loud voice, pointing to it.

"Is that the bowl you found full of berries?"

"Yeah. When I came to the cabin by myself, it was washed and put away on a shelf. Didn't I tell you things aren't right here, Cal?"

"Maybe Mr. MacGregor has a brother or a sister who's staying here. This doesn't prove anything."

"He didn't have a living soul to his name—no parents, brothers, sisters, or anyone. He told me that one time when he said I was lucky for having so many brothers and sisters."

"Well, it's probably a hobo who's camping out in here and—"

Calvin can't finish talking because we hear a twig snap outside the window.

"Hide!" Calvin hisses at me.

"Where?"

"Under the bed!"

We dive underneath the quilt-covered bed and scootch close together. My teeth are chattering and I put my pointing finger in my mouth to stop the noise. We hear the window raise and footsteps so light I can't hardly imagine they're really feet walking on the wooden planks. I move a little bit so's I can peek from the bottom of the quilted bedcover. What I see are two slim brown feet a little shorter than Sammy's.

A drop of sweat stings my eye.

The feet stand by the eating table and I hear crunching. They walk over to the desk and the sound I hear makes me think Mr. MacGregor's picture in the frame is raised up and set back down. Gaw, I'm wishing I could see! The feet go to the chair by the desk and pull it out to sit down. A drawer opens and closes. Scratching noises. I don't know what they are and I'm dying from my curiosity. I thump Calvin, and he raises his eyebrows. That means he doesn't know nothing, neither. He frowns and puts a finger in front of his lips, which means I'd better stay hushed.

We wait and wait some more. Who is this keeping us trapped under the bed? How long before Mama or Dad notices we're missing? How are we getting out of here? All of a sudden starts up the loneliest sound I ever did hear. It's a cross between crying and humming, and nobody on this earth can keep me and Calvin from knowing this here is the Wood Ghost not more than ten feet away from us.

Next thing we hear is a motor drive up outside the cabin. The small feet move fast. A drawer opens and closes. Running, the feet go to the window and disappear like they never were there in the first place. I stick my head out and see the Wood Ghost has closed the window all the way.

"What's going on?" I whisper.

Calvin hushes me with a grouchy *shhh.*

I roll my eyes but do what he says. Loud banging on the cabin door gets me so full of scaredness I grab Calvin's arm and squeeze it near off. More hard fisting on the door, followed by the sound of wood splintering.

CHAPTER Thirty One

Floyd and the Haint

You ever wonder why it is you like home a whole bunch better when you think you might never make it back there? I believe it's because you're about to stare death in the face, and that's how I'm feeling when I see cowboy boots kick the door near off its hinges. I don't have to see nothing of the rest of him to know it's Floyd who's busting up Mr. MacGregor's pretty cabin door.

The boots walk inside and stop with the pointy ends aimed right at me and Cal. I see the barrel of a shotgun resting on the planks beside Floyd's boot, and my ears feel like they been doused in Mama's hell-fire peppers they're burning so hot. Boots clank all around the room and down the hallway. They come back and carry that man as he roots around the cabin like a dadgum boar in the woods.

"Where are you, you damn fool?" Floyd says out loud but kind of under his breath.

He opens cabinet doors and slams them shut. Loud crunching says he's eating some of those cracklins on the table. I dream of busting his head with an iron skillet for treating Mr. MacGregor's things so rough and disrespectful. He plunders through the desk, opening and banging drawers shut. It's quiet for about a half a minute. Floyd grunts, and a piece of white paper drifts to the floor. Cal stiffens up when a corner of it comes under the bed.

We don't move to even blink our eyes, but I can't help but see the white paper is a pencil drawing of the picture in the frame. Only this time there's another face beside the girl, and it's a boy with long straight hair and dark eyes.

Floyd gets hisself a big drink from the faucet that's inside. He burps louder than War, who near makes me sick with the terrible loud burps he does just to get to me. The boots walk across the room and stop beside the bed. I'm shivering, on account of I'm sure Floyd is about to find us. In a crash of creaky bedsprings, a lump the size of our hitch wagon falls on the bed and near squashes me and Cal. We spraddle out flat as Johnny cakes so's not to get kilt by this idiot man who's decided to throw hisself backasswards on the bed.

"I'm gonna find you, wait and see. And when I do… we'll take up where we left off." Floyd laughs out loud. The sound of it sends chill bumps up my back.

It has to be Mr. Leroy he's talking about. My breath hangs in my chest, and I'm feeling a cough tickle building up. My eyes are watering something fierce trying to hold back from coughing. I'm about to let it blow when the most terrible sounds come from outside. I never did hear a real dead haint, but now I think I have because the awfullest moans and screeches and growls outside the cabin make me know something ain't of this world.

Floyd throws his legs off the bed. Cal's brains are about to spill out his ears since his head is situated under Floyd's hind end with Floyd in that sitting position. The sounds keep on coming from outside, and law, they're scary. Now, I don't know if I'm more scared of Floyd, or what's outside. I get rid of my cough and Floyd doesn't hear me do it. He's too busy being scared.

"N-n-no don't get me haint! I know Jesus, I do! I never meant to do nothing. You hear me? You gotta believe me. Listen to this." Floyd breaks out singing, "Jesus loves me, this I know…" in a shaky voice that sounds like a runny-nosed kid.

The scary howls get louder, and Floyd jumps off the bed. Cal puts his hand on his head and lets out a big breath. I strain my eyeballs to see what's happening, but all I see are those boots.

"Haint, my mama drug me to the church ever Sunday. Don't that prove I know Jesus and angels and all?"

The noises go on outside the cabin. Floyd lets out a strange choking sound and runs across the room. I see his feet jump over the broken door on the floor and disappear. In a jiffy, his truck engine starts up and gets fainter while he drives off none too slow.

"Calvin," I whisper. "I want to go home."

"Stay still. Let's see what happens."

What happens is the Wood Ghost's feet come hurrying through the broken door and stepping over the pieces on the floor. He cries out and now he's gone back out the door. After a few minutes of quiet like you never heard, Cal hisses, "Let's get the hell out of here!"

We scramble out from under that bed and run as fast as we can out the broken door and up the hill. I grab Cal's arm and help him go faster. When we get back to the bob wire fence, we're both breathing hard but we don't stop there or at the Y-spring for a drink or nowhere else till we see our yellow house in front of us.

We both bend over to breathe, and I have to hold my

side since it's paining me so bad. "What was that sound we heard while Floyd was squashing my head?" Cal says

"The Wood Ghost, I reckon. But I don't get it. He never sounded so terrible scary like that before. In the cabin, his noises were sorrowful. In the woods, he usually sounds scary, but lonesome, too. What we just heard was different."

"Let me get this straight. Are you saying those skinny brown feet are the Wood Ghost?"

"You know it's so, Calvin. You heard him, too."

"I don't know what I think."

I shrug my shoulders. "Me, neither. I'm more confounded than when we started out. You suppose Floyd kilt Mr. MacGregor? He said he didn't mean to do it." I'm working myself up, and I have to stop walking and take deep breaths.

"We don't know what he's talking about. A man like him… no telling what all he's done he's ashamed of himself for. I'll figure a way to talk to Tommy about it, but not yet. Right now, all Tommy thinks about is asking Martha Henson to the folks' chili supper."

"Is that the truth?"

"All he talked about last night."

"That was quick, wasn't it?"

"Yep."

"Anyways, what are we going to tell the folks about us being gone?" I ask.

"Nothing. Just nothing. You go back first and tell them you went to look for berries and they're all gone and that's the truth, anyhow."

"Shoot, they probably won't believe me. I've done that once already. What are you going to tell them?"

"I'll circle around and come out of the chicken house with the rake like I been working all morning. I already raked the floor last night when I went to shut them up, and I'm the one who let them out this morning."

"Gol-all-Friday, Cal, you're sneaky. How do you think up stuff like that?"

"I'm slicker than calf slobber, that's how." I grin a little at my brother trying to be funny, but both our heads are too full of Floyd, haints, and our own crimes to keep on smiling.

I mosey on to the house by myself. First one to spy me is Snipe, and he comes aiming at me from my left side. Lately, he and War don't hang together so much so he's been teaching Jay Bird how to use a slingshot and work the dogs in a hunt.

Snipe says, "Where you been? Mama was about frazzled calling you. She said she might have to switch your legs for going off and not telling her."

I'm not cheerful hearing that, but I know what we did was important, and I'm not sorry. Now, I'm fixing to lie again, and hell sure must be happy this morning with me and Cal's lies and a big old fool like Floyd messing up Mr. MacGregor's cabin and admitting he did something terrible but we don't know what yet.

"Went to check on the blackberries is all. They're all gone except for the shriveled-up brown ones the birds won't even eat."

"It's too late for berries, sis."

"Guess I was just hoping."

We climb the crooked cement steps on our front porch and creak through the screen door. Jean and Mama are washing the breakfast dishes, and I sit down with a leg on each side of the bench and wait for my whooping. Snipe walks on through the kitchen. He looks over his shoulder at me and pushes hisself out the kitchen door. They may be mean, but my brothers don't like it when Mama switches me.

Doodles shoots me a big grin from across the table where she's using a stubby purple crayon to draw on a half-used Big Chief tablet from my last school term.

"Glad you decided to come on home, Biddy," Mama says. She's drying a glass and doesn't look at me. Jean doesn't look up, neither.

"I just went to check on some berries, but it's too late for them now," I lie.

Mama stops drying and puts the towel down. She sits down in a cane-bottom chair and looks me square in the face. "Bid, I want to tell you something now, and I want you to listen hard. You listening?"

"Yes, Mama."

"You worked this summer and earned money for doing it, so you're getting to be a big girl now. You're almost too old for switching. Almost. Anyways, after today, I don't aim to know where you are every minute of the day. You understand?"

I nod, wondering what she's getting at.

"What I want to tell you is don't ever lie to me. That can still get you a switching even if you think you're all growed-up. You're big enough to know the difference of right and wrong. If I can count on you to tell the truth, I won't be asking you about your whereabouts unless I'm worried. Now that means you should have the manners to tell somebody you'll be gone and the general direction you're heading. That's being fair now, ain't it?"

"Yes, ma'am."

"So, today, I was worried. I couldn't find you, and I didn't know you were hankering to mosey off. Next time, give me a word or two."

"I will."

Law, I'm feeling bad in my innards. Mama looks down at the dish towel in her hands. She says, "Now I know you're not a liar, Bid, so's that part's already tended to. Just do the chores that are yours around here and give us a little howdy-do about where you might be going from now on and we're square."

"Yes, ma'am."

"I saved you a biscuit and a hunk of bacon over there on the back of the stove. The egg and biscuit is Calvin's." Mama goes back to drying the dishes just like that. Jean looks over her shoulder and gives me a wink. I know right then and there Jean's been talking up my side of things to Mama.

I scoop up the biscuit and bacon and go outside so I can think this situation over. I sit down on a stump and see Cal putting the rake in the shed. I'm feeling bad way down inside myself. Mama said I wasn't a liar, and I know I didn't used to be, not one whit. This summer, I am… and she doesn't know what terrible character I'm living out right now.

To be honest, her trust hurts more than a switching.

Violent and Dangerous

"Carl's coming home from CCC camp for our chili supper and dance?"

"That's right," Tommy says. He's tuning his guitar and sitting on the edge of Mama's rocker on the front porch. It's evening on the day Cal and I sneaked over to Mr. MacGregor's cabin and I've about worked myself to death all day, along with Mama, Jean, Sammy, Cal, and the twins. What we've been up to is boiling and peeling and chopping everything from beets to snap peas, along with pole beans, peppers, tomatoes, corn, and cabbage.

When the men were through in the fields, Mama had Tommy carry her two heavy crock jars of shredded cabbage and salt in the gopher hole so it can turn into sauerkraut. Everything else went into a scalded Mason jar. She made her chow-chow and canned it, too. Lordy-lord, I never want to see another vegetable in my whole life.

Supper and those dadburned dishes are over. I brought the wet dish towels out to hang on the big tree in the front and came across Tommy. Now I'm sitting cross-legged on the porch and learning news not a single soul has mentioned to us kids.

"When is all this happening?"

"The supper and dance are in two days, Little Britches. Carl will be here in the morning. Ruby and Ed are coming to watch Doodles and Jay Bird and keep an eye on the twins."

"They are? I didn't know that, either. How will anybody else know about this chili thing?"

"I put up announcements at Stanfill's and the feed store two weeks ago and last week, too. Told everyone at the mule rodeo and everybody I see when I go into town. Mama's going to have a hard time keeping those chili bowls filled up, I'm thinking."

"Yeah, I heard about how you mentioned it at the mule rodeo. Did you ask Martha on the spot?"

"Course not. You got to keep 'em wondering."

"How will you ask her, then?"

"Already did. Rode over on Bobby this morning."

"You sure are full of surprises. Maybe since Mama thinks I'm getting all growed up, I might get to ride Bobby sometimes myself. He doesn't care if you use a saddle or not. Say, how much does it cost to eat and dance at this chili supper?"

"Just fifty cents a head, or seventy-five cents a couple."

I whistle, then look around to see if Dad's in earshot. Tommy grins at me, and I know he doesn't care a smite if I whistle my head off.

"Sounds like a lot of money. Does Carl's girlfriend know about all this?"

"Oh, sure. Carl's picking her up in Alluwe on his way out here tomorrow. Jean wants her to help her pretty up some dresses for them and Mama, too."

"Glad I don't have to wear one of those gussied-up things. Hey, you reckon Peg and Carl will get married?"

Tommy winks, and I know that's all I'll get out of my brother on that subject. I'm wondering if I should tell him any of Cal's and my secrets. Since we trust Tommy more than anyone else, I go ahead and ask him where he thinks Mr. Leroy might have gotten off to.

"That, I don't know, Little Britches." Tommy swings his guitar into the air by the neck and wraps it back up in the sheet. I guess my face was looking poorly sad 'cause Tommy says, "I'm going to town in a couple of days. I'll nose around and see if there's any news on the subject."

"All right. Why are you going to town anyways?"

"Picking up the ground-up pork for Mama's chili at Stanfill's and ice blocks over at the ice house."

"It'll be melted before you get home, won't it?"

"Nah, I'm going before the sun is up, and Mr. Arman's letting me borrow his special ice boxes."

"What's that?"

"Wooden boxes inside other wooden boxes with sawdust in between the two of them. Pretty nifty. If I put hay all around the sides and on top, we'll have us some cold ice tea to go with that chili and cornbread."

Tommy goes in the front door and everybody else in creation comes out to sit on the porch, even Mama. Dad says, "Boys, I'm going to need every last one of you early in the morning to help me scrape that patch of land one more time and nail the boards for the dance floor. I'll sand them down and put sawdust on the top."

Mama says, "Biddy, you and Sammy are borrowing us some tin cups, bowls, and spoons from the Frosts and the Mannicotts. They know about it, so after breakfast tomorrow, hitch up Old Blue to the little wagon and take Doodles and Jay Bird with you."

"Why can't I do that?" War says.

"Because we need you to help us here, old pal," Allen says.

That suits War just fine, since it's Allen saying so. War got a whooping from Dad yesterday for out and out sassing Mama with a mean voice, but he's been pretty good for a while, other than that. What I know is Snipe doesn't like being with him anymore, and I keep thinking about what he said about finding something. He clams up every time I try to get it out of him and even said he was making it all up, but I don't believe him. He knows something, and I may have to pin him to the ground till he hollers *calf rope* to find out what.

Mama says, "War, soon's the men get the timber laid for the dance floor, you and Snipe pull the herb pots from alongside the garden fence and put them on the ground by the four corners of the dance floor."

"Which ones?" Snipe asks.

"The rosemary and spearmint. Bring the pots of marigolds, too."

"Why?"

"Mosquitoes. They don't like the smell of those herbs or marigolds," Calvin says.

Jean says, "Mama, we can make our chili up early the day after next. Tomorrow, when Peg and Carl get here, she'll be helping me fancy up some dresses for us to wear. I've got some organdy I bought in Oklahoma City last year, and some pretty ribbon we can use. I'm going to fix you up, too."

Mama waves her hand. "Now don't go doing nothing fancy for me. I'll be in the kitchen working anyways when I'm not playing the pipe organ."

"And singing, Mama. Yes, you have to look pretty as a picture!" Jean says. Mama half hides her face with the side of her hand, but I see she's grinning.

"All you kids get your chores done early so you can get a bath and look decent by the time folks arrive, which is around six," Dad says. "I want you helping out, but don't do much talking. Those folks are here to listen to the music and dance and eat. They don't need no kids pestering them. If this goes okay, we'll have one or two more before the cold weather sets in. Good money, Doobie," and he looks at Mama when he says that last part.

"And if you don't scrub out those dirty ears and fingernails, I'll get the rag after them myself," Jean says, but she's smiling so the boys don't look like they're ready to take off running to the woods.

Doodles pops up on the porch from the bottom of the tree holding two jar lids full of acorns, some whole and some halves. "I'm making acorn pie for the chili supper," she says.

Mama just rocks in her chair smiling, but I ain't used to so much going on. I reckon Dad has it in his head to get those doctor bills paid, and he's doing it.

"Looky down yonder," Jay Bird says, pointing to Blackberry Road.

"It's Ruby come early," Mama says, grinning ear to ear.

"No, it isn't, Ma," Allen says.

"He's right," Cal says, "wrong color car. Hey, it's John."

"John?" Mama says. "Well, I'll be. I shore like that young man."

Jean says, "I like him, and I haven't even met him. Isn't he the guy who keeps Dad from thrashing Doc Silvers?"

That sets everyone off laughing. Most of us stand up and wait while he pulls up to the front of the house and stops the car. When he gets out, Mama says, "John, come up here. Are you hungry? I can fry up some eggs and potatoes for you right quick. Got some left-over biscuits in the house, too, and plenty of milk."

"Oh, no, ma'am. I've had my supper, thank you kindly. I'm just passing by and thought I'd come see my patient. You doing splendidly, Allen?"

Allen salutes, touching the side of his hand to his dented forehead. "Splendidly, sir. I look like a monkey, but I don't care. At least you and Old Sawbones left me a nickel's worth of brains."

John throws his head back and laughs. It's a nice laugh that reminds me of Mr. MacGregor somehow. He climbs up the lopsided concrete steps and hands Dad two bundles of light green-gray leaves kind of shaped into a log and tied with a leather cord. Dad lifts one up and takes a deep nose sniff. He examines the leather cord knots and feels the bundle with his hands. "Sage. Dakota tribe?" he asks.

John breaks into a grin. "Dang right! The gossip in town is you know your Indian tribes, and you sure do. I was driving in from around Fort Sill, and I brought you those to burn for your party. If you have any cedar or juniper to smudge-smoke with them, you might keep those mosquitoes from eating everyone for supper while they dance."

"*Pilamaya,* John," Dad says, taking another whiff. I step over and take a smell, and I like it so much I stick my nose closer and smell it again. That starts a line of kids all having a big draw of those good-smelling sage logs.

"And you're coming to our chili dance too, John, and I won't hear otherwise," Mama says.

It might have been my imagination, but I thought I saw John steal a look or two in Jean's direction. Jean… who hasn't said one blasted word since he came.

"If you twist my arm like that, Mrs. Woodson, I just

might have to," he says.

"What you doing all the way over there by Fort Sill, John…" Allen says, but I don't hear any more, since I stretch and put my mind somewhere else. The folks and John are cooing and carrying on and it's a nice sound in my head on account of I'm looking at John and Jean and that idea comes back to me from before.

All of a sudden, I say, "John, did you meet our big sis, Jean, yet?" and I push her out front so John can see how pretty she is.

"I don't think I've had the pleasure," he says, and his eyes shine like he's real glad to meet her. He sticks out his hand, and they shake hands. Jean turns around and gives me a big-eyed I'll-get-you-for-that glare, but the way I see it, anything goes to stop that business with the sheriff. Looks to me like John might be the best cure for it.

Everyone settles back down on the porch, either sitting or squatting, and John is the center of it all. Different ones keep asking him this and that. A mosquito buzzes in my ear. I swat at it and it's like that old blood sucker puts a notion in my head I can't ignore. Soon's it gets quiet again, I say, "John, do you know anything from the town gossip about Mr. Leroy?" Everything gets quiet.

"Why, yes, I do, Miss Biddy, but I'm not so sure it's good news for little ears."

"Tell us…" I say in a voice so tiny it sounds near to nothing, "… is he dead?"

John looks around at all the young'uns. Mama says, "Doodles, Jay Bird, War, Snipe—go inside."

"Oh, Mama," Snipe whines, and Dad stands up. All four kids go inside lickity-split since that's how it is at our house. If Dad stands up, a whooping might be on the way. Soon's the screen door closes, Dad walks over and watches through it till the kids are out of earshot. He comes and sits back down.

John looks down at his spread apart fingers. "The word is Mr. Leroy was being transported from Nowata to Bartlesville last week. The sheriff's transportation truck experienced a flat, and while the deputy was in the process of fixing it, they say Leroy jumped from the back end, beat up the deputy, and escaped. There's a reward being posted for any news of him or for his capture. They have deemed him extremely violent and dangerous."

I can barely get the next words out but I do. "Do you know what deputy was taking him to Bartlesville, John?"

"I believe I heard it was Deputy Floyd Brewster."

Chapter Thirty Three

Chores on Chores

You don't have to say a word. Some of you are thinking Mr. Leroy is a bad criminal now and should be hunted down by sniffing dogs. If you think that, you're not the only one. John told us the sheriff already hired tracker men and their hounds, and they haven't come up with anything at all, though they sure are trying. Now everyone in town is all aflutter about it, John said, and here I am beside myself.

The bad news about Mr. Leroy sends me in the house to be alone. I get a drink from the bucket and see Snipe and Calvin both coming at me, but I wave them off and go running up the stairs. I don't want to see nobody right now. I have a little talk with Charley-Bird since I don't know if he heard our talking on the porch or not. Charley and I both know whatever happened on that road from Nowata to Bartlesville, Mr. Leroy is innocent and Floyd is a danged liar.

I pretend to be asleep when Doodles comes up and tucks herself into the covers beside me. Pretty soon, here's Jean getting in the bed and she whispers, "Bood, I have a surprise for you in the morning. Are you asleep?"

I don't answer.

When I wake up, Jean is gone already, and it isn't hardly day yet. The bed is smoothed over, and on top of the quilt is a pink dress and a pair of fancy shoes—not white, but close to it—with a strap that goes over the top of the foot. I never saw nothing so special in all my borned days.

Are they mine?

Who else? They're too small for Jean and too big for Doodles.

I lift the dress and see it has a swishy skirt. I hold it in front of me and look in the mirror. I almost bust out bawling since I never had a pretty dress like this before. And the shoes! I don't know what to do but just sit down in the floor and rub my hand over them and that pretty dress.

"What do you think?" Jean says from the doorway. "I made it for you the day you went to the mule rodeo. Remember all that measuring we were doing and you hated it? This is what it was for."

"It's the best dress in the world, sis. I don't rightly know what to say."

"Say you love it."

I giggle. "I do. I love it, and where did you get the shoes? They're city shoes like Cousin Evelyn would wear."

"The extra money she put in your envelope this summer bought the shoes and the material for this dress. You earned it, Biddy. You worked, and you earned it."

That's the exact time I decide working and getting money for it is something I want to do from here on out, maybe my whole life. Like I said before, I might start with ironing if I have any life left in me after ironing our washtubs full of clothes. 'Course, Mama does a bunch of that herself.

Right now, I'm feeling shy. "Won't the boys make fun of

me if I wear this getup for the chili supper?"

"Let them try. I'll grab the soap and rinse their mouths out!" Jean laughed. "Come on down to breakfast. Mama wants you to make gravy."

Soon's I get downstairs, Calvin *psssts* me over to him in the front room where nobody's hanging around.

"Biddy, we got to lay some plans," he says.

"I have to make gravy."

"Right after breakfast. Meet me in the hen house."

"I have those d—, I mean danged dishes to do."

"Take some table scraps and say you're taking them to the chickens."

Snipe comes around the corner. "There you are, Biddy. I gotta tell you—"

"Biddy! Where'd you get off to, girl? Come make your gravy before I burn the biscuits waiting for you," Mama hollers from the kitchen.

Snipe and Cal and me just look at each other. I shrug my shoulders and go in the kitchen.

It doesn't do nobody no good for nothing except to keep their heads down and get the work done on this day. Snipe cornered me while I was scrubbing the breakfast dishes and said never mind, he didn't have anything to tell me after all. Before I could grab him and pound the truth out of him, Mama came in the kitchen and shoo-ed me and Sammy out to hitch up Old Blue and our small wagon to get to the Frosts and Mannicotts with not a minute to waste getting those utensils for the chili supper.

So, here I am, sitting by Sam on the buckboard seat with Doodles and Jay Bird hanging onto the side boards in the back.

We get even with the ditch and where the Y-spring is beyond that, and I wish something terrible I could tell Sam about the fearful time Cal and I suffered in Mr. MacGregor's cabin yesterday. I'm feeling a little spooked about what Floyd must of done and Mr. Leroy being lost to who knows where and even the Wood Ghost, whoever he is.

Mrs. Frost sends us on our way with metal plates, small crock bowls, and a pie-dough cinnamon roll she made for us kids. We don't get two shakes away from her place before we divide it four ways and don't say a word until it's all gone. It's so good, it rolls our eyes back in our heads. Mama made one of those things one time, but sugar's been too scarce the last few years for such extras.

The Mannicotts swarm out of their cabin like ants on a stepped-on anthill and ask about Tommy and what shenanigans are going on at our place. Mrs. Mannicott hands me a feed sack clanging with metal utensils while all of the eight younger kids climb in the back of the wagon with our young'uns till there isn't an inch of space left. I look back and see Doodles and Jay Bird packed up against the side boards with big grins.

Mr. Mannicott goes to bragging to his missus about Old Blue and the tricks he's seen him do and what a fine mule to plow, pull a wagon, and chew tobacco and that there ain't never been such a great mule in this part of the country before. Billy and his younger brother Dodson, who's Calvin's age, are standing by their mama and dad grinning. "I'll be seeing you'uns tomorrow evening," Billy says. "Dodson's coming, too. See, Dodson's sweet on Rebecca Russell, and word is she's coming to the chili supper with her ma and pa."

What happens next is Dodson throws hisself on Billy and they go to the ground fisting and grunting and slapping.

"Here now!" Mr. Mannicott hollers real gruff. "You boys

get up from there and go soap down those leather harnesses."

They throw a few more punches before they jump up with their noses so close you couldn't stick a maple leaf between them.

"Well, we better be getting back, sir. Our dad gave us chores on chores to do before the folks come tomorrow night," Sam says, throwing me a look like he's ready to skedaddle.

Mr. Mannicott says, "Kids, out of the wagon now!" and they jump over the sides like little mice. Now all the Mannicotts smile and wave as we drive off. I look back and wave, and soon's I turn back around, I make a face at Sammy. "Shoo-ee, that was a mess. I'm glad we don't have so many little young'uns as that."

"You ain't lying," Sam says.

We're just about home when we hear the lonesome-est sound in creation drifting in from the woods. Sammy pulls on the reins to make Old Blue stop. The sound raises the hairs on the back of my neck, but it's so darned beautiful I want to jump down and follow it. Doodles scrambles up and sits on my lap.

"W-w-what is that?" Jay Bird asks, scooting up close to the buckboard seats.

"Somebody trying to tell us something," I say. What I don't say is I'm going to find out who's saying it… and why.

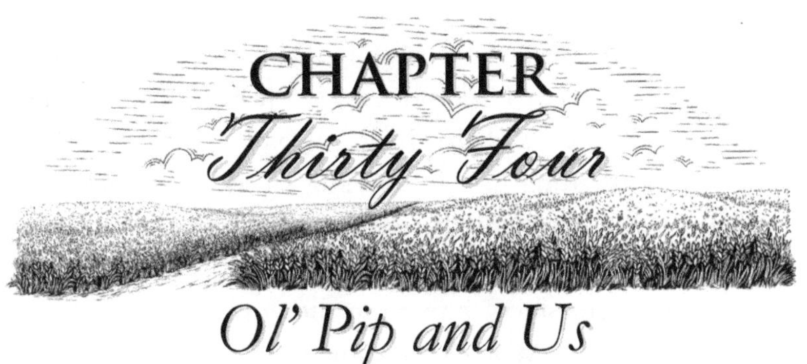

Ol' Pip and Us

I never told you this before, but Mr. MacGregor read to us every day after we played outside in the schoolyard after eating our dinner. The book he read was called *Great Expectations.* It's the dangedest book with hard words that don't make a lick of sense till you listen real hard and then they kind of melt away till all you hear is what's happening to that poor Pip, good and bad. Imagine a book so fine as that having a girl named Biddy in it! Every time Mr. MacGregor read out that name, everybody looked at me and snickered.

Why am I thinking of that book right now? Because when dinner time rolls around the next day, and the sun is high in the sky, we—the Woodsons—have a slick wood dance floor out past the front porch and it's fancier than anything I ever imagined except in a book like that *Great Expectations.* Guess ol' Pip and us have a few things in common these days.

Ruby and Ed came last night, and Ed went to hammering and sanding timber for the dance floor with Dad and Tommy. Allen is sweeping up sawdust and putting it in cans. When Carl and Peg came this morning, Carl jumped right in, and in no time, that floor was put together and ready to be covered in sawdust.

Right after that, the boys put the herbs and marigolds along the corners like Dad said. Peg and Jean finished up eight crepe paper flowers in light shades of pink, blue, and yellow, tied them with string to thin kindling sticks, and stuck them into the pots around the dance floor. They were the biggest ones I ever saw, big as dishpans, and Jean says she's been working on them since she was in the gopher hole watching Tommy when he died on us but came back.

Kerosene lanterns are put all over the place on upturned wood boxes with one on an upside-down washtub. Four deep holes covered up with crisscross sticks of wood are dug out a short way from the dance floor but close to each corner to smudge the sage and cedar and keep the skeeters away.

Here we are outside, sitting on the front porch, eating cold biscuits and fried pork chops with our fingers since we all want to stare at that fancy dance floor.

"Throw your chop bones away and not on the ground when you're done. Biddy, you sweep up this porch when we get finished. I don't want no crumbs nor dirt on it," Mama says in a strict voice.

"Yes, Mama," I answer in a faraway voice on account of I'm in a state of bewilderment staring at the crepe-paper flowers, the marigolds, and knowing we're having a party at our humble house. Nothing like this has ever gone on at the Woodsons' before.

Before the men get cleaned up, they have to carry Mama's pipe organ out to the porch. Now, if you ever saw a mother hen guarding her baby chicks, then you know how Mama watched over this situation. "Be careful, Tommy, don't hit the sides nowhere. Ed, lift your side some more. Watch close, Carl. Allen, hold that screen door wider."

This is how Mama carried on till the organ was outside facing the dance floor, which is to say it was facing our little Blackberry Road coming up to the house. A cane-bottomed chair was carried out and put behind the organ, and Mama brought out her one and only oil tablecloth and covered her precious organ with it. She looked at it for a few minutes, then wiped her hands on her apron and went inside. I never see Mama that fussy except about her pipe organ. She got it from her Mama, I think, but I don't rightly know since I never met my grandparents on any side. Calvin tells me it's really a reed organ, but not to tell Mama because she won't believe a word of it.

The boys take their baths first this time and they do it outside with Allen and Calvin making sure they scrub up while me, Doodles, and the women are in the kitchen finishing a heap of chili and big pots full of beans and chipping ice for the sweet tea. Ruby makes dishpans and crocks and bowls full of sweet tea and stores it covered on the kitchen table.

Dad is tuning his banjo and fiddle on the front porch, and Tommy is practicing songs and yodels in the gopher hole. Snipe keeps trying to talk to me, but he gets sent on another chore every time he comes in the house. All of us do.

Our work is done, and the females are taking turns bathing and washing up and getting ready while the men arrange stumps for sitting around outside. They are warned to stay out of the house and not to get a single piece of dirt on themselves or they'll be thrashed. Tommy is shooed out of the gopher hole so I can take my bath in there since I won't do it no place else with others around.

Jean brings Mama her nicest dress she wears to special things, and she's gussied it up with a ruffle all along the edge of the high sleeves and around the collar.

"How did you do that?" I ask.

"Just a strip of organdy hand sewn into puckers then sewn on by machine, Bid," Jean says. "It's easy. I'll show you how next time I sew."

Next, Jean and Peg get dressed, and Jean has used her see-through organdy stuff to sew something around the top of her dress that looks so pretty I can't stop looking at it. Peg has a big bow sewed on the front of her dress and you guessed it, it's organdy, too. Doodles has a new dress Jean and Mama sewed out of flour-sack material with little flowers on it. They've cut a horse head shape out with button eyes, button nostrils, and a red thread smiling mouth sewed on the front. Doodles is twirling around the house like a princess in one of the stories Allen reads us.

I'm just a staring at all this so hard I forget I'm supposed to get into my new dress after my bath. When I remember, I'm scared and Jean picks up on it. She says, "Biddy, come upstairs with me."

"I think I hear Dad calling me," I lie. "I'm supposed to—"

"No, you don't. Come along now, Bood, I want to show you something."

I follow her up the stairs with my bottom lip poked out on account of I want to run off barefoot to the woods and hide out until the chili supper and dance is over. Upstairs, she tells me to sit down on the bed beside her.

"Listen, I know you're shyer than all get out. We all were at your age, but it's high time to get over it. You're growing up quick and becoming a young woman faster than I like. Now, I want you to put the dress and shoes on and come downstairs. Do you want to borrow some of my new anklets?"

I shake my head since I have new ones Mama bought me

in town when I had the stomachache. Lordy-lord, I'm considering bolting out of there, but I look at Jean's face and see stubborn all over it—my own kind of stubborn. I wouldn't put it past her to follow me into the woods and bring me back home by the ear. That's Jean.

"See you in a few minutes," Jean says in a nice enough voice, but her eyes are saying *don't try to pull anything.* "I have things to fix your hair in Mama's room. Ruby's good with hair, too."

"What's she going to wear?"

"She's keeping the kids upstairs most of the night, but she's still wearing a dress she wears to church. I saw it. It's long and slim, solid blue with blue and white checks on the cuffs of the sleeves and collar. It's pretty. Hurry on down now, Biddy, so we can finish you and concentrate on the food and the guests."

First one who sees me creeping down the stairs is Carl. He whistles, and I run back upstairs. He hollers up at me, "What have you done with my sister? You sure can't be our Biddy!"

"Oh, leave her be, Carl, or she'll never come down," Jean says. "Besides, you men are supposed to be outside."

"Go now," Ruby says, shooing Carl outside and joining Jean at the bottom of the stairs. "Get down here, sis. No more fooling around. It's just us girls."

My face is stinging while I come down those stairs. For half-a-cent, I'd run off and never be seen again. Mama comes over and smiles big. "Biddy, girl, you don't look like a young'un much no more."

I don't know what to say so I don't say a word. I go into the bedroom and let Ruby brush my hair and put part of it back with a ribbon. I don't like it, not one bit. I shake it loose, and she scolds me. I let her fix it again. Soon's I slip through the front door, I pull the ribbon out and stop in my tracks. Every eyeball of every one of my younger brothers is gawking at me when I come outside. "What are you staring at?" I say to War, who's sitting in Mama's rocking chair.

"At a baboon," he says and sticks his tongue out.

It doesn't take me a hog's jiffy to cross over to him, jerk him up, and bind his hands behind his back. I'm considering throwing him off the porch when Jean sticks her head out the door. "Biddy… hey, what are you hooligans up to? Stop pestering your sister, or I'm coming out there. Bood, we need you in the kitchen."

I give War a warning glare and let go. He falls to the concrete and scampers off before I wallop him.

Follow Me

I never gawked so much in my life as I am at the people who show up and pay money to eat chili and cornbread, drink tea, and dance their feet off. My chore is to gather the empty chili bowls and spoons from the washtub and take them in the house to wash and dry for the next people. If someone asks me for more tea, I take their cup or jar in the house and refill it with a chip or two of ice and more tea. Cornbread is on a help-yourself table with dish towels over the top of the skillets and alongside round cakes of Mama's cow butter in small crock bowls.

I don't have to collect the money for anything since that's Allen's job. My brothers doing this or that is kind of blurry since we're all wild on excitement and about how strange it is having so many people at our house.

Dad plays his fiddle for a while, then his banjo, but not too loud since folks are visiting and catching up on gossip. It's almost dark, and folks mostly stop eating, quit gabbing, and start dancing or listening to Tommy or Mama sing. Jean tells me I can stop bringing dishes in because Peg and her will take care of it.

"Go dance and have a good time," she says, so I go watch the dance floor and see that dancing with a boy isn't something I want to do anytime soon since I kind of hate boys. I like clog dancing to Dad's fiddle, and that's good enough for me.

Dark closes in all around except for where the dance floor and the chairs are. The smudged cedar and sage smell so fine, and I see lightning bugs flashing down by the creek. I'm leaning against the side of the raised concrete porch with my elbows propped up behind me when Calvin and Sammy come over and lean on either side of me.

"Whoo-ee, ain't this something?" Sammy says.

"You think this is something? One day I'll throw parties like you never saw before," Calvin says, and I believe him, on account of he wants to be a town folk when he grows up.

"Reckon Dad is making some good money tonight?" I ask.

"Yep," Cal says. "I imagine he'll clear about twenty-some bucks."

"Will that help with Allen's doctor bills?"

"Damn right," Cal says.

"When are you going to quit cussing, Calvin?"

"I don't know. You going to?"

"It's kind of been crossing my mind lately. Anyways, who wants to go to the creek?"

My brothers don't answer, just turn and start walking and I'm right between them. "Wait a minute," I say, and I pull off my new shoes and stuff the anklets in the tops. I hide them under one of the big looped roots of the giant tree lifting our front porch. Soon's I do that, we take off running like three dogs let off their collars.

It feels so good to be by ourselves and away from all the

fuss and noise. We keep trotting along the bank till we get to the old bridge. The moon rises high and makes every living thing look like silver. We slow down, then throw ourselves on the ground. Well, the boys do. I sit down different on account of I'm not in my overalls.

"You look nice in your new dress, Biddy," Sammy says.

"Hush, Sam," I say. "Hey, did you guys see John and Jean dancing? They were cutting a rug to Cotton-Eyed Joe, that's for true." I clap my hands together. "Oh, I'm so glad! Jean just can't step out with that mean sheriff."

"Biddy, why are you making up junk like that? Jean wouldn't give him a saucer for his coffee," Calvin says.

"Yes, she would. She's considering going to the Summer Festival dance with him. She told me herself, and 'bout made me vomit."

"Boy, she *has* lost her marbles," Calvin says. "Damn."

It's quiet except for the katydids, crickets, and night swarm buzzes until Sam says, "When Rebecca Russell was dancing with Dodson—"

"You call that dancing? He looked like a one-legged turkey doing a jig," Calvin says.

Me and Sam bust out laughing. Sam says, "Still yet, she kept on staring at you."

"Nuh-uh," Calvin says.

"She did, too. Every time you had your back turned tending to the smudge fires. I'm thinking she wanted you to pay her some mind."

I start up whistling real soft since neither Sam nor Cal give a hoot if I whistle or don't. Nobody says anything for a time. Too much contemplating, I reckon. I lay myself back on the grassy creek bank and stare at the round moon and be real mindful of my special dress. Clouds moving past the moon make my eyes follow along. It's peaceful, I mean to tell you.

A movement brings my attention to the bridge. I sit up, squinting and leaning forward to see. I about die of shock when my eyes settle on a boy about Sam's height with long hair shining like dew. He's standing about in the middle of the bridge, and I know for sure it's the Native Indian boy from Mr. MacGregor's cabin.

To put it another way, I'm staring straight at the Wood Ghost.

I poke Sammy and Calvin and get their attention. I point at the boy, who's by now walking toward us. He stops at the end of the bridge and makes arm signals that mean we should come over there to him.

"Wh-wh-at… who… uh… what is it?" Sam stammers.

The long-haired boy keeps moving his arm like he's scooping air up toward hisself.

"What's your name?" Calvin calls out.

The boy stomps a foot like he's getting mad at us.

"Am I imagining things, or is he dead-eye desperate for us to go over there to him?" I mumble.

"Lu-lu-luh-roy," the boy says. "C-come. Lu-luh-roy."

"Did he say *Leroy?*" I holler out, jumping off the ground faster than a skeeter's wing flaps.

The boy nods his head up and down bigger than all get-out. He turns around, but he's looking over his shoulder to see if we're coming. I don't need no more asking. I'm headed for the bridge.

I hear Calvin say, "Biddy… now, wait a minute." But I don't wait.

Coody's Bluff

The full moon is like a lantern above us. We wind through the woods following the boy, and I keep myself close to him so Calvin doesn't try to stop me. I don't need to turn around to know Sam and him are right behind us on account of Calvin's breath sounds mad like he's about to clobber someone. Sam could pass all of us, but he's being nice to Cal by lagging behind. Sam's scared too. We're going into woods we've never been in before, even further than Mr. Leroy's cabin and in a different direction.

"Bid, we can't keep following him…" I hear Calvin say, and I pay him no mind. I go faster, and I'm feeling poorly about it because I know Cal's leg is aching.

"Hey, we must be in Coody's Bluff by now. We have to head back…" Calvin shuts up since we're climbing up the side of a hill and they're hard for Calvin to climb. In a few minutes, he says, "Sammy… Bid… I'll wait down here. Get yourselves back here in short order, or I'll come with a belt. I mean it."

I turn back and kind of make out his form leaning against a tree, but I can't be sure with the moonlight barely getting through the thick branches. While I'm stretching my neck down the little mountain, Sam climbs up even to me breathing hard. We turn back around and can't see the strange boy.

"Where is he?"

"Maybe he disappeared," Sam says. "Or maybe he's a haint."

That gets my shivers back up. We wait, standing real still. A sound above us near sets my teeth to chattering. It's soft, but there's no mistake it's that horrible and beautiful sound the Wood Ghost makes and here we are maybe following him to hell or worse.

"Gol-all-Friday, Bid, that's about to make me run back down the mountain to home," Sammy whispers. "It sounds more frightful close up, don't it? Who is that kid, anyway?"

"Aw, he ain't nothing to worry about. Come on." I wish I believed my own self.

We climb higher until the trees part showing us a whole slew of tall rocks. The boy is standing at the foot of them. He looks about the size of a pea shooter compared to those rocks. I'm frightened of him, I won't lie. Still yet, I head straight to him. My heart is jumping around in my chest, and my fists are ready to use if I need to. Sammy is so close I feel his breath on my neck.

Do you wonder what I'm thinking while I'm doing all this?

Nothing. I can't think at all. All's I know is Mr. Leroy needs us.

The boy claps his hands and signals for us to follow him. He twists his body and slips through a skinny crevice at the base of the tall rocks. I'm about to slip into the crevice when I hear a rip. I stop, and heck fire if my flared skirt ain't hung up on the pointy end of a dead stick that used to be a branch. I unhook myself, and if I had half a brain, I'd worry about that torn dress a whole bunch more than I am at the present.

I twist into the crevice, and law, there's almost a real set of steps made out of rocks to take us higher. The boy is waiting at the top of them. It's easier to see him now that we're under the moonlight and not amongst those thick trees. He takes us zigzagging this way and that, and I'm wondering how we'll ever get off this hill of rocks and trees.

"Bid, I smell water. We must be right next to that Verdigris River."

I don't answer because I don't even know what we're doing here, but I'm figuring we're about to find out. We keep going until the boy steps out from underneath the durndest overhang you can imagine, and his showing up like that scares the devil and all his friends out of both me and Sam.

"Aghhh!" I yell. Sammy grabs my arm and a funny cry comes out of his throat.

"Looky here, now, we can't keep climbing all night…" I say out loud to the boy, but my words hang in the air by themselves because he scampers around the side of the overhang. I can't see very far, but I make out a dark shape that appears to be the front of a cave. The boy goes inside, and Sam and I are shaking when we follow him in that black place. Pretty soon, we come out the other end so it wasn't a cave, but a tunnel, instead.

The boy hops up on some smaller rocks to get to a big rock that's broke clean in two with a little passage between the two pieces. He cups his hands and makes a whistle that sounds like the night birds that laze around the creek on warm summer nights. He does it again and shoots through the crack in that big rock. Sammy and I go between the two pieces and there amongst tall pines and feathery Cedar of Lebanon trees is another dark opening.

Law, no one would ever find this place except by providence or accident.

The boy darts inside. We follow along only knowing where to go on account of the boy making a low sound like a whippoorwill. In a short time, I see a dim light somewhere, and I think I might have died on account of none of this feels like my life so far as I've lived it.

You probably know what we're about to find, but you don't know the half of it because that'll come soon enough. We come to a place in the cave where you can decide to go right or left if you've a mind to. Laying against a wall is a quilt similar to the one on the bed at Mr. MacGregor's place. It's all spread out smooth with towels folded and stacked up on the edge of it. The towels look like the fancy ones Evelyn had in her house with two green stripes on the ends. There's two buckets full of water—one with a dipper—and a wood box turned upside down to hold a glass kerosene lamp flaming on the low side. A bottle shaped like the mercurochrome bottle Dad keeps in his medicine chest is beside the lantern.

The boy backs into the dark and makes one of his sounds, kind of like a chirp. Sam and me don't know what to make of it, but just in a jiffy we do, because here's Mr. Leroy limping to us with the bottom of his trouser leg torn open wide on account of the top of his right leg is wrapped in gauze. When he gets closer into the light, I see a big wrinkly, washed-out blood stain on the side and arm of his gray jail shirt and a grin about bigger than his face.

"Bless you young'uns! It makes my heart happy to lay my eyes on yous," Mr. Leroy says. "My, my, my. I knowed you could brings them here, Taw. You never fails me, no you don't. You's a good boy, yessir."

The boy steps part way back in the light and squats on his

haunches. Everything about him make me think of something wild and ready to spring.

"I sees you staring at my messy shirt, Little Miz Woodson. I'm sorry for it, you knows I am. We washed it in the river once, but my blood was too set in its ways to leave. I shore wish I had a nice clean one to wear for my company—that be you and the other young man—but I can't go to my home to gets me one right now. Oh no, I can't. I'm guessing this be one of your brothers?"

It's hard to find my tongue, but finally I do. "This is Sammy. He's one of my eight brothers."

"Eight! Lawsy, Little Bit, ain't your folks been blessed?" Mr. Leroy sits down on the quilt and pats the side for us to sit down. Sam and I sit so close to each other it's stupid, right on the edge of the quilt.

"Now, I hates to say this next thing, 'cause it ain't fitting to talk about it to you young'uns, but I'm feared I have to since I needs your help. See, that Deputy Floyd done shot me to kill me dead, he did, right there on the old gravel road going to Bartlesville. Yes'em. But the Good Lord, He don't want ol' Leroy to see them pearly gates yet. No, he don't."

Mr. Leroy puts his head back and fills up the whole cave with his deep laugh.

We just as soon have turned to stone, me and Sam, since we don't do nothing but stare at Mr. Leroy and the long-haired boy squatting mostly in the dark. Mr. Leroy gets done with his laugh and the sound after that is no sound at all. Unless you count the flickering of the flame burning in the glass kerosene lamp, and yes, I hear it. The ceiling is massive big in the cave and we're like four peanuts in a sideways barrel the room is so big. The light makes Mr. Leroy's and the boy's shadows flicker big on the far wall. I'm suspecting it's doing the same to mine and Sam's on the wall behind us.

"Chil'ren, I gots shot from Floyd's gun in my side and my leg. Just grazed me, honeys. I was like David running from Saul, I was. Them bullets was meant for killing ol' Leroy, but they just go-ed right on through the skin and I'm already a healing with my special concoction salve and a little mercurochrome in that bottle over there. Yessir, I'll soon be good as new, excepting for the truth of the matter being so wrongly said by that deputy."

Mr. Leroy puts his head in his hands and shakes it back and forth. "Floyd gave my soul no rest whiles I was waiting for my trial. Real often, he was a siding up to me and whispering he was gonna save the county a big ol' sum of money by shooting me and burying me in a grave with nary a marker nor words nor nothing. Yes, that's what he told me alls the time. I prayed and prayed for that man to gets a good heart, but far as I's can tell right now, he never did get one."

"What about the sheriff… didn't he make him stop talking bad like that?"

"Little Bit, he didn't hear him do it. Floyd, he thought it was an amusement to be saying them things to me and no one else a knowing 'bout it. I'm reckoning he had all intentions to shoot me dead on the ways to Bartlesville."

"But why, sir?" Sam asks, getting up on his knees and leaning in since he's getting so excited by all this.

"I don't rightly know for certain, but I thinks it's because they had that rabbit foot of mine and nothing else but the cutlink young Master Calvin brought in. That cutlink was a confusion to the sheriff, 'cause it don't belong to nobody round this neck of the woods, no sir, and there it was in the pump building same as my rabbit's foot. Y'alls brother, Master Calvin—such a nice boy, he is—well, he told me all 'bout that cutlink when he came to visit me in the jail.

"I heared the sheriff talking about that thing real low to his deputies when he thought I couldn't hear. I got the ears of the Lord hisself, chil'ren, so I heared them mumbling 'bout it right often. I believe somebody wanted me to pay for the killing of poor Scottie, all neat like, and just forget about that cutlink and what it be doing in the pump building."

"But your rabbit foot was in the pump house covered in Mr. MacGregor's blood!" Sam busts out saying.

Mr. Leroy nods toward Taw. "Hush now, son, and let's don't talk too harsh about that part. Time enough for that later."

CHAPTER Thirty Seven

The Drawings

I'm listening close to Mr. Leroy, but I'm feeling powerful worried about Calvin alone on the mountain and us so late and the folks probably going to whip us forever for being gone so long, especially at night. I stand up and pull Sammy's arm till he's standing, too.

"I knows you got to go, but if you'uns can wait just a minute or two, I wants you to see something. Let me doctor this old leg first since we don't want it to bleed out. Forgives me for talking so, chil'ren. Taw, would you get my medicine bag? I thanks you for it."

Mr. Leroy takes a pint jar full of something dark out of his medicine bag and unscrews the top, setting both beside him. He unwraps the gauze off his leg until it gets right to the wound and that part looks stuck to his leg with blood. He snips off the long piece of gauze with scissors and reaches into his bag to take out a spoon. He drips syrupy stuff on the piece of stuck gauge, then screws the lid back on the jar. The jar stuff looks almost like Mr. Leroy's Herb Whiz, but it isn't as dark.

Next, he wraps his leg with a few turns of new gauze and

cuts it off from the rest. He rips the end in half and ties it in a bow in front. "There, now. Almost good as new. Angel chile…" he says to Taw, "… go gets Leroy your drawings."

Taw goes into the dark and comes back carrying pieces of paper. They look like the paper Mr. MacGregor keeps in his desk drawer. Mr. Leroy lays them on the quilt. It's quiet, and questions are rising in my head same as cream in a milk bucket.

"Mr. Leroy, how do you talk to, uh, Taw? The only time I ever heard any words come out of him was him trying to say your name and 'come' so we'd come find you."

"Did the little fella do that? My stars, that's fine! Finer than a striped Sunday suit, it is. I been working with him at my own house and here in the cave, and he'll get it right one of these days. Smart as a whip, he is. Just gives him and the Lord some time, that's all."

"What's wrong with him?" Sam asks.

"Why, ain't nothing wrong with this lovely creation—just some hard times has made him different. I gots acquainted with him quite some time ago."

"How?" Sam asks.

"Firstly, I leaves him food outside my little house and shows him I ain't out to harm him none. After some whiles, he gets better to come in and see me inside my little house or come sit by me while I'm fixing my flowers outside. 'Course now, he's even better with people since he took to helping me so much in my times of need.

"We can talk about that soon enough, but chil'ren, I needs a powerful favor from you'uns. I gots to get myself cleared with the law—the good law, not that Floyd kinds of law. Mind you now, I'm not a rattling on Deputy Hank or Deputy George or any of them others. They treated me decent, they did, and I'm not shore about the sheriff, but I got my druthers, so I don't want you'uns telling him 'bout me when you goes back to civilization."

Mr. Leroy's eyes grow bigger than shooter marbles while he talks.

"What I knows is decent men don't kill innocent folks, no sir. They ain't even supposed to kill guilty folks with no trial nor evidence to reason it by. We all knows that.

"I want you'uns to take these here drawings and find someone to trust to help me get free. My poor sister's most likely wringing her hands till they bleed a worrying about me. Oh, that dear woman don't deserve this pitiful situation, no, she don't. I know she had to returns to Selma by now, beings that she's so active in her sermons and helping folks when they gets hard up and all."

"Where did the drawings come from, sir?" Sam asks.

Mr. Leroy nods toward Taw. "He's the one. That little twig can draw most anything his eyes set on. Never seen me anything like it, chil'ren.

"Clear as I understands it, Taw was running through the woods free as a little wildcat like he always is. He was headed for Scottie's cabin when he comes across a fancy town man leaving the pump building lickity-split. It don't seem right for a fancy-pants man like that to be in the woods, but there he was, anyways. Taw told me the story by jumping around and acting it out. I thinks I got it right that the town man was in a big hurry to get out of them woods. Taw followed him all the way to a car parked on the road, but the man never did see Taw since he hid in the trees and bushes."

That reminds me of how something was following alongside me in the woods before the tornado, but I don't say nothing since I'm so interested in Mr. Leroy's story. Still yet, now I figure it was Taw all along.

"When Taw goes to Scottie's cabin, no one's around. He moseys around a bit, but no one shows up. He goes back in the woods to sing his special way and play. Next thing he comes across is Deputy Floyd running out of that very same pump building and going to his truck parked on the road. He comes back with something long in his hand. It's all dark time now, you knows, but Taw, he's still a watching from behind the bushes and trees like he's part of the woods, and by gracious, he *is* part of them.

"Deputy Floyd goes back in the pump house and comes out looking all around. Taw don't know what in tarnation when Floyd goes hightailing it straight to Scottie's cabin. I can't understand all that sweet boy tries to tell me 'bout it, but it seems Floyd just tears up that cabin a looking for something or other. Taw hears him inside pulling out drawers and slamming doors. It scares the boy so much he lays low till the next day.

"When he gets back his nerve, that little thing goes back to Scottie's, and nobody is home again. He tries to make everything all nice again so Scottie won't see what that deputy did to his pretty cabin. He hears people a talking in the woods, and next thing he sees is the law taking our Scottie's…" Leroy lowers his voice to a whisper and leans into us, "… his dead self out of the pump building."

He hands the drawings to me, and I take them closer to the light of the lamp. Sam is pressing in to look over my shoulder. The first one is Floyd with a mean look on his face. The second one is a shovel.

"Why draw a shovel?" I ask.

"Have a look at that last drawing there and see who was carrying that shovel along with a few sticks of wood."

I look at the third drawing, and dang if it isn't the man in the backseat of that fancy car I saw in Nowata back when I had the terrible stomachache.

Lanterns in the Woods

My head is overflowing with supposings and questions, but I know I can't wait no longer to get back home. The worst thing would be folks discovering where Mr. Leroy is hiding out before we have a chance to get him clear.

"Let's go, Sam. Mr. Leroy, I don't understand all this yet, but I'll see Taw's drawings get in the right hands. I don't particular know who that is yet, but I'll find out. Promise me you'll stay hid here till I come back."

"I promise."

I roll the drawings up tight so I don't rip them going home. Mr. Leroy gives me a rubber band out of his medicine kit to keep them rolled up.

"Might try asking Mr. Henson to help us. I knowed him a long time, and he's a decent gentleman, he shore is. Smart as a buggy whip, too."

"Who is that fancy man in the drawing, sis?" Sam says.

"I'll tell you later. Mr. Leroy's going to get in trouble if we stay here any longer." I look at Mr. Leroy looking all hopeful and small inside the huge cave and him shot up in two places by that devil deputy, and I feel close to blubbering. "Charley-Bird is doing real good," I say, fisting a stray tear off my cheek. "He-he's my little friend."

"I knowed he would be, Little Bit."

His sweet grin fills me with sad and a streak of stubborn, too. I know from that minute on, I'll help Mr. Leroy get cleared with the law if it's the last thing I ever do.

Me and Sammy help each other remember the way back. Since it's so interesting and we never been anywhere like it before, we make it a game. We hightail it out of the cave, through the split-rock passage, over the small rocks to the tunnel, around the side of the overhang, and down the rock steps. We go through the skinny crevice where I ripped my dress skirt and head down the side of the mountain. The whole time, we're telling each other the way to go.

"Calvin!" I call out halfway down. No answer. "Cal, where are you?"

"You don't suppose a panther got him, do you?" Sam says.

"He'd have his hands full," I say, but I'm feeling fearful for my brother.

"Calvin!" I call over and over as we go down the mountainside. "Where did we leave him, Sam, about here?"

"Naw, I think it's further down, Bid."

I don't know what to do. Is Cal kilt, or did he fall off in a canyon or something? I stop with my heart pounding in my chest. I don't know how long we been gone or what time it is, or nothing.

"Looky there!" Sam says.

In the distance, lights are coming closer, moving up the mountain.

"Sam, you know I'll beat you within an inch of your life if

you tell about Mr. Leroy and Taw, don't you?"

"I'm not a baby. I won't tell nobody nothing."

"Pssst! Over here!" Calvin hisses at us.

We skittle over to where we heard our brother and find him scrunching down behind a rock covering a lantern with his arms and hands. "Calvin… I, well, I'm sure glad you're not gobbled up by a panther," I say.

"You two are going to get a whooping, that's for true," he says. "If Dad doesn't do it, I will. I told you to come back quick, and you ignored me. I had to go get help in case you were laying hurt or half-dead. They don't know anything except we went for a walk and you two didn't listen to me and got lost."

"Calvin, we—"

"Shut up, Biddy. Just follow along with everything I say."

I don't like Calvin talking to me that way, but I know I have to get out of this mess somehow, so I don't argue.

"But Cal, Mr. Leroy—" Sam says.

"Sammy, I swear I'll knock your block off if you don't hush and follow my directions. Don't say a word, either one of you."

Cal goes to shouting. "I found them! Hey-hoe! Over here!" He lowers his voice. "Sam, act like you hurt your ankle. Sit down. Start rubbing it."

Sam drops to the ground.

"Pretend like you're in big pain, Sammy. Moan." Cal whispers as the lanterns light up everything like it's daytime.

Out of all that bright light, we're suddenly swarmed by Tommy, Dad, Ed, Carl, and several of the men who came to the chili supper. Sammy moans pitiful like, and I act like I'm tending to him.

"What happened?" Dad says.

"They got separated from me, like I told you, then Sam fell and hurt his ankle. He can walk a little at a time, then he has to rest. Biddy's been helping him down the mountain," Cal says.

"Uh-huh," Dad says. He goes over to Sam and feels around his foot and ankle. "Can you walk?"

"A little," Sam says with a groan.

"Let's get him home," Dad says, and I can't read if he believes our lies or not.

Tommy and Ed get on either side of Sam and lift him with one of his arms around each of their necks. They're tall and Sammy ain't, so his feet are dangling in the air when they stand up straight. They walk right off with Sammy's feet hanging limp. He looks over his shoulder at me and Cal. He lets out a whimper and winks.

CHAPTER Thirty Nine

One is the Killer

Dad ain't taking no more chances of kids getting lost so he puts me and Calvin in the middle of the men carrying lanterns. I have the rolled-up drawings hid in the folds of my skirt and law, it's hard going down a mountain with one hand on my dress. As we go along, first this man then another takes off in the direction of his own house until by the time we get to Hoot Creek, it's all us—meaning just family.

Calvin keeps looking at me sideways, and I can read his mind. "It's a doozy, Cal," I whisper to him behind my hand. Since he's so restless in his innards, he's going crazy not knowing what Sammy and I found out and where we went off to when we followed the boy.

Me? I'm shaking scared and wondering who to trust to help Mr. Leroy and not turn him in before we know who the killer is. If I told Dad, would he think we should tell the sheriff? I decide right then and there, I'm going to trust Tommy 'cause he won't tell no one anything if I ask him not to.

I don't know who that Taw kid is, but he sure can draw his heart out. What I know is, there were two men in the woods at the same time, and one of them kilt Mr. MacGregor.

All the outside fires from the chili supper have been doused, and no one is up but Mama and Jean at our yellow house. We come in the kitchen door and Jean cries out at the sight of me. "Your dress! Oh mercy, Bood, are you half-dead or what?"

"Nah. Just bone tired." I plop down in a chair by the kitchen table, rolling the drawings under the table all secret like. Jean shakes her head and clicks her tongue, and I can't tell if she feels sorry for me or if she's mourning over that pretty dress she made me and the dirt I know I'm wearing on it.

Mama says, "Well, a fine kettle of kindling this is. You three go off during the chili supper and get yourselves lost and worry us half to death. Didn't I tell you to let us know when you go to wandering around the countryside?"

I look as sorry as I can and say, "I'm sorry, Mama, we were just going for a little walk by the creek and…" I don't say no more since I'm trying hard not to lie to her. "Jean, I'm sorry to you, too, on account of my new dress looks so poorly. It was the prettiest one ever in the whole world, I swear."

"Don't swear," Jean says, and her voice sounds none too friendly.

"My new shoes and anklets are fine, on account of I left them under the Huckleberry tree roots by the front porch."

Jean shakes her head and mumbles something off to the side.

"You can put him down now," Dad tells Tommy and Ed when they walk into the kitchen. "Go to bed, Sam. We'll talk about that ankle in the morning after you and Calvin milk all the cows yourselves. I'd say three is a pretty fair hour for starting. Early milking cures bad ankles." Dad walks out of the kitchen and closes his bedroom door behind him.

"Well, that's in about four hours," Jean says, looking at her watch.

Mama says, "Ed and Ruby have the bed upstairs in your room, Biddy, so you can sleep on the floor in the gopher hole. Jean and Peg are bedding down in there, too. Let's not bother your dad no more tonight by making him share the end of the bed with more than Doodles. You can bet we have some talking to do in the morning."

Everyone heads off in a different direction. Mama goes in her bedroom and closes the door. Ed goes upstairs. The boys, including Carl, remind me of cows bending a knee to kneel down and sleep as they fall into their beds laid out in the front room. I'm surprised Jean hasn't made us all get washed up, but she goes on into the gopher hole. Tommy gets a drink from the dipper in the water bucket, and I look around to see if anyone can hear me.

"Tommy, I need help," I say in a low voice. "Something awful is happening, and I don't trust no one."

"Huh?" he says, choking on water. He has a cough fit and gets over it. "Is somebody doing something to you, sis? Just point, and they'll be sorry they were ever born."

"Nothing like that. Come over here by the light so's I can show you something. And just whisper, okay?" I fetch the drawings from under the table and put my arm over them so they don't curl up. Tommy bends down to see them.

"Well, the only one I recognize is that ugly Deputy Floyd's mug. Who's the other one?"

"Remember the fancy car we saw in town that day with the woman who blew smoke out the window?"

"Why sure. Who could forget that?"

"Did you see one of those men in the back when he looked up?"

"Nah, I was concentrating on smoothing my hair back after my scuffle with Squirrel."

"That man…" I point to the drawing of the fancy man, "… was in that car. I won't ever forget his eyes and the look on his face."

"You don't say. How is it you have a drawing of him, Bid?"

The time I've been dreading has come. Is Tommy for sure the one I need to tell all my secrets to?

"If I tell you, you have to promise to keep it between us and take me to Mr. Henson first thing in the morning."

"Mr. Henson? What does he have to do with anything? You know I'm starting to court his daughter, don't you? Whoo-ee, can that little girl dance. Did you see her tonight?"

I roll my eyes. "Tommy, listen. Mr. MacGregor was kilt, and one of these here men did it."

Tommy frowns. "That's some pretty serious talk, Little Britches."

I nod and look my brother square in the eyes. "I'm telling you something now, Tommy. Mr. Leroy's life depends on this, and he told me to get Mr. Henson in it."

"*Leroy* told you?" Tommy scratches his head and pulls the bench close to my chair. "Okay, sis. I'm listening."

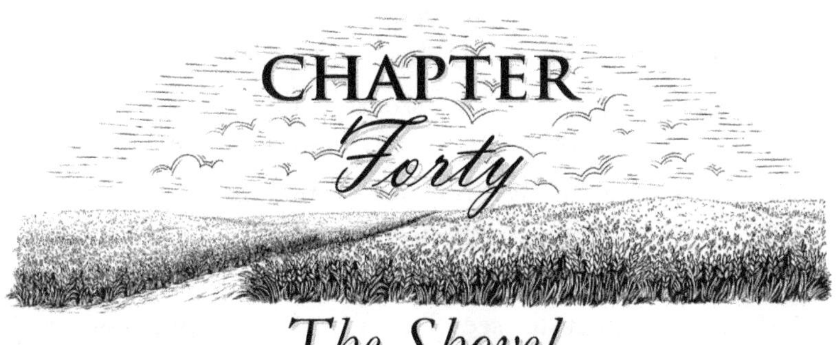

CHAPTER Forty

The Shovel

If Mama wasn't so partial to Tommy, I wouldn't be sitting here on the buckboard seat of the wagon headed to the Henson's house. I know Calvin will be pressing Sam to tell him everything that happened last night in the cave. That's all right if they don't let the rest of those big ears hear anything since we can't trust the young'uns to keep secrets.

I lost Mr. Leroy's rubber band somewhere, so the drawings are rolled up and tied with a new piece of string I borrowed from Mama's sewing basket. I don't even know what Tommy told our folks this morning, but they let me go and didn't ask me nothing.

Last night, Tommy heard most everything I could remember. He was worried about it, and should be. He said it went along with what Cal had already told him about Mr. Leroy and Floyd that time they went to the jail to show the sheriff the cufflink. He admitted he hadn't put his thinking cap on about the situation like he'd told Calvin he would, being that he was busy dying with pneumonia and courting a new gal, but now he was ready to make it right.

He agreed Mr. Henson was the proper one to go to,

allowing how he has lots of friends in the city, including some lawyers, and also because Mr. Leroy trusts him so much.

Traveling on the road alongside the woods, I know I won't hear Taw's beautiful and scary sounds since he's tending to Mr. Leroy in that cave. Still yet, sometimes this morning, I feel like the thicket has eyeballs looking at us while we roll by in our wagon.

I don't expect to see Sheriff Murphy's prisoner truck when we pull up to the Henson's, but there it is, all the same. I pull in my breath, and Tommy tells me to act grown up and don't let on that we have any news or secrets.

We're headed up to the front porch when the sheriff comes out the door of the house followed by Mr. Henson. He still has on those dadgummed sunglasses, and I reckon he sure must be hiding some evil eyes behind them. How do we know if Floyd is the only one who knew about trying to kill Mr. Leroy? We don't. For all we know, the sheriff was in on it and Mr. MacGregor's murder, too.

The sheriff nods his head. "Hey, Tommy, what are you up to this fine morning so bright and early?"

"Here to see Mr. Henson about the next mule rodeo. You?"

"A little official business this morning. Say, if it isn't Miss Rose herself. Still got that yellow bird, or did he fly away?"

That makes me mad, but I don't say anything.

"Tell that pretty sister of yours I'm looking forward to the festival next week."

She'd rather eat a raw snake than be seen with the likes of you.

I say that in my mind, but all I say out loud is nothing. One thing I do is stare a good mean one in his eyes. Or, at his sunglasses. He knows how I feel about him.

"Tommy, come on in," Mr. Henson says shaking my

brother's hand. He looks me in the eye. "I don't believe we've been introduced." Tommy tells him I'm his next to the youngest little sister and my name is Biddy.

"And here I thought her name was Rose," the sheriff says. He grins through those big teeth of his and gets in his truck. When he drives off, we go inside. I'm struck dumb at how pretty and big the Henson house is, bigger than our cousin Evelyn's.

"Can we talk privately, Mr. Henson?" Tommy says.

Mr. Henson looks surprised. "Why, yes. Let's step into my office." He leads us to a room with gobs of books in a shelf on a wall. Not as many books as Mr. MacGregor had on his wall, but close to it. It has a desk catty-cornered on a big, thick rug in one side of the room, a fireplace, and three chairs all matched up with swirly blue and white material. He closes the door.

"Please, have a seat," Mr. Henson says.

Soon's we set down, Tommy says, "Mr. Henson, my sister has stumbled onto some truths, and she doesn't trust anyone with them except you."

"Why, I'm flattered. What can I do for you, Miss Biddy?"

"First thing I want to know is, are you good friends with Sheriff Murphy?" I ask.

"I wouldn't call us good friends. We are acquaintances."

"What's he doing out here this morning if you aren't friends?"

"Biddy, it's not nice to talk to Mr. Henson like that," Tommy says.

"It's quite all right, Tommy. Actually, he came to tell me about the capture of another of the Bonnie and Clyde gang. Do you know who Bonnie and Clyde are?"

"I know what my brothers tell me about them. I don't

rightly care about robbers."

"I understand. This particular fellow, Method Anthony Ray, has evaded the law ever since the shootout that killed those notorious characters. He tried to form another gang and didn't have any luck. Tate said he attempted to rob a bank by himself up in Woodward a couple weeks ago and got caught."

"What does that have to do with you?" I ask.

"Biddy…" Tommy shoots me a settle-yourself-down look. Mr. Henson raises a flat palm toward Tommy.

"I don't mind her curiosity, Tom. The wife and I believe curiosity is one of the greatest gifts given to children and young folk." He looks me square in the face. "Let me explain what this has to do with me, Biddy. You see, I have this habit of engraving my belongings. It stems from when I was a youngster and didn't have two sticks to rub together most of the time. As I worked and saved to buy things, I'd engrave my possessions with my first initial and my whole last name."

I don't care about all that, so I start looking around the room. Not for long, because Mr. Henson says, "So, it was easy to identify that something found in Method Anthony Ray's car in Woodward belongs to me."

"What is it?" I ask.

"A shovel I lent to Scott MacGregor to dig out the foundation for the shed he was planning to build this summer. How that shovel wound up in the hands of that crook, I do not know."

My hair about stood on its end hearing that. Tommy and me look at each other. I untie the string on my rolled-up drawings and walk over to put one of them on the desk. "Is this your shovel, Mr. Henson?" I ask.

Mr. Henson looks at the drawing. "Well, I can't be certain. Don't most shovels look the same?"

"Yes, but this shovel was carried by a fancy man who was in our woods at the time poor Mr. MacGregor was kilt."

"You don't say. How do you know this?"

I look at Tommy, and he nods his head. "Do you mind if we sit back down, sir? Biddy's got an earful for you."

The Truth of It

We come out of Mr. Henson's office and who should spy Tommy but Martha Henson.

"I had a wonderful time last night, Tommy. What brings you to our house today?"

She sure does know how to flutter her eyelashes when she's talking to my brother. After a few goofy words back and forth between them, we load up in the wagon to go home.

Mr. Henson walks outside with us and tells us he'll speak to the officials in Bartlesville and get the drawings to Woodward, and he won't say a word to Sheriff Murphy until we're sure of our facts and figures, whatever that means. He tells us he'll get word to us soon's he knows anything more. He didn't let Martha hear any of our secrets, so I'm thinking we can trust him. The way I see it, we have no other choice.

I'm so tuckered out I fall asleep on the buck seat and 'bout fall out of the wagon. Tommy catches me by the overall strap before I tumble out. I look at him with such weary eyes, he says I have to go straight to bed when I get home.

"In the daytime?"

"Yep. I'll talk to the folks. It'll be fine. You go inside the house all smiling and head for the gopher hole."

I don't believe it will work, but I do what Tommy says to do. I don't remember anything but putting my head on the pillow. Next thing I know, Doodles is standing by the bed shaking my arm. "Time for supper, Biddy."

Supper?

Supper is cold cornbread and milk, roastnears, fresh pickled beets and onions, and fried okra. I'm so hungry I don't even look up till my plate is slicked clean. What I notice when I look up is a bunch of questions on the kids' faces. The youngest ones don't know what's been going on at all, but they know it's something. Somebody's told them not to ask me questions, but I still see it in their eyes.

Calvin and Sammy know enough to be double-dog curious about what else has happened, but they seem awful tuckered-out quiet from their all-day chores Dad gave them. Working like that might be better than a whooping, but maybe not.

I'm guessing the grownups, from Allen up, know things since they're not being nosey and are kind of nice to me, besides. That Tommy is a miracle. He can soothe Mama, Dad, and Jean with one hand tied behind his back.

Mama joins Jean and me in cleaning up the supper mess, then Mama says for me to go on upstairs and sleep some more.

"Mama, she needs a bath by now," Jean says.

"Tomorrow is fine," Mama says.

I don't think I can sleep since I slept so much already. I refill Charley's seeds and water and tell him about Mr. Leroy. He fluffs his feathers and cocks his head while he listens. Pretty soon, I'm yawning my head off. Doodles comes up and we sack out. I don't wake up till I hear Jean calling us down to breakfast.

The next few days, I stay busy and worried about Mr. Leroy in that cave by Coody's Bluff, and if he has enough to eat, and if he wonders if I'm helping him or not. I've been knowing Mr. Leroy since I was knee-high to a bug, so I want him to be all right and back to making his Herb Whiz for all the women around these parts like he used to do. My heart is longing to see him that way again.

We're three days past waiting for word from Mr. Henson when Snipe sidles up to me while I'm outside hanging wet clothes on the line.

"I don't care what War does to me, I'm going to tell you something."

"You're big enough to defend yourself, Snipe. Don't let him push you around."

"It ain't always that easy, sis, but listen… I been trying to get worked up to tell you this all summer, so here it is. It was me and War that found Mr. Leroy's rabbit foot in a tree out in the woods. It was wrapped in a square of plaid material inside a hollowed-out tree knot all covered up with leaves and twigs. Why we come to find it was War stole a skinny jug of Dad's blackberry wine and was looking for a place to hide it. We saw that hole in the tree, and War sent me up there to see if the hole was deep enough. I was digging around to get the leaves out when I pulled out that piece of cloth. Inside it was a fancy rabbit foot."

"You stole some of Dad's blackberry wine? How could you?"

"Don't get all mad, Biddy, and you'd better not tell on me."

"I might do it, Snipe. That's a bad one."

Snipe looks down.

"I won't tell if you promise never to do it again," I say.

"I promise."

"Even if War says to?"

"I don't do what he says anymore."

What I know and don't say is Dad will find the jug of wine missing soon enough, and it will be *Katy, bar the door* when he does.

"Why did you boys put the rabbit foot in the pump house anyhow?"

"It was an accident. We go in there all the time to play and hide out. Last time we did was the day before Mr. MacGregor got kilt. It must have fell out of War's pocket since he was hanging upside down from the rafters in the ceiling. We were in there one day before the murder. When War heard the sheriff say they was blaming Mr. Leroy for the killing 'cause of that bloody rabbit foot, he 'bout went out of his noggin. He said he'd do all kinds of mean stuff to me if I told. I wanted to say something, but War said Dad would find out we'd stole the wine and been in the pump house and who knows what all. He thinks he has enough on me to keep me from telling, but he don't. I know what's what now, and I want to come clean."

I sit right down on the ground beside my basket of wet clothes to ponder this situation. Mr. Leroy was blamed for a terrible murder just because his rabbit foot was in the pump house? Now, I find out it was all my devil brothers' fault and none of the bad things had to happen to that good man if War and Snipe had told the truth.

The truth. No lies. Truth.

A little voice in my noggin tells me I'm just as bad since I been lying so much this summer. I shake my head and tend to the matter at hand, which is my brother.

"Snipe, I'm ashamed of you to both ends of the earth.

You can't never say it was right to hold your tongue and let that poor man go through hell and high water just 'cause you wouldn't stand up to War. Just think of it… he could have been hung for a killing he didn't do! Why, I ought to tell on you this second and let you get walloped for a whole day since…"

I shut up on account of Snipe is bawling so hard he can't even stand up. He sprawls out on the ground beating his fists in the dirt. While I'm figuring what to do next, I see Mr. Henson's car coming down Blackberry Road to our house.

I leave my brother to his suffering and run to get Tommy from the field. I tell him about why Mr. Leroy's rabbit foot was in the pump house, and he whistles. Snipe has taken off somewhere, and I'm not surprised. We come through the kitchen door just when Mr. Henson is coming in our front room. Mama and Jean are bringing him in and asking him if he wants some sweet tea or a bowl of beans with some leftover cornbread from the noon meal.

"No, thank you, Mrs. Woodson. That sounds delicious, but I just finished a big lunch. I'll sure take a raincheck, though," he says, smiling. I don't know what a raincheck is, but Tommy asks Mr. Henson to come sit at the kitchen table. Mama and Jean go outside, and here we are with privacy until Cal and Sam come walking in.

"Uh, wait outside, fellas," Tommy says. Calvin starts to jaw off, but thinks better of it. No one bucks Tommy any more than they do Dad.

Soon as they're gone, Mr. Henson says, "Well, I have very interesting news. Let me start by saying that after you left a few days ago, I took the drawings up to the officials in Bartlesville myself. They contacted the police in Woodward, and a courier was quickly sent to take the drawing to them.

This morning, we heard back that the young lad's drawing was an exact replica of the man caught robbing that First National Bank of Woodward a few weeks ago. When Method Anthony Ray was shown the drawing of himself and found out that someone saw what he did in the woods near Nowata, he broke down and told the authorities the whole story."

"So he kilt Mr. MacGregor?" I say, jumping out of the chair.

"Perhaps not. He claims that he and part of his gang, which happens to have included Bonnie and Clyde and Henry Methvin, were driving from Everly to Dallas by way of Nowata. It was their practice to take backroads to avoid county sheriffs and policemen in general. While doing so, their car got stuck in the mud on Wayne Road. Mr. Ray went to find a shovel and some boards to get them out of the mud. He saw Scott's cabin, and Scott offered to help. Scott told him he kept his tools and some lumber out of the weather in a pump house not far away. When they got there, Method claims he merely knocked Scott unconscious to buy time for the gang to get away. He says the gentleman was very nice to him, and he left him his cufflinks by way of a thank you. Apparently, they're expensive cufflinks."

"Gol-all-Friday, you believe that, Little Britches? It was the true Bonnie and Clyde and some of their gang we saw that day in Nowata. Who in thunder would have thought it?" Tommy's grin looks like it might split his face. "Mr. Henson, how did that Method fella keep from being shot up with Bonnie and Clyde?"

"It appears he stayed behind in some little town to visit a girlfriend and had plans to join the gang in a few days," Mr. Henson says.

"Do you believe him? I mean, about not being the one to

kill Mr. MacGregor?" Tommy asks.

"I might, son, if I can clear up a matter. Biddy, you say the lad who did the drawings saw this 'fancy man' and then another man, who is obviously Deputy Floyd, in the woods the same night?"

"Yes, he told Mr. Leroy—I don't know how since he can't really talk—but he said he saw Floyd go in the pump house pretty quick after the Bonnie and Clyde robber left. Floyd left for a short time, went back in the pump house, and then hightailed it to Mr. MacGregor's cabin. He tore it up inside like he was looking for something. Taw stayed hidden outside until Floyd left, then he went in and fixed everything back in the cabin until it was clean again. He didn't know Mr. MacGregor was already laying dead in the pump house."

Mr. Henson pulled a watch on a chain out of his pocket and looked at it.

"Right about now, a search warrant is being issued to search the home, truck, and personal effects of Floyd Brewster. We shall see what turns up. Hopefully, Miss Biddy, you will soon have good news for your Mr. Leroy."

Bug-Eyed Crazy

Mr. Henson leaves, and it's for sure I got lots to think over. I don't want nobody bothering me, neither. I walk down the gravel road to the spring, feeling like I growed up about ten years since school let out. I'm skipping more than walking till I climb the hill overlooking Mr. MacGregor's cabin. I only want to sit there on the hill and look at it, not go in. 'Course, it wouldn't be hard to with the door all busted in by Floyd. Tommy told me not to worry about it since he and Allen would go fix it later today so no forest critters get inside.

Soon as Mr. Henson left, Tommy went to tell the grownups and Cal the whole truth of everything. I slipped out the door and took off before Sam or anyone else could find me. Oh, listen, I did tell Tommy first to let Mama know I was going roaming a little and I'd be home in a bit. See, I'm trying real hard to live up to her image of me being a truthful girl.

Looking at that pretty cabin so snug and tucked into the edge of the woods, it's hurtful knowing Mr. MacGregor won't ever be inside again reading a book, taking a drink of water from his nice inside faucets, or getting ready to teach us at the

Armstrong School. What will happen to Mr. MacGregor's things and his pretty cabin, I don't know, since he's got no family left.

It starts to sprinkle a little, and for some reason, I get a yearning to go through the woods from Mr. MacGregor's cabin to Mr. Leroy's little place. I've never been that way before, and it sounds like something I might want to try while I'm so deep in my thinking.

The path from Mr. MacGregor's place to Mr. Leroy's place turns out to be cut deep, like it's been used a whole lot. The woods themselves are thick as tater soup, and I'm glad I don't have to hear no Wood Ghost sounds today. It might scare me in such heavy timber, even if I knew it was Taw. The sky all clouded up makes it darker and darker as I go.

Walking along the path, I'm thinking about how Allen didn't die from that mule kick this summer and how much it grieved all of us to see him hurt so bad. I told you before, we don't hug in our family, but that doesn't mean we don't like each other a whole lot, especially if one of us is ailing.

Anyways, Allen told us yesterday he's going off to the West Texas State Teacher's College this fall, and John, the almost-doctor, is going to sponsor him. I don't know exactly what that means, but I think it means John wants to pay for Allen's schooling since we suffer with almost no money in our family. That's sure to get Jean looking at John with different eyes, now isn't it?

What else should happen right after Allen's accident is Tommy dies but won't stay dead. That doctor was so grieved about him living when he said he wasn't going to, he up and quit doctoring in Nowata. We all say good riddance that he's gone, on account of he never belonged here in the first place.

I'm thinking a body could near suffocate with so many

trees arching over and right beside the trail to Mr. Leroy's place. For no reason at all, I ponder how that cigar-smoking woman smiled at me, and imagine… she was a bank robber… Miss Bonnie herself! She was about to be kilt soon after that. I wonder if she was wearing her lipstick redder than a rooster's comb when they filled her body with all those bullets. That's an ugly thought, so I stop thinking about it.

It feels good knowing Mr. Leroy is about to get cleared of all law-breaking crime and is coming back to his home. I'll miss Charley-Bird something terrible, that's for true, but he belongs with Mr. Leroy. I figure he's kind of Charley-Bird's dad.

I come around the side of Mr. Leroy's place and feel heartbroken to see all his moss rose and assorted flowers in the painted white tractor tires brown and weed smothered since Miz Abernathy had to go back to Selma and couldn't wait no longer. The whole place looks about as lonesome as anything I ever saw, sitting there so quiet and alone in the tall trees.

I sit down on the tiny porch step and have myself a cry. I know Mr. Leroy's going to be all right, but that doesn't stop the tears coming. Part of my bawling is about Mr. MacGregor, and the rest of it's because I've been due a crying fit for a time now but always have that pack of brothers around and can't have one. I let the tears come hard and drop on my overalls.

Who knows why I do what I do, but I decide to pull the weeds and dead flowers out of the middle of those tires. I get a heap of stuff out and gather it up to scatter on the edge of the woods. I come back and smooth the dirt flat in each tire. I'm careful not to harm the moss rose, since I know my mama harvests the seeds off hers ever year and saves them in a white envelope.

I stand up admiring my work with my hands on my hips. I whistle out real loud and say, "That looks fine, Biddy girl. Mr. Leroy will be right proud."

I whistle again, but right then is when I get a shivery feeling up my back and neck, like something's out in the trees watching me. I pick up a stick, but I know a stick won't fend off a wild animal. I look all around me in the woods and hear lots of normal bird sounds, even a woodpecker hammering his beak on a tree. Then it goes real quiet. I back up toward Mr. Leroy's house with my eyes circling all over the place and thinking of a plan to get home.

If I run through the woods to the rope and wood bridge, it's all wooded, but scattered-out trees once I get away from Mr. Leroy's place. The other way home is back the way I came from Mr. MacGregor's house. Once I leave there, it's open land to home. The bad part is how thick the trees are from the shanty to the cabin, and that bothers me right now.

Why I got myself in this situation, I do not know, but I'm thinking I won't do it no more. I got too many brothers who want to tag along with me to get myself afraid like this. Letting anyone besides Calvin and Sammy hang around with me is a plan I never made before. I figure maybe I'm getting a little horse sense, or am I losing some of my stubborn streak?

I figure on running all the way to the bridge over Hoot Creek, and I'll be home in no time after that. It's still spitting scattered rain and it feels cool to my skin. I take off down a worn path in my usual fast run. Next thing I know, I'm splattered on the ground with the wind knocked clear out of me. I lay there trying to get my breath, but I can't since I fell so hard on my chest and belly. I allow I hooked my foot under a tree root and that makes me laugh at myself for being clumsy. It dies in my throat soon's I see pointed cowboy boots walking toward me.

"How's that feel, girly-girl? Bet you're wishing you had more sense than to nose around other folk's business, now ain't you?" Deputy Floyd says. He takes hold of my shoulder and jerks me up to a sitting position. Even if I hadn't taken that hard fall, I'd still be out of air on account of Floyd looks so bug-eyed crazy.

CHAPTER Forty Three

The Big Bluff

Floyd's hair is flopping all over the place like he forgot to paste it down. A big part in the middle looks like someone plowed through his scalp and scattered the long pieces to the wind. His tan shirt is half tucked in and half out, and his matching tan pants are streaked with dirt. One pant leg is tucked into the top of a boot but the other is hanging loose and wrinkled.

"You don't fool me, you little sharecropper trash. You know where that no-good Negro man is, don't you? You're here gathering things for him. I been keeping my eye on you, don't think I haven't. You was too fond of him, which I seen the day we arrested him and I says to myself that I was gonna keep you in my eyesight. Yessir. I got my spies, and I know you took off the other night and everyone was out looking for you. You been helping hide him, ain't that right?"

"No, it isn't right," I say with my lips pulled tight so's he can't tell I'm scared to death.

Floyd's face comes swooping down on me like a bat out of a cave. It lands right in front of my face and twists into rubbery skin. His eyes are bloodshot, and his breath smells like corn liquor. I know what that smells like since I've smelled Dad's homemade corn liquor before.

"You're damn right lying to me. He ain't getting away scot-free. He'll pay, and you're gonna help me or else."

His spit is landing on my face while he yells, and I feel like I'm close to retching. More than Floyd's ugly face and spit, what's eating away at me most is how I know who the killer of Mr. MacGregor is, and it's the man kneeling right in front of me.

He knows it, too, 'course he does, so why's he still trying to blame it on Mr. Leroy?

Floyd stands up keeping his big, round eyeballs dead on me. He turns around and slams his open hands against a tree trunk. It must have hurt bad 'cause he yells out most fiercely. Next thing I know, he's kicking that poor tree with his sharp-toed boots. "Damn almighty! Dammit to hell! It ain't my fault! Don't tell me that. It ain't my fault!"

I haven't never been around a real crazy person before, but I got my instincts. They tell me to be still and don't rile him up more than he is right now. Floyd drops his hands to his sides. He's turned away from me toward that beat-up tree, but he's talking just like somebody's in front of him. I can make out his words, but it's like there's two people talking 'cause he says things like, "You didn't, neither," and, "Yes, yes, I did," then, "He don't know. We won't tell him." But it's just one Floyd saying it all.

That quick, I'm thinking how I'm sure in a pickle. A murdering man has lost his mind, and here I am his prisoner all alone in the woods with no one to hear me scream for help. No matter how much I kick myself inside my head for winding up like this, it doesn't change one thing about it. Just knowing I'm in a predicament so peculiar and dangerous brings my stubborn streak clear up from somewhere and turns my face hot.

I stand up slow and quiet and take a few steps away. Floyd's still having that talk with hisself and doesn't turn around. I take a side step and turn around. I glance over my shoulder. Still safe. I'm a hair from shooting down the path when I fall under the weight of that man. Tackled, like the boys do each other when they rassle.

I turn over slapping, scratching, biting. I'm screaming my lungs off, too, but he's getting the best of me. I grab his nose and bend it to the side. While he's hollering about that, I do what the older boys taught me to do if I ever found myself in a bad spot—knee him in his privates. He yelps like a kicked dog and rolls over holding himself. I wiggle over and get on all fours. I'm raising up when I'm flattened from behind.

"You ain't going nowhere, Miss Uppity!"

My thinking is going fast, and it says I'm getting out of this mess, 'cause no fool man is going to get the best of me. I don't get a chance to have no more thoughts before Floyd jerks me off the ground and shakes me with both his hands like I'm a rag doll.

"You're taking me to that damned colored man, you hear? I know you know where he's hiding. My spies tell me you was up by Coody's Bluff the other night. It's against the law to help a fugitive, so you might just get arrested for helping him, missy."

He shakes me till I think my brain will come un-sewed from my skull. Even with my mind rattling around like that, I'm thinking how ignorant Floyd is. Something else I'm thinking too—about how Cal told me one of these days someone is going to show me how it really is. Well, Cal, today is that day, but I ain't taking it laying down.

"You k-k-killed Mr. Mac-Mac-Gregor, and you kn-kn-know it!" I stutter out. Floyd stops his shaking.

"What did you say?" he growls.

"I said Mr. Leroy is a good man, and *you're* the one who's trash!"

An open hand slaps my face so hard my eyes roll back in my head. I taste blood.

"Watch your mouth, Miss High Horse. I ain't fooling with you no more. Where's he at?"

I put my fingers on my lip and bring it away with blood on it. Floyd doesn't give me time to answer before he pulls and drags me through the woods toward Coody's Bluff. Seems like his "spies" told him where they found me and Sam the other night, so that's where we're going. What I figure is he heard about Sam and me from town gossip since he's too stupid to have spies.

Floyd's grunting and mumbling and jerking me around like I don't weigh nothing at all. Nobody can treat me this way and get away with it. That's what I'm pondering, along with a sort of plan—a bluff—to throw Floyd off so I can run away. Before we get to the place where the men brought the lanterns to find me and Sammy, I say, "We have to climb up to the top of that other little mountain and head left to the Verdigris River. That's where he's hiding, down there in a small cave you can't see from the top."

Now, you and I both know to find Mr. Leroy, we have to head to the right to go through the crevice, up the rock steps, around the overhang, through the tunnel, between the split rock, and then we'll get to where he's hiding out.

Thing is, Floyd doesn't know that, and he never will.

My step is light now, as I lead Floyd on a path I've never been on before. My lip is swelling, my shoulders ache, my arms are 'bout pulled out of their sockets, and I probably don't have two inches not bruised or scraped, but I press on because I have to. I smell water and know we're close to the river.

"Stop here. I need to sustain myself," Floyd orders. "And don't try anything, you hear?"

I nod and lean against a tree while he takes out a small silver flask from a pocket inside his shirt. He tilts it up and sucks on the opening. Streams of liquid run down the sides of his mouth. He puts the flask away and wipes his lips with the back of his hand. He snuffs his nose and spits, then unzips his pants and starts peeing right in front of me.

I almost die. My face burns as I turn away. I've never seen such a rude thing in all my life. Not my brothers or dad, nor no one I ever knew, would have that kind of backward manners in front of a female. The picture in my head of my brothers beating this nasty man into a pulp gives me comfort as I plug my ears so I don't hear him wetting the ground.

I'm in the hands of a dangerous killer who has no care for anyone, specially girls or Negro folks or sharecroppers. I'm considering he knows he's beat as far as the law's concerned, so he wants to take Leroy and probably me with him on his trip to destruction.

Those are big thoughts, but that's how you start thinking when you know you're staring death in the face.

We get to the top of the mountain and look down over the river. I try to spot something that looks like it could be a hideout for Leroy to fake Floyd out. Nothing yet. The river is narrow in spots, and we start stepping down the rocky path leading to it.

"Where's the cave?" Floyd growls.

"You have to get closer to see it. You don't think he's stupid, do you?"

"Shut your damned mouth! I don't like you females thinking you got smarts over me. You're ignorant white trash, and that's all you'll ever be. You got that?"

I don't answer.

"I said, you got that?"

"Sure, I got it, Floyd," I say because the look in his eyes right now is *off*, like a rabid animal. How do I know what that looks like? Carl told me about it, how an animal with rabies has eyes that have no life in them no more, just a blank stare like Little Orphan Annie's eyes in those funny papers, only worse, on account of the danger right behind the dead look. That's what I'm seeing in Floyd's eyes right now, so I go along with him.

We come to an open flat place still a long ways from the bottom. Floyd goes over to the ledge and looks to the right and to the left. He turns back to me with hate boiling on his face. "You think you got one over on me, don't you? There ain't nothing down there secret enough for a man to hide in."

"It's further down past that bunch of trees, Floyd, I promise."

"You're lying. You know what? I'll take my belt to you and see if you get a better memory. Once you're bleeding real good, you'll take ol' Floyd where he wants to go." His lopsided grin turns me sick inside. He unhooks his belt buckle, and in one quick pull, the belt is in his hand.

"No wait! I mean it! His hideout is down there! Right behind—"

Slap! The belt whizzes through the air and wraps around my legs. It stings terrible bad, and I howl. Another slap of the belt catches me around my chest and my cheek. I know as sure as I've ever known anything that I'm in for a beating that has no justice anywhere in it.

I go to screaming like I screamed on that boat when Mr. Borino tried to get an advantage over me. I scream and grab for the belt when it hits me across the arms. *Shoosh,* the belt goes across my back so hard I stumble. I choke and heave like I'm about to vomit. Floyd laughs out loud, and the sound echoes off the sides of the hills around the river. He stops waving his belt and stares at me with a look I don't like.

"Say, you look right pretty bawling and jumping around while I thrash you. You ain't no little girl, neither… you're 'bout a woman. I'm seeing that, now. Making me feel real good to watch you carry on so. Uh-huh. You ready for some more, honey?"

"Please listen to me! Mr. Leroy's right down—"

"I'm done listening. A good man-whooping is what you need."

His belt lashes out and snaps me across my belly. His arm is raised again when the most frightening and beautiful sound I ever heard in my life comes flowing through the air and circles around where we are, down by the river, and back up on the sides of the hills.

"Wh-what's that?" Floyd says. His belt hand drops to his side. The sound gets louder. It's filled with terrifying sadness and dread. Floyd drops the belt and goes to shaking. He hugs himself with both arms. I remember how scared he was in the cabin when he heard those sounds outside. This time, the unnatural cries are even scarier.

It's my chance, and I take it.

"That there's the Wood Ghost, Floyd. He flies through the air seeing who's evil. When he finds anyone evil, he dives down and…"

"Shut up! You're lying, anyways. Ain't no such thing as a Wood Ghost. It's just a wounded animal or something. Let's get back to your beating." He raises the belt back into the air.

"But I thought everyone knew about that kind of haint, Floyd." I yell, dodging the slash of leather coming at me again. I start talking real loud so's he doesn't miss my words while he tries to whip me. "Haven't you ever heard that ghost before… by yourself in the woods? Bet you have."

"M-m-maybe. But I know better than—"

The sounds get louder, and I am chilled to the bone with the beauty and terror of it.

"Floyd, if you're a good man, you got nothing to worry yourself about. But… if you're guilty of sins, the Wood Ghost will—"

"What're you talking about? *He'll what*?"

I don't answer. I put the most worrisome look I can gather on my swollen face. I suck in my lips and shake my head.

"Tell me, or I'll keep belting you till you do!" He loops the belt double and shakes it in my face.

"Okay!" I scream. "I'll tell you." I drop my voice to a whisper to start off and raise it louder and louder while I say, "If… if you have sins… sins you hide from other folks, the Wood Ghost will swoosh through the air and… with his sword… chop off your head!"

The longest wolf-sounding cry of horror comes from the woods, and Floyd's teeth start chattering. He's shaking so bad spit runs down his chin.

"I ain't letting no haint chop off my head. He can't get me in the water, and you're coming with me!"

"We can't clear the rocks, Floyd! We'll never make it!"

Floyd has me in an armlock. He drags me with him toward the edge of the bluff.

"No, please, Floyd! I don't want to die!" I dig my feet in. He jerks me harder. We are ten feet away. I grab onto a spindly tree.

He clamps his hands over mine, and finger by finger loosens my hands from the small tree, and I'm screaming at the top of my lungs, "Help! Let me go!"

Seven feet away. I bite him on the arm. He yelps and slaps my face one way, then the other. He pulls me toward my death.

Four feet away from the edge. I'm crying out to the Almighty to overlook my summer lying and tell my family I'm sorry I died so poorly.

We are on the edge of the bluff looking down at the river and the rocks jutting out of the water that will sure enough kill us.

A shot rings out. Then another one. Floyd's face looks like he wants me to explain what's going on. His arms go loose, and I slip out of them quick as lightning. Part of the bluff gives way under my foot, and I near faint away with fear. I grab onto ground, and Floyd's legs to claw past him. Wheezy and bubbling sounds are coming out of him.

I'm almost past Floyd, crawling on my belly. He grabs my foot.

I scream and scream, beating the ground with my fists. From the thick trees, I see Sheriff Murphy running to us. He whacks Floyd's hand with the side of his hand until Floyd lets my foot go. The sheriff scoops me up and lays me under the little spindly tree that couldn't save me before.

"Don't move, Rose Woodson," he says.

"Look!" I yell, pointing at Floyd who's standing by the edge with blood all over the whole front of his shirt. He has a rock in his hand.

The sheriff levels his gun toward Floyd. "Floyd Bingham Brewster, you are under arrest for the murder of Scott Patrick

MacGregor."

"You ain't taking me nowhere, Tate. I'm going by myself." Floyd stands there staring at us, kind of teetering back and forth. He turns and laughs out over the empty space in front of him. Law, it's an awful sound. In the next blink of an eye, he steps off the bluff.

My mouth goes drier than shoe leather. Sheriff Murphy walks to the edge and looks over the side shaking his head. He comes back over by me and squats, still gawking at the spot where Floyd has just kilt hisself.

He takes off his sunglasses and rubs his eyes. "My Lord," he mumbles. "Are you hurt bad, Rose?" he asks, staring at me.

I 'bout faint, 'cause that sheriff is looking at me with some of the kindest eyes I ever did see. They been hiding there all along behind those dark sunglasses.

Angels is Rejoicing

It's hot, and I don't care. Sammy and me are almost at the tall rocks that made Taw look as short as a pea shooter about a week ago. Cal and Allen are waiting for us halfways down the mountain while we go deliver our messages.

The way Allen sat down in the shade and leaned hisself against a tree with his book in his hands, we aren't in any hurry. We don't go by how Calvin acts about such matters, since he's so restless. He wants everything to happen quicker than a skunk's squirt. I reckon he'll just have to walk around and fret and wait.

I can't hurry anyways, since I'm still so sore from the beating Floyd gave me. I got a heap on my mind, though, and I decide to get started talking about some of it while Sammy and I make our way to that cave.

"Sam, I got something for you to remember, and it's important."

"What is it?"

"I'll tell you, and here it is. Don't believe nothing from nobody till you look them in the eyes. That's where the truth is."

"You talking about Sheriff Murphy again?"

"Sure am. I had him all wrong, and I blame those d—, I mean dadgum sunglasses. I never could see his eyes to know if he was good, or what. Truth is, he might be an odd one, but he's not bad or mean. He saved my life, Sam, up there on that bluff."

"You want Jean to step out with him, then?"

"She can if she wants to. Who tells Jean anything anyhow?"

Both of us have a laugh right then 'cause our sister will make up her own mind and always has. Thing is, I got nothing against the sheriff no more.

It's slow going with all my injuries. The family treated me like I was near kilt when they saw all my bruises, and especially those welts from Floyd's belt. To be honest, it felt pretty good to see how hard it was on my brothers, every last one of them—even War—who had a shiner when I got home. We all know what that was about, and good for Snipe, I say.

Anyhow, my brothers wanted to beat Floyd to dust, but how do you beat a dead man? It was something to see how all-fired mad they got, so I guess I might stop hollering and complaining about my brothers so much from here on out.

"Sam, you like our front porch?"

"I suppose so. It works for a porch, don't it?"

"Admit you like to look at that big rough side facing the gravel road."

"Shore I do, especially the ol' black beetle with two missing legs sealed in there."

"And the leaves and little gravel pieces stuck all around him?"

"I guess so."

"That side's all wrong because there was a wind storm

while that part of the concrete was still wet, Dad says."

"That sounds about right."

"You know how Doodles likes to stack her jar lids and bottle tops and buttons between those Huckleberry roots on the big tree and the part of the concrete those roots done and raised up near three foot?"

"Yeah."

"Those roots raise up the porch and make it all lopsided, and we still like it. Then there's that hollered out hole Snipe and War like to hide in. That hole makes no sense to be there on the smokehouse side, but it's there, just the same."

"So?"

"Carl says somebody who was learning about concrete didn't finish learning about it before he made the yellow house's front porch. It's square and dull-colored gray, crooked something awful from tree roots, and it has a hole that's stupid to be there."

"What are you getting at, sis?"

"I'm coming to it. See, that porch is ours for now, and we're danged proud to sit on it, and we admire it, too. What if… I mean, maybe… that kid Taw is kind of messed up like our porch, not perfect, but dandy just the same? He sure can sound nice with his sounds when he wants to, that's for certain. He tried his best to save me from ol' Floyd with his forest language, didn't he? I appreciate that little fella for that, I sure do.

"And draw? Shoot, I've never seen a better drawer than Taw. He's wilder than green onions, but he's special at the same time."

Sam gives me a strange look, but it's pleasant, too. We're quiet while we slip through the skinny crevice which is a sight easier in my overalls than that dress I had on before. I'm wiping sweat off my forehead like it's water.

"I didn't know we come so far when we was following that boy last time," Sam says.

"When you have to hurry to keep up and it's dark, too, it doesn't seem so long, I reckon. Go ahead and call him Taw, Sam, okay?"

"Okay, sis. Think we ought to start making some bird sounds or something like Taw uses for talking? I can do a pretty fair meadow lark and a blue jay."

"Good idea, Sammy. Let's wait till we get closer to the cave."

We don't take more than two more steps when Sam says, "Looky there," and he's staring straight at Taw watching down at us from a tree.

We don't say nothing, and neither does Taw. He curls down, sure-footed like a cat, and leads us the rest of the way to the cave. We barely get inside before Mr. Leroy is hurrying to us with that big smile and his white teeth glowing all over the place. I run to meet him. I try to talk and can't.

"Well, now, Little Bit, you shore do have a sweet count-a-nunce a coming out of you ever where this fine day the Lord has made for us. But what in the world has happened to you, baby girl? You gots bruises and scrapes and lines of red all over your face and neck."

Out of nowhere, I'm bawling like a big baby. I hide my face in my hands.

"Now, don't yous kids worry none. If we gots bad news, then we gots bad news. Ol' Leroy still likes you. Shoot, he even loves you with Jesus's love, and everything is all right this morning and ever day. Come sit down, chile. You looks hot and overcome, and I feel worrisome with all those marks on you."

He walks toward the quilt and we follow him. Sam whispers, "What's got into you? Want me to tell him?" I shake my head, and Sam and me sit down. Mr. Leroy dips a tin cup into one of the water buckets and brings it to me. I notice he's barely limping, and I sip from the cup and feel myself settling down. I offer the rest of the water to Sam, and he gulps it down and wipes his mouth with the shirttail sticking out of his overalls.

"I been doing lots of thinking in this here cave while you's been gone. Nothing much else to do, ain't it so?" Mr. Leroy laughs his cave-swelling laugh. "Anyways, I done had me a grand life with a good mama, God rest her lovely soul, and a sweet sister who's a 'vangelist, and a fine younger brother before he died of the croop. I been walking with that Savior a long time and making my tonic for the womens, and I've had things just fine, young'uns. If they locks me up and says lies against me, the One who matters most knows them lies ain't so.

"Looks to what ol' Joseph went through a being sold to slavery by his own brothers. Naw, I reckon I got it a heap better than those Bible gentlemens. What I'm saying is, I'm all peaceful. I's ready to go see the sheriff now."

I look into that face so full of good and say, "Mr. Leroy, you're free."

"Free? I is?"

"Yep. Nobody no how has a thing on you no more."

Mr. Leroy jumps up shouting and raising his hands up. "Oh, sweet Jesus. You's set me free! The angels is rejoicing today, chil'ren!"

CHAPTER Forty Five

Blackberry Road

When Mr. Leroy settles down from his singing and thanking the Almighty, he goes behind a little wall and comes out with three round store suckers. "Taw sneaked in my little house again a few days ago and brung us my stash of suckers, young'uns. This here's to celebrate my being loosed from bondage."

Taw sticks one in his mouth. It makes a big lump in his cheek. I tell Mr. Leroy I'll tell him later what my wounds are from, but first, he has to learn how his rabbit foot wound up in the pump house. While I tell him, his eyes grow big as silver dollars.

"But how did your rabbit foot get in the tree in the first place, sir?" Sam asks.

Mr. Leroy looks down. "I'm shamed to talk about this bad habit I gots, but yous chil'ren deserve to know all the truth of things. It ain't right to have worldly superstitions, but I gots me one. Every summer I puts my pretty white rabbit foot in a hollered-out tree knot somewhere tween my house and the pump building.

"Why do's I do it? Foolishness, I allow, 'cause it ain't

Godly to believe in good or bad luck. I been a doing it for so long, and it never did disappear on me till this time. I can't see how those boys ever found it."

"Nothing is safe from those two, not even our Dad's… uh, belongings," I say, catching myself before I tell on Snipe when I promised not to.

"It do feel good to know the whole truth of how that foot gots in the pump building, Little Bit."

"There's more, Mr. Leroy," I say, "and it's about the killer."

"You means they done and caught him?"

"They sure did, but first, did you ever hear of Bonnie and Clyde, the bank robbers?"

"Can't say as I have."

"You never heard of the most famous robbers in history?" Sam says kind of loud and jumping up from the quilt. "Don't you know they robbed banks all over Oklahoma and Kansas, and maybe the whole United States? Whoo-ee, they're famous, all right, and they're dead, shot to pieces over in Luzianna."

"Why my goodness gracious, Master Sammy. You shore do knows a lot about them robbing folks. You say they's dead?"

"Shot fifty times, and their car, too," Sam says.

"And Tommy and my mama and I saw them drive through town," I say. "They were supposed to leave town, but they had some car trouble and had to see a mechanic. That's how I come to see them in Nowata the day after Mr. MacGregor was kilt."

Sam throws hisself down on the quilt. "Some people have all the luck. I never got to see Bonnie and Clyde or the fancy man Taw drew on paper."

"What you means by all this? Did them Clyde peoples harm our Scottie?" Mr. Leroy asks, and I go ahead and tell him all about the time I saw Bonnie smoking a cigar and blowing smoke circles out the window. How that fancy man was in the back when their car drove through town, and how they'd gotten themselves stuck in mud the day before, and how the fancy man went to Mr. MacGregor's cabin to borrow a shovel and lumber to get unstuck.

Taw creeps closer while I tell the story. Mr. Leroy's face changes and his eyes get big, then they squint, as I talk, and I can tell he's confounded.

"Hurry up, Biddy, and tell him about Deputy Floyd or I'll do it," Sam says.

"Hold your horses. I'm getting to that part."

I tell how the law from Bartlesville swooped down on Deputy Floyd's house and truck and everything else and found the other cufflink like Calvin had, and a watch and ring they think he stole from Mr. MacGregor's cabin.

"Why woulds he steal from Scottie?" Mr. Leroy asks.

"Mr. Henson told Tommy that Floyd liked to gamble and he wasn't good at it. He said he'd been in hot water for some time, which I think means he owed money. Anyhow, from some of the things they found in his house and truck, they believe he was behind most or all of the house and barn robberies around Nowata and Alluwe when folks were gone to church, or grave visiting, or to town. He kept his stolen money and some of the other things hidden in the pump house behind a big fake tin patch in the wall."

"Gracious! Is he the one who…"

I nod my head. "He found Mr. MacGregor knocked out by that robber man, whose name is Method Anthony Ray, and he made up his mind right then and there to go ahead and finish him off and rob his cabin. He was looking for cash and jewelry, but Mr. Henson said Mr. MacGregor kept his valuables in the bank like anyone with any sense should. Shoot, we don't have none of those valuables, so I guess we aren't worth robbing."

"What *we's* gots is more valuable than what's *they* gots on this earth, Little Bit," Mr. Leroy says, and I know he means the Almighty.

"Anyways, Floyd heard about Sam and me up on the mountain that night we came to see you, and about the men coming to look for us with lanterns. He decided I was helping hide you, so he came after me and—"

"He took a belt to her something awful, and shook her, and tackled her, and slapped her, and almost kilt her, the dirty rat!" Sam yells out.

"You don't mean it!" Mr. Leroy's eyes fill with water. "I feels terrible… like it's my fault, chile," he says softly.

"Naw, it's no one but Floyd's fault. I'm all right. Don't fuss about it," I say, but I like him fussing about it.

Sam says, "Turns out, Floyd's the one who smashed in Mr. MacGregor's head with a lead pipe he fetched from his truck."

Mr. Leroy cuts his eyes over to Taw. "Be gentle now when yous talks about Scottie. This poor boy here is still a grieving smartly for his grandfather, he is."

"Who's that?" I say.

"Why Scottie MacGregor, naturally."

I melt into the quilt like candle wax and wish I could slap my own self. How could that wild creature be Mr. MacGregor's grandchild? Sam is staring at me with his mouth open big enough to hold two horse apples, and I'm sitting here dumbstruck.

"But Mr. Leroy, this here boy is a Native boy. And he's, uh, well, he runs wild in the woods and makes noises that aren't real language."

"That's all true enough, Little Bit, buts we just gots to be patients and kind to him. He was all alone with his…" Mr. Leroy leans in to us and says in a whisper, "… his dead mama, and no one to tend to him for 'bout two weeks till the doctor comes out to check her condition and finds this terriblest situation.

"He was just a little swatch of a boy, no more than three year or so, and he took to the woods shortly after that time. He's been gathered up and sent to more places than you can shake a stick at, but he always escapes and comes back to these here woods."

Mr. Leroy's whispers are getting louder, and Taw is staring at us with dark, shiny eyes.

"But how is he Mr. MacGregor's grandkid?" Sammy asks.

"Why it's Scottie's own girl's boy, honey."

Sammy and I look at one another and back at Mr. Leroy.

"I sees yous don't know that Scottie's daughter worked with the Choctaws when her college was out for the summertimes. Worked on fancy edgy-cation papers about them peoples, too, and first thing you know, she winds up and marries a Choctaw man. Scottie told me all this once we got acquainted real good. Said it was the sin and sorrow of his life that he didn't accept his girl's Indian husband. He said his heart was to be broked till all eternity since he'd been so stubborn about it."

"Where is Taw's Choctaw daddy?" I ask.

"Taw's daddy got kilt in a logging accident pretty soon after they married, up in Washington state, or somewheres like it. Scottie's girl, her name was Grace, moves herself back to our own Okie-homa to finish her college. But you knows how folks can be mean if you's not like them? That's what happened to poor Grace MacGregor. Nobody was nice to her with a little Indian baby, and she took to working in other folks' houses, and not in nowhere fancy. She stopped her schooling, too."

"Where was Mr. MacGregor?" I ask.

"Bartlesville, chile. Being an important man at that Pump Company, and not knowing one little thing 'bout his girl and her baby being in so much trouble and all alone."

"How did he find out?" Sammy asks.

"A letter comes to his house right after his wife passed on. Came out of Heaven, I thinks. Some folk at one of the schools that tried to take on Taw found it in his things. It was all sealed up and ready for a mailing, but it never gots mailed."

"Why not?" Sam says.

"'Cause it was stuck in the little boy's suitcase all those years. It slud down behind the material inside, and weren't never found till a kind lady at one of the state schools found it. She writes Scottie and sends him the letter she found. The lost letter was from his girl, Grace, and it broke Scottie's heart in two, it did. The kind lady lets him know his girl is gone from this earth now, and she tells him Taw is there at the school.

"Scottie… he hurries to that school faster'n you can blow a match out, but little Taw, blest his heart, has run off again to these here woods. Scottie wastes no time moving here, and that's when him and ol' Leroy gets acquainted, and we was good friends, I'm telling you. Bestest friends, maybe. Never a kinder man than Scottie, excepting how he didn't allow for Indians back then. His heart never did get over his Grace, but he loved Taw, and Taw loved him. It didn't take long, neither, for thems to be closer than two biscuits in a skillet. It was in their blood as kins, yessir, it was."

I don't know what comes over me hearing Mr. Leroy's stories, but I decide right then I'm not cussing no more. Being in that huge cave listening to his rich, kind voice and how fond he was of Mr. MacGregor, and still is of Taw, and feeling the pleasure he's taking in being free again, just works something over in my insides. Mr. Leroy is *the truth*, and my heart is full of being good and not lying from here on out.

Making our way back down the mountain with Mr. Leroy, Sam, and Taw hanging back in the trees but still with us, I ponder about Mr. MacGregor saying the fortitude of the children was his joy. I think he was talking about how strong his own grandson was, surviving by himself in the woods for so long. Maybe he meant us farm kids, too, 'cause he had a powerful feeling for all of us, that's for true.

This summer of 1934 proved Mama right about a Blackberry Road being like life—how it has some sweetness and plenty of thorns to go with it. For me, the best thing I found out was how none of us is worth two plug nickels without other folks watching out for us. Guess that means all us here in our neck of the woods need each other a whole bunch, and something tells me, we always will.

The End

About The Author

Jodi Lea Stewart

Jodi Lea Stewart's writing reflects her life starting in Texas and Oklahoma, moving to an Arizona cattle ranch next door to the Navajo Nation, and resuming later in her native Texas. As a youngster, she climbed petroglyph-etched boulders, bounced two feet in the air in the back end of pickups wrestling through washed-out terracotta roads, and rode horseback on the winds of her imagination through the arroyos and mountains of the Arizona high country.

She left the University of Arizona to move to San Francisco, where she learned about peace, love, and exactly what she *didn't* want to do with her life. Since then, Jodi graduated *summa cum laude* with a BS in Business Management, raised three children, worked as an electro-mechanical drafter, penned humor columns for a college periodical, wrote regional western articles and served as managing editor of a Fortune 500 company newsletter.

With an Okie mom and a Texas dad, an eclectic mix of Native Americans, Southern Belles and Gentlemen, not to mention Cow Punchers, as her life companions, Jodi walks comfortably through the hallways of anything Southwestern, Southern, and beyond. She currently lives in Arizona with her husband, a crazy Standard poodle, a rescue cat, and numerous gigantic, bossy houseplants.

Jodi is a member of the Southwest Writers and New Mexico-Arizona Book Co-op.

For more information about the author, visit her website at **https://jodileastewart.com/**, or visit these other sites:

Facebook Profile:
https://www.facebook.com/jodi.lea.stewart

Facebook Page:
https://www.facebook.com/AuthorJodiLeaStewart/

About Me:
https://about.me/jodileastewart

Amazon:
https://www.amazon.com/Jodi-Lea-Stewart/e/B0085YFWZ6

LinkedIn:
https://www.linkedin.com/in/jodileastewart/

Dedication

This book is dedicated to my mother, Vivian Ozine Woods-Myrick (top row, far right), the real "Biddy," and to her siblings, my ten aunts and uncles. For the background of Blackberry Road, I borrowed the flavor of their incredibly colorful stories from childhood growing up as children of a real Oklahoma sharecropper and his wife who not only survived tough times with barely two dimes to rub together, but who also managed to instill morals and ethics into their offspring.

Family reunions back in the day were rich with tales and laughter about "the good old days." Thankfully, I always had a pen and paper handy to jot down the stories from those now nearly forgotten times.

The plot, characters, and mystery in this book are mostly fictional, but I'm not saying what is or isn't.

Vintage Sharecropper Recipes

Recipe List

MAMA DOOBIE'S FAMOUS CHICKEN NOODLES

You won't believe what she does next. She up and wrings a chicken's neck and fixes chicken and noodles especially for Tommy. She says it cures what's ailing you, and most times, it does. I'll tell you this, none of the rest of us gets sick eating that pot of chicken noodles for supper, no sir. Especially with Jean's cornbread with cracklins and a pot of beans, besides.

- Fresh chicken, your own or store-bought (about two large breasts or 2-3 cups of meat)
- 4 eggs
- ¼ tsp. salt
- All-purpose flour

Boil chicken until done. Don't discard broth. Remove any bones or skin. Skim if desired. Cut or pull chicken into small pieces and return to broth. Whip eggs and salt with fork. Add flour in large amounts until dough is almost crumbly (about 2 cups). Divide dough into 2 equal balls for ease of handling. Roll out the first ball with plenty of flour until thin. Add more flour and fold in half. Keep repeating. Roll thin, add flour, and fold in half until the layered dough is approximately 5x8-inches big. Roll it up like a jellyroll and slice crosswise in thin rings and push to the side. Repeat with the second ball of dough.

Separate the "rings" of dough gently. Add a few at a time to the boiling broth and chicken. Stir and lift the noodles gently as they cook to keep them from sticking together. By the time all the noodles are added to the pot, they should be done. Don't overcook. The noodles will be a clear yellow when done.

FRIED PORK CHOPS

Here we are outside sitting on the front porch eating cold biscuits and fried pork chops with our fingers since we all want to stare at that fancy dance floor. "Throw your chop bones away and not on the ground when you're done. Biddy, you sweep up this porch when we get finished. I don't want no crumbs nor dirt on it," Mama says in a strict voice.

"Yes, Mama," I answer in a faraway voice on account of I'm in a state of bewilderment staring at the crepe-paper flowers, the marigolds, and knowing we're having a party at our humble house. Nothing like this has ever gone on at the Woodsons before.

Roll pork chops in flour seasoned with salt and pepper. Fry in bacon grease until browned on each side.

DAD DOOBIE'S TATER SOUP

You should know our eating table about fills up the whole tiny kitchen, and we like it because this family loves eating about more than anything else. A long bench goes down the whole length of one side of the table, and the rest of the seats are cane-bottomed chairs set edge to edge around the other three sides. My dad grew up with the Indians in the Indian Territory, so he knows how to weave the cane-bottoms and fix them when they get holes.

Note: Men, make this soup when your missus is bearing children and can't cook no supper for the ones already here. Go ahead and mix up some cornbread to go with it so those hungry bellies get filled up.

- 1 qt. potatoes, peeled and chopped into small chunks
- 1 lg. onion, chopped
- 2-3 slices fried bacon, chopped

- Salt and pepper
- Cornmeal
- Chopped green onions, optional

Peel and cut potatoes. Add water to cover plus 4-5 inches. Cook potatoes with onion. Add a couple of tablespoons of bacon drippings. Salt and pepper as needed. Before potatoes are done, add bacon pieces. When potatoes are tender, mash slightly and thicken with cornmeal. Sprinkle chopped green onion on top.

PINTO BEANS AND SALT PORK

Everyone sits down, and Jean starts the tater bowl on the end where Dad is. He looks around and takes two tablespoons of taters, a Johnny cake, a few radishes, onions, a handful of red lettuce to rip up and drip bacon grease on to make wilted salad, and a dipper full of beans on top of everything but the salad. That's how it works. You figure out how many mouths are eating and take the right amount so's everyone can eat. If you don't respect that, you get sent from the table hungry. Usually, we have enough food to have a pinch of a second helping, but it has to be after everyone else has had their first go.

- Dried pinto beans
- Large onion
- Salt pork, 2-3-inch piece, cubed
- 1 Tbls. chili powder
- 2 cloves garlic, sliced or mashed
- Salt and ground pepper to taste

Go through beans and pick out rocks or sticks. Rinse and drain. Dump beans in a heavy pan and add water to cover plus 5-6 inches. Add cubed salt pork, chili powder, salt and pepper. Bring water to a boil, cover pan but not tight. Stir and add more seasonings as desired until beans are tender.

HOT BEAN DUMPLINGS

Jean wipes her hands on the towel around her waist, and we drift inside to the smell of boiling beans. Mama drops little pieces of dough in the top of the bean pot, and she's made us some sweet tea. I reckon it isn't so bad to be home today and get Mama's hot bean dumplings and tea, and the boys don't get any.

- Left-over cooked pinto beans made juicier by adding more water
- Red or green peppers to make beans hot, optional
- Biscuit dough rolled out thin and cut into 1-4-inch strips (dumplings)

Bring beans and juice to a rolling boil. Drop biscuit dumplings into pot and heat through. It doesn't take long. Serve immediately.

CORN AND TATER SOUP

- Dad Doobie's Tater Soup
- 2-4 ears of corn

Make Doobie's Tater Soup recipe and add corn cut off the cob before thickening the soup with cornmeal.

PORK CHILI

I never gawked so much in my life as I am at the people who show up and pay money to eat chili and cornbread, drink tea, and dance their feet off.

- 2 lbs. coarsely ground pork

- 2 med. onions, chopped
- 2 cloves garlic, smashed
- 3-4 small fresh tomatoes, chopped
- 3 Tbls. chili powder
- 1 tsp. salt
- 1-½ Tbls. black pepper
- 1 tsp. oregano (fresh is best if you have any handy)
- A hot pepper, optional
- Water

In large Dutch oven, cook ground pork, onion, and garlic until meat is brown and onion and garlic are tender. Drain fat. Add tomatoes, chili powder, salt, black pepper, oregano, and a hot pepper if desired. When it bubbles, reduce heat and add about 1-½ cups water. Cover and simmer until it's cooked through. Add left-over pinto beans if you got any.

BARLEY SOUP

I clamp on the last pieces of washing with clothes pins and run to tell Mama we got company. She's having Allen lean up so's she can fluff his feather pillow. After she smooths his quilt and tucks it around him, she brings him a bowl of barley soup. He sticks out his tongue once she's turned around.

- Pork shank bones
- 1 onion or 4-5 green onions, chopped
- 2 cloves garlic, sliced
- 2 fresh tomatoes
- 1 mild green pepper
- 2 small zucchinis
- ½ head cabbage, shredded
- 2 turnips cut into 1/8's
- 1 cup uncooked, soaked barley
- Salt and pepper to taste

Boil shank bones with salt, pepper, 1 clove garlic, and ½ the onions until meat is tender. Rinse and soak barley in warm water for about 15 minutes. Add barley to meat and broth. Cook about 30 minutes. Add rest of vegetables and cook 10 minutes or until tender.

WILD ONIONS AND EGGS

We're all being quiet with our heads low till we get some food in our bellies, except Mama asks who went down by the Groff place to gather the wild onions we're eating along with our wilted salad. Calvin raises his hand. That makes Sammy raise his, too. I see Calvin look at me pitiful since I'm feeling so mournful about Mr. MacGregor. I know he took a table fork down there and pried those sweet-smelling onions out of the dirt just for me.

- Wild onions, lots
- Eggs
- 6 pieces bacon, chopped and fried.

Go to the woods or fields and gather wild onions using a fork to lift them out of the dirt. Wash and cut them into pieces, heads and stems both. Fry bacon pieces. When almost done, throw in the chopped wild onions and fry a minute or two. Drain and set aside. Fry or scramble however many eggs you want. Serve them with a spoonful or two of the bacon and onions. Mighty good with biscuits and a side of dandelion greens or Lamb's quarter greens boiled and seasoned with salt pork and a splash of vinegar.

FRIED RABBIT

Dress out like a chicken. Roll in flour, salt and pepper. Fry until gold brown in lard or bacon grease.

STONE-JAR SAUSAGE

When I come banging through the front door, I see Mama's cooked a big breakfast of hen eggs and some of her red-hot stone-jar sausage for Dad, Ed, and Tommy. Seems late to be eating breakfast, but then I recall Dad was going straight to the fields early this morning before it rained again. He works up a powerful appetite when he works in the field before eating.

- Sausage patties seasoned with red pepper
- Large stone jars (crockery jars)
- Rags to cover the jars

Mama Doobie makes her stone-jar sausage in the fall during hog-killing season. She seasons her sausage liberally with home-grown red pepper. Then she forms the sausage into patties and fries it. She drops the cooled meat, along with the grease, into stone jars and ties clean rags over the top. She stores the jars in the cellar. When she wants to cook up a batch of sausage, she takes a pan into the cellar and fills it with as much meat and grease as she wants for that time. She dumps the whole clump into an iron skillet and heats it until it sizzles, red grease and all. Stone-jar sausage is a wonderful treat in the long winter months.

LAMB'S QUARTER GREENS

Two bowls of Lamb's quarter greens swimming in salt pork and black pepper are on each end of the table along with pitchers of cow milk. Mama's canned hot peppers and chow-chow are in the middle of the table with forks in the jars.

- Lamb's quarter leaves and stems
- A small hunk of pre-fried salt pork
- Bacon drippings
- 1 clove garlic
- Part of a hot pepper, optional
- Black pepper
- Salt to taste

Wash greens. Boil in salted water and pre-fried salt pork until tender, less than 10 minutes. Rinse. Fry garlic and pepper in bacon drippings. Add greens and fry for a few minutes. Salt and pepper to taste. A splash of vinegar and raw onion tastes good on top, especially on the left-overs.

Use this same recipe for Sour Dock.

DANDELION GREENS

- Dandelion leaves
- A small hunk of pre-fried salt pork
- Bacon drippings
- 1 clove garlic, sliced or mashed
- Part of a hot pepper, optional
- Salt and pepper

Wash greens. Cut off the bottom stems. Boil in salted water and pre-fried salt pork until tender, less than 10 minutes.

Rinse. Fry garlic and pepper in bacon drippings. Add greens and fry for a few minutes. Salt and pepper to taste. A splash of vinegar and raw onion tastes good on top, especially on the left-overs.

FRIED TATERS

Mama hands me the bucket. "Finish filling up the drinking bucket, Biddy, and peel us a big stack of taters for supper. No telling what'll happen around here before we know it," she says, and she was right.

- Peeled potatoes, cut into small pieces
- 1 onion, chopped
- 2-3 green onions, chopped
- Bacon grease

Heat bacon grease in a large iron skillet. Add potatoes and onions and fry until crispy brown. Stir and turn over with a spatula while they cook.

HANDS-ON WILTED LETTUCE SALAD

A big pan of garden lettuce, wild onions, and radishes still wet from scrubbing the sand off them sits by Dad's plate. A paring knife handle is sticking out of the end of the pan.

- Fresh garden loose-leaf lettuce
- Radishes
- Green onions, garden-grown or wild
- Hot bacon grease (best with bits of fried bacon in it). Serve in a metal cup to keep it hot.
- Salt and pepper

- Cider vinegar in a bottle with a sprinkler top

Wash and drain lettuce, radishes, and green onions and put into a large bowl, pan, or platter. Place on table with tongs. Everyone serves their own salad and cuts it up how they like it on their plates. Drizzle on hot bacon drippings, add salt and pepper and a splash or two of vinegar.

*Mama Doobie's favorite lettuce had red, curly edges.

FRESH CUCUMBERS AND ONIONS IN VINEGAR

- 4-6 small to med. cucumbers; garden-grown is best
- 2 small or 1 large onion, sliced

Liquid Mixture: (amounts approximate)
- 1 cup water
- 1-½ cups vinegar
- 1 tsp. salt
- 1 tsp. pepper
- ½ cup sugar

Slice cucumbers and onions and add to liquid mixture. Store covered in refrigerator. Refreshing side dish.

FRIED OKRA

We were all tired and hungry, and thankfully, supper was almost on the table when we got home. Right in the middle of eating, Mama says, "Daniel Frost stopped by today. Said his missus has been up in Lawton tending to her sick ma. Oh, and Mr. Leroy is missing." My fork just falls out of my hand.

- Pick a good mess of fresh okra, washed and rinsed, cut into ¼" slices

Roll in cornmeal, salt and pepper. Fry in grease until slightly crispy.

FRIED CABBAGE

- 1 head cabbage
- 1 onion, thinly sliced
- 2 pieces bacon, chopped and fried
- Salt and pepper

Fry bacon. Shred cabbage by cutting with the grain in thin strips. Slice the onion. Add cabbage and onion to the bacon and drippings. Stir to coat. Add lots of black pepper. Salt to taste. Cook open in the skillet until cabbage is desired tenderness.

SQUASH AND ONIONS

Mama left orders for me to start supper early, and I wonder how she knew I was coming home a week early. It's raining cats and dogs now, but Dad's had the boys gather some cabbage, peppers, and squash from Mama's garden on the backside of the house before I got home. I get busy frying up cabbage and onions in bacon grease with just the tip of one of Mama's ungodly hot peppers in it. I boil up a mess of crookneck squash in salted water with some of the green onion stems and wash the lettuce and radishes for wilted salad. I have the cornbread almost mixed up and the grease sizzling and ready to go in the big iron skillet when the dogs and geese make a racket. I can't look out on account of all the pots and pans I have working on the stove.

- Yellow crookneck squash, zucchini, or both
- Onion, white or green, chopped
- Water
- 1 Tbls. bacon drippings
- Tip of a hot pepper

Cut squash into chunks. Chop onion. Add to pan with a bit of bacon grease and the tip of a hot pepper. Boil until squash is tender.

ROASTNEARS

While I'm eating, I'm thinking that harvesting all that field corn by hand is going to be hot work. I guess I don't mind since the Woodson family sure does love it's roastnears. When the first mess of corn comes ripe every summer, we take it to the creek and boil it up in pots over an open fire for supper. If you want cow butter smeared on it or salt and pepper, you're welcome to it, but most of us slick it down our throats with just a shake of salt. We eat till we're ready to pop. If we have any left over, Mama bakes it slow the next day into parched corn. She throws it up on the cook stove when it's finished. In no time at all, it disappears.

- Corn on the cob
- 1 tsp. sugar. If using a big pot, use 2 tsp. sugar.
- Salt and pepper
- Cow butter, optional

Pick the corn. Shuck and remove corn silk. Cut off ends. Boil water. Add corn and bring water back to a boil. Boil for about five minutes. Remove from water or drain pot immediately. Season with salt and pepper or cow butter if desired.

PARCHED CORN

Shuck and remove corn silk from fresh corn. Put in 450-degree oven about 25 minutes. Put left-over boiled corn on the cob in 450-oven for approximately 10 minutes. Salt and eat. Very chewy.

FRIED CORN

- 4-5 cobs of fresh corn
- 2 thick slices bacon, chopped and fried
- Bacon drippings
- 1 med. onion, chopped
- ½ cup mild canned green chilis, chopped and drained

Chop bacon and fry. Cut corn off cobs. Add corn, onion, and green chilis to skillet with bacon and drippings. Stir occasionally until desired tenderness.

FRESH PICKLED BEETS AND ONIONS

Supper is cold cornbread and milk, roastnears, fresh pickled beets and onions, and fried okra. I'm so hungry I don't even look up till my plate is slicked clean. What I notice when I look up is a bunch of questions on the kids' faces.

- 1-quart boiled beets
- 2 onions, sliced
- Liquid Mixture: (amounts approximate)
- 1 cup water
- 1-½ cups vinegar

- ¼ tsp. salt
- ¼ tsp. ground cinnamon
- 1/8 tsp. allspice
- ½ cup sugar (or to taste—the mixture should have a balanced sweet/tart taste)

Leave 2 inches of stems and the tap roots on beets. Wash and boil covered until tender. Mix water, vinegar, salt, cinnamon, allspice, and sugar and put into a bowl. Slice and quarter (or dice) boiled beets and add to prepared liquid with sliced fresh onions. Store covered in refrigerator. Perfect for any summer table.

SUNSHINE DILL PICKLES

- 1 qt. vinegar
- 2 qt. water
- 1 cup salt
- ½ tsp. Alum
- Dill, dried or fresh, to taste
- Medium-sized cucumbers, 3-4 inches long

Mix vinegar, water, salt, and alum. Bring mixture to a boil. Add dill and let cool. Pour into sterilized Mason jars filled with cucumbers. Set in the sun for three days.

SAUERKRAUT

When the men were through in the fields, Mama had Tommy carry her two heavy crock jars of shredded cabbage and salt in the gopher hole so it can turn into sauerkraut. Everything else went into a scalded Mason jar. She made her chow-chow and canned it, too. Lordy-lord, I never want to see another vegetable in my whole life.

- Fresh cabbage
- Non-iodized salt
- A sprig of dill, optional

Core and shred cabbages. Mix with salt. (SEE NOTE BELOW) Layer cabbage into a big-mouthed crock jar. Add a few springs of fresh dill, if desired. Fist or tamp each layer a whole lot to bruise it and make sure no air is between the layers. When the crock is one-half to three-quarters full, push a plate tightly over the top of the packed cabbage. Use a sterilized stone to hold the plate down. (Mama Doobie used washed bricks, but that was a long time ago.) Tie a clean rag tight over the top. Store it in a cool place. Throw it out if anything black or pink grows on top of it. White or gray is okay—just skim it off. Check often. Sample in 2-3 weeks, but it might take 6-8 weeks to make the sauerkraut, depending on your tastes. Drain and can in sterilized Mason jars, or keep refrigerated up to 6 months.

Note: Per modern guidelines, use 3 Tbls. non-iodized salt to every 5 lbs. of shredded cabbage. For every half-gallon of non-chlorine water added (optional), use 3 Tbls. non-iodized salt.

BIDDY'S MILK GRAVY

I don't know why everybody loves my milk gravy so much, but they do. I've been making it on top of the stove since I was so short I had to stand on a stool. Burned my belly and arms lots of times, but I still like to do it.

- Drippings and crumbles from fried chicken, rabbit, pork chops, bacon, or sausage
- Flour

- Milk
- Salt and pepper

Remove meat from skillet and set aside. Pour most of the drippings into a can, keeping 4-5 tablespoons in the skillet. Leave in any crumbles from whatever meat was frying. Add flour and stir into the drippings. If it separates, that isn't good so add a little more drippings. Brown the flour to a light golden brown, stirring constantly. Add milk, stirring constantly. Add most of the milk at once, at least a quart, and keep stirring. Let it bubble up until it has the right consistency. Add more milk if necessary. You want it to be like a thick sauce. When it's just the right thickness, pour into a bowl and serve.

Note: Leave the gravy a medium thickness because it thickens more on its own. Half fresh milk and half canned milk in equal amounts gives the gravy a better flavor. Be sure to brown the flour before adding milk or it will taste pasty.

DAD WOODSON'S FAVORITE RED-EYE GRAVY

We're about to sit down to a fine supper of roast pork, red-eye gravy, cornbread, cucumbers and sliced onion in vinegar, and a mess of snap beans with bacon when the dogs start barking.

Fry pork loin or ham in an iron skillet. Pour grease out of skillet and save. Re-heat skillet. When it's hot, pour ½ cup of liquid coffee into the skillet to scald. When it quits cracking and popping, add the grease back in the skillet. Serve over milk gravy (about a teaspoon on top) or over biscuits. Tastes delicious with ham or pork of any kind.

CORN-BREAD GRAVY

When we have gravy, whoever calls dibs first on the gravy bowl gets to sop up the last of the gravy with bread.

Fry any kind of meat. Remove all but ½ cup of drippings. Stir in cornmeal until it thickens. Brown until it looks slightly scorched. Add milk or water to dilute and keep stirring. Mixture should be fairly thick. Bring to a boil and serve over cornbread.

COTTAGE CHEESE

Let milk sit out in crock bowls until clabbered. Put into a cotton cloth bag and hang on the clothes line. Let it drip until it turns into cottage cheese. When all the "juice" is gone, season with salt and pepper and serve.

COW BUTTER

Cornbread is on a help-yourself table with dish towels over the top of the skillets and round cakes of Mama's cow butter in small crock bowls.

Skim cream off top. Shake in a jar until it curdles. Drain off liquid and put into a bowl. Use a wooden paddle to press curdles against side of bowl to get all the milk out. Salt and shape. Keep cool.

CORN BREAD

I'll tell you this, none of the rest of us gets sick eating that pot of chicken noodles for supper, no sir. Especially with Jean's cornbread with cracklins and a pot of beans, besides.

- 2 cups cornmeal
- ½ cup flour (or 1-½ cups cornmeal and 1 cup flour)
- 1 tsp. salt
- 3 tsp. baking powder
- 2 rounded tsp. sugar
- 1-1/3 cups milk (or 1-1/3 cups buttermilk to which ¼ tsp. soda has been added)
- 1 egg, slightly beaten
- 4 Tbls. bacon drippings, lard, or oil
- 2 Tbls. melted and hot grease for bottom of skillet

Combine dry ingredients. Mix egg, and melted fat in a bowl and beat well. Add to dry ingredients. Add milk or buttermilk a little at a time. Mixture should be thin. Stir well and pour into iron skillet with smoking-hot grease in the bottom. Bake hot, about 450-degrees, for 25-30 minutes until golden brown on top. Turn skillet upside down on a dish towel or leave in the skillet. Cut and serve.

To make cornbread with cracklins, pour ½ cup boiling water over a cup of cracklins broken into small pieces and add to wet mixture. Bake as usual.

JOHNNY CAKES

Jay Bird takes two Johnny cakes all at once, and Dad mumbles, 'Key-yoh' real low, but Jay Bird hears it for sure and puts one cake back.

- 2 cups cornmeal
- ¼ cup flour
- ½ tsp. baking powder
- 1 tsp. salt
- 1 Tbls. sugar
- 1-½ to 2 cups boiling water
- 2 Tbls. bacon drippings or melted lard

Measure and sift dry ingredients in bowl. Heat water to boiling. Pour water and bacon drippings over dry ingredients. Drop by tablespoons into deep fat and fry. Or shape in your greased palm and place on a greased baking sheet and bake 30 min. at 450-degrees.

I can't answer him about those books because my eyeballs have hooked onto something else—the chipped bowl sitting on the table filled to the brim with pork cracklins.
"Look," I whisper in a loud voice, pointing to it.
"Is that the bowl you found full of berries?"
"Yeah. When I came to the cabin by myself, it was washed and put away on a shelf. Didn't I tell you things aren't right here, Cal?"

To make Johnny Cakes with Cracklins, make the Johnny cakes recipe but omit the bacon drippings. Add ½ cup boiling water to cracklins broken into small pieces. Add cracklins to the wet mixture and fry or bake just like regular Johnny cakes.

BISCUITS

Mama sent them off with cold sausage patties and biscuits and our biggest jars full of well water. She pointed me to the heap of dirty clothes she'd gathered from everywhere in tarnation. Oh, law, did I ever cuss in my own head about that.

- 2 cups flour
- 1 tsp. sugar
- ½ tsp. baking powder
- 4 Tbls. melted lard or bacon grease (or oil)
- Buttermilk or milk to moisten

Melt 4 Tbls. lard in skillet or pan. Mix flour, sugar, and baking powder. Add ½ melted lard and enough buttermilk or milk to make a dough. Knead lightly and roll out to about ¾ to 1-inch thick. Dip biscuit cutter in flour and cut out biscuits. Dredge one side of each biscuit in hot oil, turn over, and place with sides touching in the skillet. Bake at 450-degrees for about 15 minutes or until golden brown. Makes one small pan of biscuits.

POOR DOOBIE

Note: Fix this when all those hungry bellies are growling and there ain't much food to be had.

- Left-over cornbread
- Bacon drippings
- 1 med. onion
- Black pepper
- Sage
- Vinegar

Cover bottom of an iron skillet with bacon drippings and heat. Cook onion a few minutes. Fill skillet with left-over cornbread crumbled pretty fine. Add sage and black pepper to taste. Sprinkle on vinegar. Stir all the time until heated through. Bake a few minutes and serve.

MAMA'S CHRISTMAS CAKE

The screen door closes behind them and we all stand there looking at Rebecca, but I'm not lying, the idea of that sweet cake Mrs. Russell brought us is stuck in my mind. We never have cake except at Christmas when Mama makes her candy cake with the melted candy frosting.

- 2 cups flour
- 3 tsp. baking powder
- ½ tsp. salt
- ½ cup lard (nowadays, shortening)
- 1 cup sugar
- 3 egg yolks, set whites aside for the meringue icing
- ¾ cups milk
- 1 tsp. vanilla

Sift flour, baking powder, and salt three times. Work lard with spoon until fluffy. Add sugar gradually to lard. Continue to work with spoon until mixture is light. Beat egg yolks with a fork until thick. Add to sugar mixture. Add flour gradually, alternating with milk, beating each time until thoroughly mixed and full of air. Stir in vanilla. Bake in 2 greased and floured 8-inch pans at 375-degrees for 25 to 30 minutes or until a broom straw, toothpick, or match stick stuck in the middle comes out clean.

Cool. Remove from pans. Spread meringue between layers, on the sides, and the top of the cake. Sprinkle crushed peppermint candy and other Christmas candies on top and sides. Put in stove and watch. Take out when candy starts to melt. To cut, put tip of knife in the center of the cake and tap hand to break through light candy crust on top.

MERINGUE FOR CHRISTMAS CAKE & PIES

- 4 egg whites (add 1 egg to the 3 whites left over from making cake)
- 3-4 Tbls. sugar
- 1 tsp. vanilla
- ¼ tsp. salt

Note: Nowadays, ½ tsp. of Cream of Tartar helps make stiff peaks in the egg whites. You guessed it… Mama Doobie didn't have any such spice in her kitchen way back when.

Beat egg whites and salt (and cream of tartar) until foamy. Add sugar a tablespoon at a time. Beat until stiff. Spread inside layers, over the sides, and on top of the cake. For pie, spread on cooled pie filling. Seal onto the pie crust. Bake 10-12 min. at 375-degrees. Cool away from drafts.

CRUSHED CANDY TOPPING FOR CHRISTMAS CAKE

- 1 long, fat peppermint stick
- 1 cup of ribbon Christmas Candy or any type of hard Christmas candy

Crush candy with a hammer inside a tea towel. Spread over Meringue Frosting.

RAW APPLE CAKE

I look up and she smiles so nice I decide I'm not ashamed no more. I take the drink and sip it. I want to swig it down all at once but I don't, be-

cause I think that might be what a hillbilly does. I'll tell you right now, it's the best thing I ever tasted that wasn't cake or hard candy.

- 4 cups apples, chopped fine
- 2 cups sugar
- ½ cup melted lard (or oil)
- 2 eggs, beaten
- 2 cups flour
- 2 tsp. baking soda
- 2 tsp. salt
- 1 tsp. cinnamon
- 1 cup nuts or raisins (or ½ each)

Mix apples, sugar, and melted lard (or oil) and let stand. Beat 2 eggs and stir into mixture. Add flour, baking soda, salt, and cinnamon with nuts or raisins. Bake at 350-degrees for about 40-45 minutes. Test with a broom straw, toothpick, or match stick to see when it's done.

CRAZY CAKE

- 1-½ cups flour
- 1 cup sugar
- ¼ cups cocoa
- 1 tsp. soda
- ½ tsp. salt
- 1 tsp. vanilla
- 1 Tbls. vinegar
- 1/3 cup melted lard (or oil)
- 1 cup water

Sift flour, sugar, cocoa, soda, and salt into a round skillet. Add vanilla, vinegar, melted lard (oil) and water. Mix well by hand. Bake 35 minutes at 350-degrees. Test with a broom straw, toothpick, or match stick to see when it's done.

PIE CRUST

- 1 cup flour
- ½ cup lard (shortening)
- ¼ tsp. salt
- ½ cup or more ice-cold water
- (Double recipe for a 2-crust pie)

Mix flour and salt together with a fork. Cut lard into flour with two kitchen knives. Handle lightly and make into small crumbs. Add water gradually and mix with a fork until dough is barely sticking together. Gather into a ball and roll out evenly on a floured surface. Turn once. Roll thin. Fit into pie pan. Cut off excess with a knife. Crimp edges. Puncture sides and bottom with a fork. Bake at 350-degrees about 25 min. or until golden brown.

Note: If filling the pie crust to bake, don't puncture sides and bottom with a fork.

PIE-DOUGH CINNAMON ROLL

Mrs. Frost sends us on our way with metal plates, small crock bowls, and a pie-dough cinnamon roll she made for us kids. We don't get two shakes away from her place before we divide it four ways and don't say a word until it's all gone. It's so good, it rolls our eyes back in our heads. Mama made one of those things one time, but sugar's been too scarce the last few years for such extras.

Use left-over dough after making pies. Roll dough out thin. Dot with cow butter. Cover top with lots of sugar and cinnamon. Roll, tucking in ends before the last roll. Put into a pan seam-side down. Bake until browned. Slice and serve.

BANANA PIE

He charges Mama twenty-five cents and tells her to feed me overripe bananas for a few days to get me cured. I like that, because we never get bananas except when Mama makes her special banana pies at Christmas time.

- 2 baked pie crusts
- 4 small bananas
- 4 cups milk
- 2/3 cup flour or (4 Tbls. cornstarch)
- 1-½ cups sugar
- 4 egg yolks (save whites for meringue topping)
- 2 tsp. vanilla
- Dash of salt
- Meringue topping

Make and bake two pie crusts.

Filling: Dissolve flour or cornstarch in ½ cup of the milk. Add rest of milk, beaten egg yolks, sugar, and vanilla. Cook until it thickens.

Cover pie-crust bottoms with sliced bananas. Pour filling over bananas. Top with meringue and bake about 10-12 min. at 375-degrees.

MAMA'S RAISIN PIE

- 2 cups seeded raisins
- 1-¾ cup water
- 6 tbsp. flour
- 1 cup sugar
- 1 tsp. vanilla

- 2 Tbsp. vinegar

Cook raisins in water. Mix flour and sugar together. Add gradually to cooked raisins, stirring constantly. Cook until thickened, about 5 minutes. Add vanilla and vinegar. Pour into unbaked pie crust in 8-inch pan. Cover with top crust. Crimp edges together. Make slits in top. Doobie made an "R" in the top, along with more slits. Bake 400-degrees for 40 minutes until crust is golden brown.

VINEGAR PIE

I went with Mama three times to that revival, and I never did get alone to talk to Miz Abernathy about none of this. Those revival folks sure do know how to bake up some cakes and pies, but that doesn't tell us where Mr. Leroy is.

- 1 baked pie crust
- 1-½ cups sugar
- 3 Tbsp. flour
- 3 Tbsp. vinegar
- 3 egg yolks, well beaten
- Cow butter (the size of a walnut)
- 1-½ cups boiling water
- Lemon juice, to taste

Stir together sugar, flour, vinegar, egg yolks, and cow butter. Add boiling water and cook until thick. Flavor with lemon juice. Pour into a baked crust. Cover with meringue and brown in oven 10-12 min. at 375-degrees.

CUSTARD "PIE"

Note: Makes its own crust

- 4 eggs
- ¾ cup sugar
- 2 cups milk
- 4 Tbsp. flour
- 1 tsp. vanilla
- ½ tsp. cinnamon
- ½ tsp. salt
- Dash of nutmeg

Mix all ingredients and pour into a greased and floured 9-inch pie pan. Bake at 450-degrees for 15 minutes. Reduce heat to 350-degrees for another 15 minutes. Insert a knife through middle to test for doneness.

DEWBERRY OR BLACKBERRY COBBLER

"Blackberries are still green, but some of the dewberries are coming on right now. Birds will get them if we don't. Saw them yesterday when I went to check on the spring. Probably a big enough mess there to make a good-size cobbler," Dad says. A big old grin goes around the table with us thinking of a first-out dewberry cobbler.

- Dough for two pie crusts
- Few quarts of dewberries or blackberries
- 1-½ cups sugar
- Cow butter
- Cinnamon, optional

Make two pie crusts in one bowl. Roll out 2/3 of the dough on a floured surface. Put into a rectangle pan. Fit into sides and press bottom down lightly. Leave dough hanging off the sides of the pan. Add the berries. Sprinkle on sugar and dot with cow butter. Roll out the rest of the dough and put it in the middle of the berries. Bring up the sides and make it look as pretty as you want to. Make sure there are slits or spots not covered so the cobbler can breathe while it cooks. Sprinkle a little cinnamon on top. Bake 10 minutes at 450-degrees. Reduce heat to 350-degrees and bake until crust is golden brown.

BLACKBERRIES WITH COLD BISCUITS

"Warren, you ain't been up at the spring bothering those berries, have you?" Dad asks.

War shakes his head. I figure he learned his lesson from that whooping he got last summer for eating most of the first ripe ones and stomping on some of the ground vines just to be ornery. Truth is, he didn't cry during that licking, and it made me bawl...Dad is serious about food for his family, and War shouldn't have done what he did. Still yet, I cried for that no-good brother of mine.

- Use home-canned blackberries, gooseberries, dewberries, huckleberries or peaches

Crumble biscuits on plate. Pour on home-canned blackberries with juice. Spoon on sugar if the fruit was canned with no sugar. If you don't have any sugar in the house, use sorghum or honey.

FRIED APPLES

Slice apples leaving on the peeling. Coat in sugar and fry in bacon drippings. Remove from skillet, sprinkle on cinnamon, and serve.

RAISIN PUDDING

Batter:
- ½ cup sugar
- 2 tsp. baking powder
- ½ cup raisins
- 1-½ flour
- 1 tsp. vanilla
- ½ cup milk

Mix all together and pour into a 1-½ quart baking dish.

Sauce:
- 1 cup brown sugar
- ½ cup softened cow butter
- 2 cups boiling water
- Pinch of salt

Mix and pour over batter. Bake at 350-degrees until nicely browned.

SPRINGTIME SASSAFRAS TEA

He learned his healing secrets from the Choctaw and the Cherokee and other Natives, and that settles it for us. When he says we need to drink sassafras tea every Spring to thin our blood and keep us strong, we drink sassafras tea. When people come from miles around for his herb medicines, they lift him high to all who'll listen.

- Sassafras roots (one large or 1-12 small roots)
- Fresh cream and sugar

Come spring, go to the woods and dig up a large sassafras root. Wash and scrub it until all the dirt is gone. Put into a big pot and cover with water. Bring to a boil and boil until the water turns pinkish-brown. The pinker the water, the stronger the tea. Dip out a cup of tea and doctor it up with fresh cream and sugar. Keep the root in the pot on the back of the stove. You can add more water a time or two for more tea.

DAD DOOBIE'S STOUT COFFEE

- Ground coffee
- Water
- Medium-sized saucepan

Put several tablespoons of ground coffee in a pan. Fill with water and boil until it gets to the desired strength. Add a splash of cold water to settle the grounds down before serving. Don't toss out the grounds. Save and add more grounds the next morning. Add water and boil. When the pan is about half full of grounds, throw grounds into garden dirt and start over. This coffee will get up and walk out the door, so keep a lid on it!

Progressive Rising Phoenix Press is an independent publisher. We offer wholesale pricing and multiple binding options with no minimum purchases for schools, libraries, book clubs, and retail vendors. We offer substantial discounts on bulk orders and discounts on individual sales through our online store. Please visit our website at:

www.ProgressiveRisingPhoenix.com

If you enjoyed reading this book, please review it on Amazon, B & N, or Goodreads. Thank you in advance!

CPSIA information can be obtained
at www.ICGtesting.com
Printed in the USA
BVHW080521220223
658930BV00001B/15

9 781950 56073